RIPE FRUIT SOON SPOILS

MELANA MORRIS

Library of Congress Control Number:
2023909630
The Library of Congress has catalogued Melana Morris for this publication as follows:

Morris, Melana R.

Ripe Fruit Soon Spoils / Melana Morris

ISBN 979-8-218-95349-2

1. Contemporary Romance – Fiction.

2. Generational Trauma.

3. Adult Love – Fiction.

4. Paranormal.

5. Religious – Fiction.

245

Acknowledgements

ILLUSTRATION BY DANIELLE ROBINSON

DIGITAL BY BARB HICKS

*"When wild imaginations run free,
creative stories are birthed." ---MRM*

INTRODUCTION

This book started as a short story for an urban anthology. As time passed, life happened, and the project did not occur. I decided to expand the story and create a manuscript so off the wall crazy; I pray Jordan Peele, M. Night Shyamalan, *and* Boots Riley finds this book one day just randomly scrolling literature platforms, looks at the cover of this book, and it stimulates their interest.

The relationships in my life and the craziness of my imagination fuel every word between these pages. I thank everyone for their lessons and unsuspecting contributions. This book was therapy for me in a lot of ways. It gave me a chance to sort out unresolved feelings about a lot of things and a lot of people. It allowed me to let off steam without revealing the contributors. It was easier to do here.

I come to realize that time is the most precious commodity anyone can have. The time we spend with our loved ones, the time we work on our jobs, and the time we give to others. No one cares to waste it in the beginning when there is plenty to go around, but as time passes, it becomes more and more precious.

I spent over ten years developing this manuscript. That is a lot of time to give to anything, just like when I gave myself to different relationships. It was a bittersweet relevance. I held on to people not worthy of my time but soon realized they created characters and storylines. I allowed people to stay past their season. How much of myself I gave to them to keep them close: my heart, my time, and my body—the very things I can never get back. It made me think of everything I allowed just so they would love me. I sacrificed a lot of myself, thinking it would help hold on to them.

I was angry about a lot of shit. Raising two children by myself, being a full-time college student, working over sixty hours a week in a hair salon made me bitter. More upset at myself for thinking the men whose children I bore, would be there for me. I bitched for decades. Often lashing out because I was mentally broken. I destroyed a lot of close relationships; some unreconcilable to this day.

I ignored warning signs when I fell in love, and was so gone in one relationship, God had to speak to me in the bathroom to snap me out of my blind spiral. He told me the person I wanted to spend my life with would never happen, and didn't. That crushed me. I was in a dark space for a long time and it created dark scenes within the book. The vibe we shared was unlike anything I had ever encountered with anyone; and if he's reading this, he knows exactly who he is. When you can literally feel someone right before they come back into your life again or when they are thinking of you is rare. I gave everything in that relationship, and to come out of it with nothing blew my mind. I'm not the first woman to empty her cup, and I won't be the last. Every person who has fallen for love has dealt with a letdown or two, playing its ugly game.

That became the premise for this manuscript. How people would do anything, depending on how desperate they are, to find and keep love. I took the essence of every man that abused my love and loyalty, and rolled them into one character.

And in this book, Maximus Negus Dubois is that character.

The tale goes back and forth, learning from the two main characters' perspectives. At times, an omniscient view shows an overview of the situation: how the characters see life and how they operate, and multiply, within it.

Take a whimsical trip through your mind, religious beliefs, and sexuality as you discover a world no one knew existed. How funny that it does, just not from this angle.

Melana

CHAPTER 1
Planting Seeds

Centuries ago, on some faraway island, there was a tribe of women called the Declotae. Their appetite and grandeur held them in the highest esteem in the Caribbean Sea. Conquerors feared them because of their power and their punishments. Their name, derived from the most horrid means of death known to man, was rooted in the Art of Decapitations. It was a sure way to signify an idiot's defeat and end any chance of returning from the dead. One season, a swift change in universal governing between the islands forced the women to change their methods to less vulgar, separating practices.

Known all around the globe for their sexual tastes, the Declotae was always ready to fuck. Their soft and natural beauty boasted its appeal and demanded instant respect of the pussy. The sweetness in the maiden's smiles tempted with soft turns and never revealed more than an interest to catch an eye. They displayed the normal lusts of the flesh: puffy breasts, thick thighs, and long hair. The Declotae had all the desirable attributes men drooled over. They became lost in the shape of their hips and how their eyes smiled back to get attention. They flashed like lightning, quick and white, and if caught gazing a split second too long, were mesmerized and enslaved forever. Many men have tried to dictate how things would go from their moment forward, thinking their dicks were good enough to barter or withstand the needed task at hand.

The Declotae was often compared to the Roman 300 by how they assimilated in numbers. They proved their greatness on the battlefield by moving as a unit. The elder matriarchs governed and fought. The younger maidens did more domesticated tasks to homestead their fortress. Built like little brick houses, hot and solid, they ruled with iron fists and protected the island's entire sea wall. Even though they only stood at an average height of five feet, they towered with superhuman strength.

Swift in their artistry of the sword, they cut bullshit off at the knees. Each Declotae knew her role. Sexually, they baited and switched. They were using the younger, fresher, tenderoni to lure the prospect—only to change in the cunning, more experienced cougars for the cause and purpose. It was an old strategy used as far back as the French Revolution. Their battle moves were crafty in strategic attacks when drawing the enemy in from one angle and striking by surprise from another. The Declotae's practice worked in any situation that fits its purpose and they perfected its undefeated record. Known for rolling over their opposers with great power, the women protected the Guff of Souls and their precious commodities, so many have tried to stake a claim.

In their intricate design, the exotic beauty of the tribe lured men in like suckers. They used their curvy bodies to hypnotize victims as they walked with the Caribbean breeze, once their eyes twinkled back, or even when they played in their long, dark hair. It took vanquishers' minds away from the mission to conquer and behead. Many have tried to separate the wealthy-crowned maidens to prove their journey and victory. That assumed thought process also lured men to their untimely, worthless deaths.

Often viewed as fragile, the women's lack of intellect to guttural things made them easy to misguide. Some called them a tribe of stupid hoes because of their fabled deep vaginal canals. Some called them the tribe of weak bitches for their dramatic mental breakdowns when faced with handsome conquerors. They instantly became feeble in the knees and swooned over well-endowed holders. Their naiveté was another layer to their strategy no warrior considered into the equation. The women only played dumb to get what they needed. Their purpose held a greater meaning in the universe and cared less what the three-legged mutants thought about them.

Though the Declotae suffered much, their resolve never waned. With strength and tenacity, the tribe adjusted to the winds of change to stay afloat. At any cost, every maiden committed to their purpose no matter what they sacrificed personally: dreams, another way of life, doing other things, or exploring other worlds.

The power of creation lied within the fruit of Declotae wombs.

The sweetness of their vaginal walls held pussy power.

The kind of pussy that gripped large cocks.

The kind of pussy that vibrated at a three-point seven on the Richter scale during orgasms.

Their sugar boxes gave blow jobs from the inside.

That skill sucked men in even further.

They stroked their shafts with perfect grip and flick, and the explosion of semen that squirted millions of seeds deep into their raspberry, pink-lipped purses produced life in abundance forever.

Many men have tried to overtake the Declotae because of their phenomenal love-making skills. They were plotting to undermine their intelligence based on opinions and naysayers from across the globe. Thinking they could pimp the tribe out. Judging the women to be loose and whorish, dumb even, because of their wet pussies that dripped with sweet goodness. Not expecting them to be as witty as they were. Their beauty ran deeper than what the men could see on the surface. It was an iatrical part of who they were. They were playful, nurturing, easy to talk with, didn't nag, and easy to love. They sublimated peace. Men have killed each other to only smell the fragrant aroma of the purest pussies in the universe. And to taste it, have sent plenty to early graves. Some have even laid down, face up, and boldly awaited the ten thousand milligram sugar drip to fall gingerly upon their desperate tongues.

It caused them to shake like epilepsy.

They went into Diabetic comas.

Dying instantly with their tongues left dried, shriveled up, and as black as night.

So many have concluded that if they could seize the Declotae, they would control the Guff, which meant controlling everything—including the universe. The Declotae held the world in their hands, and travelers from distant lands knew it. It was a three-for-one in many respects. A triangle love affair that would ring on forever.

The women colonized the globe for reproductive reasons and returned to their island once a year for the Gathering of Souls. It was their yearly jubilee celebration for the Guff and its never-ending rotation of life. The lusts of their flesh fed their appetites. It was a continual cycle of sin damned by their ancestor, Eve. That's what made their pussy nectar exceptionally sweet. Temptation, abomination, and lust were the main ingredients that dripped from their vaginal openings with fervor. They were the root of creation on galactic proportions. They were the fountain of life, and here, at its source, a group of travelers found their way.

One solstice, the jubilee was held during the spring and the conditions were lovely. Hurricane season had become more difficult to honor the soul's celebratory events. A week-long festival full of eating contests, duels, hot-box competitions, and water games kept the island buzzing.

"You see that?" One maiden at the north post pointed out to sea.

A shiny vessel caught her attention during the nighttime festivities one evening. It continued to go back and forth across the ocean line. Alerting the other women, she blew the ram horn to ready her tribe for whatever come that may.

At first glance, the shiny object seemed lost in its exploration. For hours, it danced against the moonlight and circled the sea. The blinding reflection from afar made it hard to configure the watercraft's size and shape. As it appeared that the watercraft had curved to leave, it turned sharply and was headed straight toward the island.

"Here comes more dummies," one maiden shouted as she started to crack her neck and knuckles.

Once again, having to defend their island and its peace, the women prepared for battle. But as the shiny object came closer, the craft's steps became evident, and figures appeared to be forming from the glare of the shine. In uniformed stride, an army of men was approaching their shore. The bronze reflection of skin hypnotized the women as they walked from the waves of the sea. Their muscular bodies proudly displayed the metallic hardness of their loins as they marched forward. They, too, looked to be impenetrable. The maidens began transforming from the shoulders and hips, cracking their knuckles to widen and lock, and spreading their toes to stick in their ears when they rolled with force. The Declotae were ready to form into wrecking balls and strike!

But as the men approached the shore, their boyish dimples eased the Declotae's defensive guard and take pause. The maidens reversed their spherical form when enticed by the display of dark, meaty warriors approaching their island. One flash of their ivory smiles froze anxious feelings and melted observant hearts. Their caved pactions enticed the maidens in an instant. When the men arrived, they subjected themselves to the tribe by bowing before them in the highest regard—denting the wet sand underfoot with their giant kneecaps.

"Forgive our intrusion," said the head warrior. His voice moved like the rushing waves before him. "We're traveling from far away and seem to be lost. We need a place to rest."

The warrior offered precious rubies and jasper that unfolded from his arms like the reddest carpets. He presented goats and oxen that steered at the women's feet within a snap. With the pickiest of palates, the tribe was not impressed by the musky herd at all. Their tongues, savoring more delicate species of flesh, were more interested in the men's meaty loins instead. Every Declotae's eye was in awe. The women were mesmerized by the thump in their groin muscles that throbbed in synchrony. Their phallus pulsed like a heartbeat and made every maiden's desire grow more.

The Declotae were also honored for their land's productivity. Their culture thrived from the eccentric-silk attire that traded well to the holistic economic yield in the Herbs. The Kush leaf, Durban Poison, and Strawberry Cough flowers flourished on the east side of the island season after season. The warrior offered newly budded flowers of the rare, exotic herb Purple Haze. It appeased the Declotae since they had heard so much about its violet leaves and hazy effects. The expense was too great to obtain the unique flower, and with this new gift, the Declotae relaxed a wee bit more.

So, they tested the herb to prove its legend. Lighting the crispy buds in Fronto leaves, the purple layers of smoke puffed into the air like lavender clouds. It was refreshing what the warriors presented to the tribe. By not coming off brazen towards the women or in the law of the land, the Declotae welcomed their approach in more ways than one.

Everyone toked for hours. They danced and laughed throughout the night. The men shared stories of their vast travels and conquests. The women shared stories about their global connections and dreams. By accepting the warrior's offer, the women agreed to see what other goods the men would need to barter and possibly be on their way in the next breaking days.

These men were strong in build and embodied seven feet of pure masculinity. Their goliath structures intimidated, but as their smiles widened, softened their tough exteriors. It made them appear like gentle giants. Their brawn physiques sparked a different fire that, once lit, could not be tamed. The spoil was in ample harvest for the women to enjoy, so they agreed to allow the lost travelers to sup for a season and parlay.

As the season changed, one turn of soil turned into four. Four multiplied into eight. Prosperity grew each year as crops rotated new seeds and vegetative growth. The warriors constructed magnificent architectural establishments on the Declotae's island. They fortressed weakened structures left from previous invasions and sublimated themselves to live peacefully amongst the female tribe. The men catered to the needs of the women by showing their leadership capabilities and, at times, overstepping the parlay to solve petty issues quickly. These men worked hard in their roles, attempting daily to prove their value and how much the tribe of women needed them present.

Not only were the lost travelers impressed by the Declotae's island and what it offered in commodities, but harmony was another bonus their environment brought to the table. Finally, at peace with their decision to surrender to the tribe, the weary travelers allowed their guards to come down. It appeased the men that they didn't have to conquer the female tribe by force to acquire all the island's goods, including the women. The warriors were just as pleased to discover that this landing was worth the trip most warned they would probably never return from. Once they found the women could assist them in their assignments, there was nothing more the lost travelers needed to ponder. This destination was well worth the risk.

So, the explorers took a different approach. They did everything from massaging feet to priming bastard sons for field purposes. Their fathers were absent, and most were at the bottom of the sea. The warriors hated a soft male. Even though the young men were well put together, their effeminate attributes forced the warriors to be harder on the girly helpers. It was obvious that women had raised them; their inappropriate characteristics were unknown to the men and confused them. The boys were demure and ginger in every respect to a woman, and this tribe of Negus warriors wasn't having it. The male species would not fall victim to such a heinous crime on their watch.

By showing the Declotae numerous combat strategies, they allied with the tribe as a joint force. The men argued that if they were to protect the island together, they would need to know certain aerial and tactical moves to strengthen their collaboration. At first, the women took offense to the nerve of the warriors believing the tribe's moves had not kept conquerors away for decades; but when the men flashed their smiles, the thought was soon brushed aside.

For months, they taught the women how to tree glide. They showed them how to move effortlessly through the foliage like a mist, guiding their arms by the waist to secure them. They demonstrated slower breathing techniques that lowered the heart rate to appear dead underwater. It wowed the women how long the men could hold their breaths. A few maidens wondered if they could eat pussy that long underwater, too, since they were showing off and everything.

Their accord was mutual and was peaceful for many seasons, but the older women knew the tricks of the enemy—they knew all too well the tricks of the dick.

The Declotae did not want to offend their helpful and enticing guests, but the women knew their presence warranted discretion.

"We cannot let our guards down, ladies. Do not make it easy for them. I know your pussies are throbbing and we are *all* in need, but we know who they are. Don't forget that." The head Declotae smashed her golden stick into the ground to get every maiden's attention. "They only want our heads and our Guff!"

So, the women gave the warriors more to accomplish in the attempt to test their worth. In return, the men did even more to gain the women's trust. They planted new vegetation for the community to thrive from: soursop to heal disease, aloe vera to regenerate the skin, and sea moss for detoxing the blood and organs from unwanted bacteria and parasites. The women loved adding medicinal trades to their roster. It gave them a more purposeful adoration no other island could compete with.

The men also showed the women how the pile of decayed twigs taking up space near the shore, if buried a few feet under the sand, would produce coal for energy in a short period.

Pressurized coal generated diamonds.

That invention delighted the Declotae beyond measure. Their heads would not be up for grabs anymore, and that discovery was priceless.

"Now what? They solved a problem for us. We need them here," one maiden declared.

"I know, right? I can be feminine with them here, not a bitch on wheels," spoke another. "Even the young men are learning *their* future roles."

The explorers also carried a special gift of gab. Pussies easily defiled without consent, wettened with ease. The men learned the art of Kama Sutra from West India and decided to win the women over with its illustrious gifts. The travelers had never tried them, and what was a better way to execute the learned strategy than here?

The approach addressed mental stimulation that coerced the flesh in response. The travelers swooned over the women with their soothing voices. They hid their agenda in witty conversation that enticed more. They jargoned facts with fallacies to make their explorations sound more interesting. The warrior's voices enchanted the Declotae with descriptive nouns and adjectives that sweetened every tale.

Whimsical in their storytelling, they were fast-talkers and spoke everything some of the younger women needed to hear. How much more beautiful they were than the older women. Telling them how much more time they had on their hands than the elders did. Showing them their side riches and how much of it they had to equally share with them, if they helped to bring the two folds together.

And with that, they promised *more*. With their swift-acting tongue work, they corrupted the Declotae's impenetrable wall. The warriors pledged loyalty, devotion, and being there when needed. The family unit was everything to the men and was something they longed for. It was a quest the weary travelers never conquered.

The travelers picked up on the women's promiscuity. The sway in their hips was one flirtatious way they tempted the men to stay put and plant roots. The Declotae's delectable kissing techniques were superior. The way their four-inch tongues released in lashes to get a cock-rise in attraction. The way their lips barely excited the outer rim of the men's ears when they hugged close to say thank you. The travelers wanted the women close forever. The essence of their natural body oils stimulated their loins like electricity. The sweet warmth of their skin softly pressed against their faces and into the traveler's hearts with each interaction.

The men swore there would be peace between the two cultures. They sweet-talked sticky notes to the women's hearts and opened the floodgates to their tingling wombs. The maidens cooed with pleasure as the travelers fucked their minds savagely and dickmitized their souls with fancy prose. It tickled ears and stimulated neurons in the maiden's brains that triggered clits to throb, pound, and tingle.

Just by listening to the poetic crack, the young maidens caved into the traveler's desires and sat on dicks to please their cervical drums. Thrashing their desires around like alligator tails. Whipping the pussy like orangutans gone wild. Bouncing in African rhythms and grinding pelvic meat in upside-down positions. They squirted sugary orgasms into their naive faces and banged balls together when they bent over to the front to touch their suckable, honeyed toes. The women's thighs were powerful enough to knock over deep-rooted trees with one kick, the same thighs known for riding dicks for days.

They fucked one another with tricks.

Both cultures drank from the fountain of covetousness.

They locked the nations together for eternity, mixing fluids to create the sex juice of the ages.

The elder Declotae, not knowing the eternal cycle their sisters had placed them in, were blind to their girlish haze as they walked about—hell, they thought it was the herb. How ignorant the maidens became in their bliss. They were twirling through the fields barefoot for hours and singing love songs. Some did cartwheels along the shoreline that left their footprints in the disappearing sand forever.

By manipulating the weaker women in the tribe, the men conspired with them and discovered their weaknesses. The young maidens were giddy in their reveal. They told the travelers how their petite frames transformed into wrecking balls and pummeled enemies during battle—showing numerous presentations to demonstrate their contortionist maneuvers quickly.

They boasted how the waves in their luxurious hair, created by the goddess Dali, whose hair flowed like charred liquid gold, strengthened their tiny frames. The explorers had only heard that the jet-black pigment of follicles that grew from the Declotae's heads glazed in small black diamonds from the mines of Africa. The story was so grand in its legend, or so the travelers thought, that no one in the universe had black diamonds stranded in the locks of their hair. The mere blessing of being in their presence was mind-blowing, and to never have been conquered was too much to imagine. It was hard to believe the tales others told, and there it was, right in front of them to triumph comfortably. The bounty rate for one head alone equaled a king's wealth. And there were hundreds of them parading about in their glee.

"This conquest would be perhaps the most profitable yet," one traveler concluded as he compacted his treasure into the soil to ensure its imbedding.

"But look at what else we would have access to," proclaimed another as he foolishly plucked a berry from its stem and basked in its undeniable sweetness.

"They are more valuable alive," proclaimed another as he also plucked a juicy berry. "Negus, these berries melt in your mouth!"

The travelers discovered the sugary raspberries growing from a fruit tree in the Forbidden Zone were the only ones of their kind in the universe. The power of sugar in these berries supplied deadly doses of nectar to unsuspecting fools. It was the grand poison of poisons. Berries so soft and juicy, they melted onto your tongue like whipped candy. The raspberries coated Declotae wombs like honey and allowed their uteruses to snap back with virgin qualities days after childbirth—no stretch marks. No bleeding. Quick turnarounds. Just back to procreating and on to the next baby. That was too perfect for the men to fathom. It fit into their puzzle without any resistance and that tale was just as unbelievable as the others.

"We could dick them down to control them and weaken their bond from the inside," another traveler announced.

"Yes, it will cause distrust amongst them," proclaimed another warrior.

"The TTT Method would work here. Don't you agree, men?" One warrior suggested during the height of their deliberation.

"Ah, the This-That-and-the-Third Method would work! We *are* planting seeds and will be here for a while. You're right!" the head warrior exclaimed with an exuberant amount of enthusiasm. "Good thinking, Negus!"

As the weeks went on, the Declotae noticed shifts in their unity. There was discord between the ages. The elders prohibited the younger women from interacting with the travelers without a chaperone. Some maidens rebelled by disappearing for days from their posts. Some were not showing up at all. One elder noticed some travelers that were in areas not privy to them and called for an assembly. When they met, the general of the warrior's army stood firm on the reason:

"We were finding space to bury more brush. We need more coal for energy and diamonds. We thought the elders understood that?" he spoke with authority and temperance.

Speechless in their approach, the women stood there and watched him sink deeper and deeper into his story. Laughing at him as he flipped at the gums, knowing his lie made no sense. Not only were the clusters gone, but the fuchsia-pink stains on his teeth and fingertips were proof enough for the Declotae that he was a liar. He was too stupid to wipe his hands to get rid of his guilt. There was no need for a male to eat the sweet berries, not unless he was a pussy himself, and from what she was looking at, his lanky frame made him look like one. His lie was brown-nosing the elders and he became a weak link that had to be circumcised from the shaft.

"Wake up!" He snapped his fingers in the middle of his explanation to take their attention away from his bulging package. "Don't you want more diamonds? We thought developing the coal solved that problem for your tribe?" he said with sarcasm, which pissed off the elders. He made his cock jump several times as he popped his fingers over and over, and accentuated the beat of his meaty loins.

The Declotae snapped out of the traveler's dick haze and realized no such understanding existed. His rock-hard cock had zoned the elder out and made her forget why she was standing there with her golden stick. She was disappointed that his punishment had to be ordered. She poked him as he walked the plank. She swatted his ass in swift strokes to make him hurry up. She shook her head as she ordered his demise.

"See. You cannot trust them. They have two heads and fail to think with either one," the elder confirmed.

"Damn," sighed one maiden. "His dick movements were good."

The warrior's order was to hold the Orb for a year, without pause, for trolling into the Forbidden Zone, stealing fruit, and for lying to an elder. They whipped his back with torrential lashings that left dangling skin slices in tattered pieces. As it healed, it dried into horrific faces that mimicked his anger and pain. They kicked his knees to humiliate his weakened strength. As he weakened daily, his forced obedience was testing his manhood. Having shit and pissed on himself daily for all to see and reminded the other men to fall in line or they would be next. He had epically failed his brotherhood. And with him were dozens that fell away because of their arrogance.

The warrior's assignments were tremendous and aborting them was not an option. So, the men aligned themselves accordingly after losing so many men and could not sacrifice more bodies. Their secret had to stay silent as the perfect time was nearing for the transfer. They had to humble themselves for a bit longer to honor the island of women the gods had placed them on to save face, but their patience was wearing thin.

"We should decapitate them all and be gone from this place! How many more must we lose?" One traveler shouted across the yard after watching his dear friend fall victim to his strange vanities. He recalled so vividly in his memory as his brigade watched another friend walk the deathly plank…

The narcissism his comrade had thinking he was the gift of dick from the Negus heavens. He thought he could withstand getting fucked all day as maidens walked by, as they pulled up their dresses, placed down their stools for more height against the giant stuck holding the Orb, and jackhammer his big dick all day. His dear friend believed he could handle his punishment. The only embarrassment was in the bodily secretions he expelled daily and having to bend over so he could get wiped and cleaned for the next fuck. The maidens jumped onto the traveler's body, hooked their legs across his gigantic arms, and embraced him close until they both released orgasmic juices that splashed everywhere. His buddy thought his knees could handle the grind of pussy meat from their orgasms rotting away at his skin, knee plate, and meniscus. It sounded good in the beginning, but a hard cock doesn't stay up forever; and once he started passing out a few times a day from the lack of blood to his cerebral brain, his friend became a vegetable. Seeing his exposed cartilage and fatty tissue disintegrating made him go insane. And once that happened, they had to attach a twig with a yellow ribbon tied around his penis to keep it erect. Milk everything out of him and snatch his fucking soul. Then once the ribbon withered away, so did the bearer.

But the warriors proposed a better idea. Instead of losing valuable men for their crimes, they could implement a chart designating how much time an offender must serve when he breaks the law. The travelers introduced the penile system with caution to the tribe, and at first, the maidens were opposed.

"How dare you make requests when you and your men are guests on our land? Stop breaking our rules and your men will be spared!"

The women murmured as they disputed his pitch; but as his words danced in their heads, they made perfect sense. The women concluded why should they sacrifice another warm-blooded specimen and give him back to the sea where he could crush the Guff's bounty?

"Okay, tell us more."

The men proposed to take shifts to uphold the rotating Orb between the gravities in exchange to alleviate the fatal sentences that came with it. As the head warrior continued to plead his resolution, he respectfully asked for co-habitation and meager genital allowances for their men.

"It would help satisfy everyone's needs? Don't you agree?" His argument had solid points. It eliminated the death factor to the penalty, unless a more serious offense was committed, and kept every phallus on deck for fucking and mass production.

The Hunch Station was propped on the cliff edge of the island and on full display. Fastened by four ten-ich diameter posts drilled into the rock, it stabilized the weight of the contraption, the Orb, and the man obligated to secure it. The punishment weathered storms in the bearer's honor and it was too great to give up on. He couldn't look like a pussy, not now. What would his comrades think? His ego and hip-work showcased for all to see. It proved his character. It solidified whether he was a man of his word or not.

A real Negus.

The travelers agreed to guard the Guff's continuous rotation and protect the innocent souls born of sin and illusion. If needed, they would fight for the Declotae. Their skill set was far more bold-faced than the women could have imagined. The men demonstrated vanishing skills and introduced the hoax for demonstration. The trick was not familiar to anyone and startled the maidens. To disappear and reappear at will, astounded the tribe. At first, their magical tricks excited them, but over time, the women became skeptical of their devilish gift.

If they had to, the travelers would take the Guff to a place where no army would ever find it . They promised to guard it with their lives to keep it safe and sound. Once again, making the women take pause.

"That disappearing shit worries me."

"I agree. I fear our feelings will get involved and then what, they vanish with our hearts and our Guff?" One maiden voiced a valid point and the others quickly agreed with her.

The elders of the Declotae tribe deliberated for hours over his proposition. The women contemplated the good and the bad; but the universe was changing and conquerors were becoming harder to ward off.

After long consideration, the elders agreed to move forward with his proposition. Securing the Orb's safety and survival was their only purpose. Like any contract, adjustments could be made if needed. The women were stuck between a rock and a hard place.

Both cautioned about the danger of the proclamation as talks went on. The responsibility of the Guff. The dedication to the traveler's assignments. Everything required to bond the deal took sacrifice from both sides. They spoke about what it would mean and how far it could go generationally.

"Your women need to be sure they can handle what we require. Our assignments are timely," the general asserted without giving specifics.

"The Guff is a huge responsibility. Your men need to be sure they can handle *our* requirements," the head Declotae warranted as she pounded her golden stick. "If not, your end will not be favorable."

"With all due respect, neither will yours," he rebutted.

The tribes went back and forth about the time the travelers would be allowed to stay on the island. They stayed up one night smoking Strawberry Cough which made the traveler's faces tingle. It exposed the little boys inside of them and made them tell silly jokes too corny to repeat. Another evening, the Sour Diesel had everyone super high and believing they were philosophers.

They also discussed pussy rations and how many days a week giving head would be required until the sun cracked the new day. Agreeing to this part was lengthy and tiresome. The Declotae demanded a two-way street. They liked having their pussies ate on the regular and was non-negotiable—but it was also something else the warriors had never mastered. Going down to perform the act was not something they practiced. Usually, dick supplied the need. The men grumbled as they talked, not sure if they would be ridiculed for being amateurs; but the women weren't having it. Fellatio was a requirement, just like a blowjob, whether they liked it or not. It would be the deal breaker.

There were mumblings and disagreeing words that filled the atmosphere until one maiden stood to her feet to make an announcement:

"You give, we give. We receive, you receive," the charter maiden stated. "We will teach you how to pleasure our pussies. They are not regular vaginas and require special care," she went on and described the importance of cleanliness and stoke direction to avoid feminine issues. "The canopies will be perfect locations to learn our bodies. The beds are huge, the posters have private drapes, and it's near the shore. It would mask the cries of orgasms against the crashing waves," she proclaimed her proposition of fellatio to the men.

And with that, the warriors agreed in fairness and the Sixty-Nine Position was created to bind the Sexual Responsibilities act of the agreement. It guaranteed both sides received oral stimulation during the allotted times.

"Twice a day, every day. Once in the morning and once at night," the charter maiden ordered and waited for the chatter to subside. "Oh, and more Purp flowers, please." She smiled and banged her tool. "I do some freaky tricks on that Purp!"

The women giggled as she spoke, nodded their heads, and demonstrated hip thrusts for humor. But before agreeing to the pact, the travelers declared replanting of more Haze required an extra sacrifice on the Declotae's behalf. They had to nurture the men by hugging them close and telling them they were loved. It surprised the women, and they were pleased to add this to the contract without any further explanation. It was sad for the women to discover the men were never emotionally cared for, not even by their mothers. It was the saddest story the warriors told the maidens. It etched empathy into their hearts. Everyone deserved to be loved no matter what their past entailed.

"That's it?" Many women whispered in disbelief.

"That's easy," they willingly agreed, speaking from the softness of their compassionate hearts.

The maidens longed to pour their love onto prospects, even if it was in vain. The men didn't know their end once their purpose was served, no matter what they agreed to. That made the women go overboard with affection while the men were still alive.

Anal sex was mutually forbidden. Even though it created another hole when vaginas and split mouths were swollen, it took a special person to withstand the paste and the smell. No one wanted to deal with that, especially the warriors. The memories shook the men to the core and made them loathe even the friendliest ass tap during athletic games along the beach shore. How adamant the men were about sodomy; it was clear they hated what it represented: degradation, shame, and submission of principle. The women felt the vulgarity in their explanations. The French enslaved them for decades and chained them to the bottom of ships like dead fish to bring them across the Atlantic, which was what they had to do to escape their stinky, perfumed tyranny.

That's where the travelers learned how to hold their breaths for a long time, discovering gills at their ribcages when some ships overturned avoiding the British enroute to the Americas. When they arrived months later in Anguilla, the Frenchmen thought the dark giants were dead, and tossed them back into the water. The men swam across the Caribbean Sea and landed on Española to escape.

They argued over the guard stations and who would be better suited for the frontline posts and competed for bragging rights in the community kitchen. They disagreed over knifing techniques between the cultures and whose was best to fortify the Forbidden Zone entry gates.

"We'll guard those, thank you," the head Declotae proclaimed with authority. "The men have no reason to walk that garden, and if one more of your shiny giants are found in that area again, your whole fucking posse will be bulldozed off our island. Don't let it happen again."

"Okay, we get it," they said in unison, regretting not stashing more berries into their loincloths for later.

So, they finally agreed through challenging remediation, some sweet talk, and setting zone boundaries. The travelers needed the women just as severely as the Declotae needed them. Neither side wanted to fold, but with some negotiation, everyone bent over. The travelers had to produce for their mysterious agenda, too, just like the Declotae, for the Guff. They were both infatuated by its innumerable opportunities to see its generational doom.

"I think we'll call this pact, 'The Declotae and Trevallier Guff Assignment Decree.'" The elder struck her gavel in agreement, and lightning cracked the sky above them as she hit the podium. The proclamation rented the seam of creation right up the middle of time.

The explorers laughed at her French pronunciation to accentuate the agreement—an all too real reminder the travelers wanted to forget. It was only one part of their dark history.

Trevallier added a spin on the vague name the women called them by. It made the travelers feel robust, more invincible, more than the Regal Negus title that was slowly rendering a negative, plebeian name. The men vowed to add it at the beginning of every warrior's title. It gave the men a majestic arrogance that flattered with wealth and mystery.

It was a new chapter in their ongoing existence, and they had plenty of chapters before this. How the warriors showed up out of thin air with no proof of who they were or their origination. They manifested their bodies and landed on the Declotae's fruitful shore to multiply exponentially and with purpose.

It was perfect how the elder Declotae whispered the sweetest utterance of "a" at the end of its pronunciation.

"Tre'-val-leeee-yaaaay," the warriors repeated the name over and over to feel it, dragging the 'a' sound to the gods and beyond the heavens. The name penetrated their souls and deep into their bones. The men nodded in agreement as they accepted the decree's epitaph.

"Yes!" The warriors liked the weight of its vagueness. It didn't say much about the men, but it told other conquerors of their worldliness. The descriptive rung freedom in the men's ears as they chatted amongst themselves. Finally discovering a name that moved them in silence. The name fit so well the travelers never changed it.

They were no longer Regal Negus, but Trevallier— travelers of the universe.

The Declotae felt safe under the warrior's care and made the maidens feel protected. They were carefree in their days and rested with the men being their guards and shields. Order was re-established. The tribe softened into ladies and redirected the misdirection within the cosmos. Relief filled the pillowing skies above the island and restored the order of man. The maidens were tired of fighting. They just wanted to fuck. They did not desire to roll in the dirt like men, always protecting their island.

The travelers excited the air around the island during their stay. The maidens put on the most naked shit they could find flying on the clothesline and fuck the man chained up, holding the Orb. Warriors rotated hourly. Twenty-four cocks got wet that day and it was wonderful for everyone.

The men performed grand stomp dances in celebration to the agreement. They couldn't believe how much pussy was at their disposal. The women performed seductive moves that dazed the warriors into a trance. They couldn't believe how many hard dicks were available to get on.

And on the last night of commemoration, a storm came through and rained on the island for eight days and nights. The pouches the travelers hid in the Forbidden Zone sank deeper into the ground like quicksand. It buried turmoil further into the core of everyone's destiny. Once the rain stopped, the men surveyed the island and discovered the plains flourishing with an overproduction of greenery that pleased everyone.

During their time of togetherness, armies from other lands tried to force assimilation on the tribe without knowing of their parlay with the men from the sea. The hidden treasures buried deep into the sand were also a guiding light; a beacon that spoke to the creatures of the land and fowl of the air monitoring the skyline. Warning other travelers not to stop here. It prohibited any foolish attacks the peaceful environment may evoke from eager conquerors. For thoughtless seekers that continued, they learned the hard way; they were a pile of skeletal remains growing plankton at the bottom of the Caribbean Sea.

Another decade passed and the universe changed the sexual code to unfamiliar acceptances and its quality of suitors, forcing close family members to procreate to keep the bloodlines pure.

Europeans started the distorted trend, and it spread across the globe like wildfire. They claimed fathers and daughters were the strongest bonds genetically. Mothers and sons came in at a close second, but they could only reproduce once without DNA mutations. While sisters and brothers were the most common unions that created an inbreeding of first cousins that were the weakest; they created pure idiots and a generational branch of cross-eyed, stuttering motherfuckers with no heart.

It was further proof that the collaboration between the two cultures would thrive beyond measure, if they followed the rules to the game.

So, one of the travelers' sons was next in line to negotiate the terms of the men being allowed to assemble amongst the Declotae tribe. His father was part of the first dozen men plunged into the sea for his pussy-ass crime and one of the reasons the decree was established.

See, the traveler's son offered more than his father had. His latest travels to the outer skirts of the universe yielded special tokens with extraordinary powers and gifts; and how he acquired the pieces was another unbelievable story too long to explain here. Not only did he honor his father's agreement within the decree, but he offered an extension of time to sweeten the deal.

"Time? You can offer no such thing. Be gone with your doubletalk," the head elder Declotae shooed him away as she spoke.

"Oh, but I *can* offer time. Both cultures would benefit from it. We would be unstoppable. We could live forever, for starters." He stood firm on his offer and boasted about his age. "I've lived longer than what you know."

His words confused the women. The young man was but an adolescent with adult-bodied privileges. The maidens whispered amongst themselves, trying to figure out his riddle, and putting his neck through the test of rings to verify his standing. His neck stretched two multiples of a giraffe's neck in length before they removed him from the circular mechanism.

They were amazed at his elastic capability. None of what he said made sense, but the test never lied in its reveal.

"Ah," they sighed at another devilish gift the man executed. The women had no conclusions to his trick, other than he was a demon.

"Liar."

"No way."

And in their assembly, the Declotae realized they needed his offer. The elders also placed their necks through the test and sighed at the numbers left.

"I don't know, ladies," said one older maiden.

"I could use some extra time. I don't know about you, sis," said another elder.

"We're never given enough time to do everything. I still have dreams to accomplish besides this," declared another maiden counting her rings.

"I'm sick of having babies, too," shouted another.

The young traveler's tongue tickled the elder's ears with feathery diction. Promising the trick of every trade, the lantern of time offered endless possibilities.

The proposition was tempting, but the elders were tired of playing games on their soil. The travelers offended too many times. It was time for him and his shiny herd of black, liquid gold, muscularly enticing men to leave their island before things got ugly. The young man's fast-moving lips blurred in a tender love song, and the women were smitten. Time was often an abstract bonus that ignorantly attracted many, especially if theirs was running out.

Not only did the Declotae need male warriors to uphold their precious Guff, but they also needed them to withstand its burden. That meant dedicating time. His offer was too appealing to dismiss. Since the travelers were only required to possess the assets of breathing and a penis to qualify, the very core of their manhood was vain in its service. The women would also seal the contract of the ages if the herd of warriors could withstand the expectation and demand of the Guff. Nobody could fuck with them, not with time on their side. The men only existed to serve them sexually, and the Declotae knew men liked to fuck. So did the Declotae. It was perfect.

The men destined for the cause had to be strong in their wit, strength, and loins. The Declotae grew tired of switching out weak prospects. Egotistic men thought they were a god's gift to the dick world. Vainly glorifying the extra finger more than their brains could handle, but the travelers had genetic codes shining all over them. Their loins pulsed with stamina. The Guff would never go dry, and the way the travelers moved, it would stay replenished. It was seamless how many men there were. Not only could they rotate daily, but there was well over a year's worth of cock meat to keep everyone satisfied. No one male would ever tire. Every ratio evened out into threes somehow and, over time, equaled out to eight—the number of completions. Strange in its oddity and how it mutated the corners so perfectly that it forced an attraction like a magnet and formed a tight lock. Sealing their bond with such evil precision, it sliced through the silhouette of love and mortified its putrid character for eternity.

"What greater gift is that? Forever?" One maiden questioned as she twirled her hair between her fingers. The mere thought of living for eternity sparkled in her naïve eyes.

"We would never die," whispered one maiden as she hid her smile behind her soft hands.

"But at what cost, ladies? I honestly don't trust him or his fancy words," one maiden alleged.

With the bounty of men at their disposal, numerous thoughts rambled throughout the island about how they could not afford to lose him because of his ignorant mouth. He offered everything they needed to rule the galaxy. Time. Men. Fulfill everyone's needs without prejudice or favor.

A warrior would only have to serve for the day, or more if he pleased, and then another quickly chained up to serve up his sausage meat with joy. He held the Orb as his hips moved in gyrations. He was creating new sexual positions for all to see. The scribes etched his poses as he pumped. They were documenting his bondage and leg work jerking hard in his manipulations to showcase his gifts.

Some traveler's dick work gossiped about the land and separated the good dick from the bad. Some battled in the middle fields to go next. One time, two brothers pronged each other to death, trying to scrape the thick pussy-paste from their blackened tongues after an eat-out contest of fresh maidens to serve for their victory.

With the last prospect only lasting a few months from the previous crime, the Declotae was eager to replace his propped assistance. His arms were frail, his dick was limp, and his replacement was dire. Most warriors knighted to carry the Orb were from the spoils of war. Their punishment for being stupid. Foolish in thinking they were superior to the tribe. Stupid for believing they were more intelligent. And here, another loser had said the wrong thing. He had lied to her. Just like the idiot standing in front of the elders talking about time.

"No one can offer that!" The head Declotae sounded more like she was trying to convince herself that he was not telling another tale.

If he were, his work would be continual, an onslaught of dedication until his weakened arms and lifeless productive parts gave way and could no longer continue. In that case, the option was definitive; there was only one. His purpose carried one role and once that was of no use, he became useless.

Some were decapitated where they stood when they reached for their swords in fear like the young traveler was itching to do. In that case, his headless body would only keep his sexual extremities strong as long as his rigor mortis continued setting in his body. When that happened, the elders allowed the fresher maidens to fuck the headless specimen first since they were furthest from death's appointed time. They were learning their pussies and who had more patience than a cock-hard corpse propped like a scarecrow? Where was he going?

"That would never happen to *us*," he asserted. "We could *never* fall victim to that. Not anymore." The young traveler's words were unsettling when they rolled off his tongue. They sent spine-tingling chills through them all. "Time is a dangerous weapon. We all could use a little extra, don't you agree?" He focused his eyes down at her, taunting his statement like he was calling her old.

"There's your double-talk again," she announced with disbelief.

His statement pissed her off, but she was cool with it. She knew he was inexperienced and was patient with the young man. Whippersnapper believed he had all the answers to everything. Yes, he was confident, but he was also stupid for stepping to the head bitch with a raggedy pitch about time.

"You saw your father fall victim to it. Your rambling speech is truly a bother. It's aggravating the hell out of me," the elder confided as she pounded her stick.

"We're a different generation. My father was his. He could never guarantee to you then, what I can now," he added with poise.

These travelers guaranteed the Declotae's Guff protection, knowing they would never fall victim to their punishment. They had no reason to lie.

This generation of travelers had a secret, though. They agreed so willingly because of what they brought to the table. The travelers knew their worth, even if stolen. That's another part of the warrior's story. The magic coins planted deep into the Declotae's soil, amongst the decayed leaves and twigs producing coal for energy, generated bonds wrapped in damnation. The pouch of gold coins the travelers acquired held its priceless secrets. The island, was crowned the bedrock—their home; and solidified the roots of their new foundation. Their magic would preserve the Trevallier to the island for generations and the generations of Declotae after them. The union would ripple through time and eventually catch up to the last survivors of its curse.

Its beacon would always draw the bloodlines to the island no matter what. So deeply embedded into their lineage, no one would ever be able to leave its curse unless the initial coins were found and destroyed. Melting the coins broke every curse bound to it. The metal would reflect in the water against the warm Caribbean moonlight and sink to the bottom of the ocean floor.

The elder turned suddenly and deconstructed her shoulder in anger. "Too bad you lied to me, young man. The time narrative is a good sell, but you won't get me with that one." She snatched the traveler by his ear and flung him across the courtyard with ease.

And before they tossed the young man from the edge for being another liar, he pleaded with them and begged the women to think twice about what they were doing. Stripping him naked for extra humiliation, they stuffed his balls into his anal canal to offset him throwing up on the way down.

"Dumb ass," they sang in unison while they watched him squirm.

"You have been here too long not to know what the fuck happens to dummies like you," one chastised.

"We are not to be fucked over. Haven't you heard, bitch?" another Declotae reiterated.

"Pussy," yelled another as she shoved raspberries in his mouth and watched as his tongue turn blood-beet red.

He spat the berries from his mouth and screamed at the top of his lungs how it didn't have to be this way. He yelled at how stupid they were in their actions. One maiden tried to defend him and sent the others into a frenzy.

"His father was a liar, and so is he! You believe a stranger than proclaim loyalty to your sisterhood?" Her anger lashed back at the young maiden with grandeur, her eyes batted in a wild fury of angst. "Your fancy talk may work for young girls..." she leaned in close to the bridge of her collagen-tight nose before she turned back to him in rage, "...but you're dealing with something far more superior than that! Fucking fast talker!"

She walked around him, sniffing his punk ass. The young traveler was afraid, his joints cracking from her kicks, his tendons hyperextending from the blows. The maidens laughed as she squatted over his knee and came like a river; the acid exposed his kneecap to the bone. Her cutdown was low. It degraded his mysterious worth. The young traveler started shedding tears from the corners of his eyes in shame.

"Wait, what is this?" One maiden wiped the streaming flow of liquid gold from his saddened eyes.

"Ha! Your tears alone will multiply our yield!" teased another. "Aw, but you're about to die. Oops, sorry," she annoyed him with her tone. The maiden didn't care about his gold tears and her empty-headed joke tickled the others around her.

"Push him over!"

"Kill him!"

"You can live forever!" he screamed in surrender. His feeble cries broke his wimpy voice.

"Ha! Unfortunately, you lost us, King Midas," the head Declotae agitated as she wiped his tears away. "It sounds like you will steal our Guff and take it where we can't access it at all! *Your* guarantee does not sound like a guarantee to *us*, mister shiny gold man from the sea!" She wiped his face and smeared the shimmer of hot glaze between her fingers. She watched his pathetic waste of flesh begging and bartering with anything he could.

"Please!" he begged once more.

His gold tears meant nothing to her, and as the Declotae attached boulders of stone to his wrists and clamped the cuffs, he continued to plead for his life. The Declotae laughed in their haunting shrill at his weak attempts to save his useless existence. His over-the-top plea was annoying the women. He was acting like a bitch, further proving how soft he was.

Their beautiful faces changed into gothic ram heads in their anger. Giving the young traveler something to vividly remember on his way to death. They pointed at his body, as it jumped around like a fish out of water. They watched him grunt as his sperm sack popped out from his golden asshole; it, too, was crying out of fear. It farted tunes of anxiety in quick, wet fire-cracks.

And when they rolled him from the island's west side, he flipped off the edge of the thousand-foot cliff and fought the air as he fell. The traveler whipped through the gravity pull at high speed, quickly drawing him closer to his death. The maidens ran to the edge and watched him fall, pointing at the boulders guiding his speed and knocking him in his stupid ass head. The rocks knocked him on the head with force, rendering him unconscious, as he plummeted through the air and to the bottom of the sea floor. The tribe cheered on his inevitable demise.

Then, suddenly, the young traveler revealed his trump card in desperation when he stretched out his leg perpendicular to his fall; he gestured in his clownish poses to gain his composure. He shocked the women and danced in the air for his audience.

The young man teased his fall and contorted his body to expound his aerial gifts in flight. His so-called demise from the cliff guaranteed his death, but proved to the maidens that he was the devil. His disappearing acts, his Neck of Rings test, and now—flying in the air like a demon. He played in the sky by diving in every direction sideways as he swooped high into the air like a bird in flight. He whistled in high chords as he zipped past them—flying through the sky like a kite high off the clouds. He sang as his movements that flustered his terrified female audience. He watched as they ran around; the maidens screamed in sheer horror and spread across the grass like ants.

The Declotae scattered the island to watch his production as fear ran through their bones. Acrobatically, he taunted his gift at will. He twirled the boulders around like num-chucks, beating their sonic boom of collision above their heads. His arms controlled his sideward fall across the sky and ocean, verbally cursing the Declotae tribe as he performed.

"I tried to tell you!" he teased. "You're dumber than me," he sang in soprano keys pitched at octaves that vibrated against their ears and popped the bubbled drums of delicate skin inside.

The maidens shrieked in dismay as the silent cries of war sang tunes of urgency. They were regurgitating the liquified nourishment from their bellies as it splashed back into the waves of their diamond-encrusted strands. Maidens threw crumbles of stone at him.

They charged at his body from the cliff like javelins, spearing their raspberries like miniature Mazel Tov cocktails. Their fiery weaponry flew as a shield, blazing at the traveler to destroy him. He would surely plunge into the deep like a ton of bricks. The berries never failed. As the maidens watched the berries flame across the sky, they watched in horror as the traveler stretched his mouth as wide as the approaching bullets drew near and inhaled the wall of sweet, blazing fire.

They disappeared into the pit of his throat and rumbled around in his belly like an earthquake. The deafening vibrations moved across the atmosphere like thunderstorms as they shook inside his body. The traveler began hula hooping his hips to swirl their alignment before he retrieved the bombs from his throat and fired them back at the maidens with fury, scorching the island with his anger.

Some Declotae exploded on impact. Some passed out instantly as they assimilated to the sonic boom of nothingness beating around them. Mouths moved, but they could not hear each other. The terror in their eyes flooded with despair with each Declotae burning on all sides of the island.

Echoes of silence blasted everywhere. Their feet shook as they ran; their knees fell to the ground in anguish, catching on fire instantly. Some maidens jumped the sheer cliffs from whence they pushed ill-fated enemies. They were, instead, catching more oxygen as they fell. They turned into shooting flames of fire as they plummeted to their end and attempted to extinguish the flames burning their beautiful, voluptuous bodies.

As he played in the air, the young traveler moved his feet around, dislocated his ankles and knee joints to separate his toes, and flicked an abnormally long toenail out towards the horizon. When the young traveler extended his leg even further, the sharpness of his nail grew longer, and sliced a clean break into the sky.

He then crashed the two aggravating hindrances of rock into rubble. The chains cuffed to his wrists melted away like candle wax as fire shot from his eyes to free himself more. The young traveler laughed wickedly at the Declotae scatter as he separated the rest of the horizon with his other toes, stepped into its dimension, and pulled the sheet of the earthly existence into it.

He pulled the realm like an angry Italian about to engage in a table flip—like a bullfighter aggravating his opponent; the grand pull of his yank warranted his impatience. He had played their games for way too long. The anger in his jerk was deliberate. He was losing good men to silly shit. Maybe they *should* have conquered the island; they wouldn't be dealing with the foolishness they were dealing with now. The young traveler, two-hundred years young, took everything with him when he yanked it into his realm. He widened the slit and pulled everyone on the island into its unsettling vortex.

"I tried to tell you that it didn't have to be this way," he spoke as he took each maiden through their due process, the ones that survived and still had some value. The elders still had some eggs to donate. The younger maidens were a gift from the heavens. His loins exaggerated, and his mouth dripped wet with each maiden's pussy hole he anticipated hammering.

And there, each Declotae vacuumed into the thin vortex was pressed, caste, and incubated. Their Guff spun wildly amidst the galactic goop, with no one protecting it, and whirled sheets of precious fetal skin everywhere.

The silent hell they helped to curse was now a part of their horrific, ongoing story. The young traveler taunted them as he hooked them into their notches. He boxed his elongated digits to freeze the frame, mentally storing their terrified faces for memory. Flash!

He mocked in his laughter when he flicked their encasements; they tinkered like wind chimes. Sharp waves of anxiety crystallized in the air as they dangled. The traveler, counting his pods with enjoyment, basked in his bounty of incubating women. It was the sweet sound the capsules made in sway. The sugary cubes of death harmonized a soliloquy of life and death, the perfect love song.

The maidens watched him adjust his small, wooden stick to the other side of his mouth from their crystal tombs. They watched as he nodded in satisfaction while he moved around them. A sigh of relief rumbled from the traveler's loins as he counted his harvest of nectar to rule the cosmos. Pleased in the hundreds of maiden's assemblies, he turned away from his large multitude of production, lifted the horizon, looked back at their terrified faces screaming and banging their embryonic tombs, and disappeared into the infinite mist of time...

CHAPTER 2
Hundreds of Decades Later

...My delicate body was new to this world. The bright lights and chilling temperature were a cold welcome to this existence. Doctors poked and shoved things inside of me to test my vitals. My skin was blue. I was here. Arriving at Magee Women's Hospital in the middle of a cold winter night, my birth mother, for one reason or another, relinquished her rights. Magee Hospital turned me over to protective services, where Allegheny County placed me into foster care. For a long time, I thought my life was a giant sleepover. Other kids were being dropped off daily, and the same adult who brought them never returned. They showed up with the clothes on their backs and tears running down their unhappy faces.

While living in a foster home, nothing was private or my own. We bathed together, shared beds, and wore each other's clothes. The bedtime stories were the same. The type of parents we would like, how much we want to be loved, and when would we be picked? It didn't matter by whom. The package had no value either; we just wanted out!

Some wished for rich moms and dads. Some just wanted to be free from where we were. I dreamed of living far away, dancing through fields of white butterflies, and hearing the ocean's crashing waves all around me. I needed to be far away from that crappy place. I never felt like I belonged, especially living there. The only thing I belonged to was the state. There was an emptiness that I could never fill. I didn't feel connected to anything. No one looked like me or talked like me, and I just didn't fit in.

From the time I can remember, my fists have been in a defensive mode. The need to protect whatever was mine was a line no one crossed without a fight. From my worn toothbrush to my dirty shoes, I had to keep safe whatever I could. I even hid my panties from five-finger thieves, and most of them had holes. That's how bad it was. Kids would steal the funniest things. We all had nothing, and they still wanted control by stealing whatever they could. There was no purpose in it, not really. Some were there longer than others and felt they had a right to do it. Taking nothing from nothing because of status, like it was a game, and they were entitled to take whatever they wanted to.

The dark house we lived in did not make it any better. The wooden floors creaked. The water ran cold. The window blinds opened halfway. The lack of sunshine inside kept most kids running through the backyard outside.

So, I lived in the foster home for a few years before being placed with the Gills. They were a friendly family. I remember being around a lot of smoke. The dad, jolly in his ways, smoked funny-smelling cigarettes. At the age of six, Child Protective Services removed me from their home. The dad had tested positive for drugs numerous times which was a no-no.

They suspected Mr. Gill had burned me with his cigar and marked my chest. I went back into the foster home for another year before being temporarily placed with the Stotts. Their drinking habits didn't have me there long, either. Benny, one of the Stott brothers, was also a sex offender, and I also had to be removed from there.

For years, the housemother told me to keep my birthmark hidden. The undocumented mark on my chest was something the housemother ignored when I arrived. She was more focused on the aesthetics of the matter, wanting everything to look its best. Funny that she missed this eye catcher. Mr. Gill never burned me. The fact was, no one noticed until the housemother brought attention to it. The mark camouflaged with my skin and sometimes hid itself as it discovered its outline and color.

The housemother was horrible about supporting our basic needs. We barely kept bread. Food was scarce at times, even though the government supplemented our meals. She would sell the home's allowance for the cash value on the street. She messed over the money with lace front wigs and eyelashes. She was always in the mirror checking out her body while children ran around with runny noses and empty stomachs. She played in her fake hair like it was hers. The children she governed over were only passive forms of income to fund her vanities. She looked the part of attracting desperate families to feel better about her insecurities and reproductive deficiencies.

She picked and prodded me all the time. Once, after attempting to wash my birthmark from my skin, she realized its permanence and pushed harder, scowling at me for its deformity. It changed periodically. The shape transformed along with my moods, causing an issue people may not want to address. The head mother made me feel inadequate because of its uniqueness. That angered me as a child. Her mean comments and nasty attitude made everything she said cold and heartless.

"People may think it's cancer," she would say. "They won't choose you if they think you're ill. No one wants to take care of a sick child."

She must have hated light-skinned people. I would be mad, too, with skin messed up from make-up that put pimples on my already dark, ugly face. From time to time, prospects would come to the open houses to check out the selection of children. Like we were on display for a child drive. We were modeling our raggedy dresses, too-small tee shirts, and tattered flip-flops. No wonder no one picked us; we looked like a bill.

I would hide my birthmark for fear of not being chosen, covering my chest a little more securely. The head mother said it looked like a devil mark and no one would adopt me because I was cursed.

"Ain't nobody gonna pick you."

"You look retarded. Funny-shaped bitch."

"Put something on that's gonna cover that ugly shit up."

"I want you out of here, too."

She said those things often. Her words would cut through me like a knife. My birthmark contorted in shape according to how I felt, and I hated her. It was ugly to her because she was ugly on the inside. The jaggedly etched outline was an anomaly, and as I grew, its erratic definition bubbled outside of the shape and perfected itself into a little red heart.

I hid the mosquito bumps growing from my chest. At first, they resembled eraser heads; and what felt like plums sprouting from my body almost overnight were firm oranges by the break of day—instantly causing attention to how different I was. Being the only seven-year-old with a bra size that made the head mother question her sensuality, the ridicule increased even more.

Even in their display, I sat in the back of every room. I was fussed at for overeating since my clothes fit more snuggly, and there was never any extra money for clothing. My pants rose to my ankles and created high waters. My backside was plumping out, and my boo-boo cat was advertising my coochie print.

I was spreading out, not growing up. I wanted to give the best representation of myself, and it was hard to show my innocence under those conditions. I didn't look like a little girl; I resembled a miniature dwarf lady-kid.

No one took the time to explain what was happening to me. They didn't know. Instead, they teased, they groped, and they said the meanest things. I had to be submissive on some level to redirect their attention. I had to humble myself, so my blossoming figure wouldn't show so much and downplay my assets to appear simple.

Sometimes, I would steal Piddle's shirts. He was the biggest boy in the house, and his queen-king tee shirts covered my bumps enough for me to feel comfortable. He looked out for me at times by stealing more food from the kitchen pantry, another cup of apple juice, or even an extra cookie at snack time.

I wanted to be chosen by my new parents—not be the last pick of the litter. The stares couples would give when it was my turn to come out were disheartening. How big both of their eyes got when they took a good look at me. The women were shocked; the men smiled wide. Every time I didn't get picked, I would disappear into a secret cubby space and cry. I needed a place where I could disappear and never have to come out and be bid on again. Even though no one showed me how to do it, I prayed every night—asking the stars in the sky to pick a mom for me and get me out of there as soon as possible. That was all that I had.

CHAPTER 3
A False Attachment

Amen! My prayers were heard, and by the age of eight, there was finally an interest in adoption. I was still young enough to be considered adorable. I grew another quarter of an inch. My short height kept me in the cute zone. I was a little light-skinned, mixed girl with pretty hair. The lady who adopted me was thickly built herself; it made more sense, that if we looked alike people wouldn't question our relationship. That made me feel good. It made me feel wanted and connected to someone.

Mary Bishop welcomed me into an intriguing way of life. Her rules were easy: I had to be eighteen to do what I wanted, I had to get good grades in school, and to never tell her business out in the streets. Her fears were many: flying, decent men, and speaking up for herself. She mastered the jack of all trades with her job skills. From sewing to science, she dabbled in any craft that yielded another notch under her belt and another paycheck. With no interest in college, she accumulated different trade skills to survive.

We practiced religion and went to church regularly. Mary was the person who taught me how to pray. I appreciated her vast knowledge of her faith and God. She didn't spare the rod and punished me when deserved, sometimes to the white meat, for not coming straight home after school. The mark on my backside was etched into my brain like it was on my body. It was a constant reminder to do what Mary said do.

I never spent the night at anyone's house, I had to stay right out front where she could see me playing, and I was not allowed to go to the penny candy store within the same block. She had better see me when she looked out of the window, or my behind would catch it. Mary had a chokehold on my whereabouts and always kept me under her armpit.

"They won't be showing your face on the news," she would say. Mary always thought somebody was doing the most God-awful things to me.

We were poor and lived in Rankin, Pennsylvania. Most of my friends were kids that lived in my neighborhood and attended the same school, Rankin Elementary.

One boy, Ian, would buy me orange taffy squares to be his girlfriend. He liked how my hair sparkled in the sun. Ian liked to play in it, especially at recess. His big, shiny head looked like a bowling ball. That's what made me laugh and want to play with him. He wasn't mean to me like the other kids were. Ian looked like a miniature bodybuilder with his protein-enriched, oatmeal-packed frame.

I would tease him along with the other kids. We measured how round his head was and how long did it take him to put on a turtleneck in the winter. On field trips to the zoo, his head would get stuck between the safety bars. The fire department freed his head for the third time and warned him not to enter that way again. They threatened to charge Ian's mom an emergency fee if they had to unwedge Ian's abnormally large head one more time.

One day, Ian wanted to kiss me. I told him no, and when he grabbed me and knocked me over, I got up and pushed him down in front of his friends. A few days later, a neighbor chastised me for being too grown and snatched me up by my handmade britches to prove it to Mary.

It was Ian's mom. She was a big woman that always dressed like a man. That confused me as a child. She was screaming all kinds of bad things about me and some bad words which I had no clue. I was a fast hussy and everything else, according to her.

"Your little girl is out here playing Hide-and-Go-Get-It with my Ian," shouted the woman-man from across the concrete lawn. Her big boobies hung over her stomach clamped with a four-pronged belt to secure her gut.

"Be glad he's hunching on girls, dike bitch!" Mary slandered the mannish woman on site.

Her colorful words shocked me. I had never heard them before or knew what they meant.

"Looks like she's going to follow in your footsteps, Mary. Just like her raggedy mammy, little light-skinned tramp." Her words cut through the air and sliced with ill intent.

"Choke on a dick, bitch!" Mary swung her finger in defiance and embarrassed the fish eater on site. I knew Mary cared for me when she defended me that day. Mary didn't believe her; she knew that wasn't my spirit and was offended that we were both called whores.

I wasn't one of those fast-switching, little project girls that started stuff everywhere I stomped while swinging my hair beads. Not like beady-headed Raven. She tortured me as a child. She would make fun of my sewing machine-made outfits at school. Her shiny, store-bought threads caught everyone's attention. I envied that. Raven knew she got under my skin and would make fun of me throughout the day with her cut-downs. She was outside twisting her loud beads around and hyping her ghetto-ness with their hard clacks.

Mary boldly confronted Ian's mom-dad. Telling the woman-man she better be careful whose kid she touches out here—she might catch a charge for being the neighborhood pedophile. Ian's mom told Mary she better be careful who she threatens because she will and expose who *is*.

The two fought in the courtyard for thirty minutes, often pulling out each other's hair. Raven's beads clacked as she jumped; some beads caught the landed punches perfectly for sound effects.

Their knees and elbows scraped to the meat as they tumbled to-and-fro against the pavement. When it was over, the curls Mary snatched from the bull dagger's head were swimming in a jar full of egg water.

Mary placed it out in the sun and waited. It brewed like sun tea. Three days later, Ian's mom was in a horrible car accident and broke one of her legs.

"Bitch," Mary mumbled when we passed her daily. They glared at one another, but the woman-man said nothing. "Bet yo ass won't snatch nobody else's kids up with that busted ass leg," Mary rambled on while she doused the lady's head with the jar's concoction one hot summer afternoon.

That's when I felt like someone finally had my back. Never having that feeling before, I rested in it. We didn't have much, but I felt loved, and that was everything.

Over the years, I watched men run over and abuse Mary. I didn't like that. The bad stuff always showed its ugly head after they moved in with us.

Mr. Vanche put a knife to her throat and forced her to blow his penis while I nervously stood in the hallway, holding one of my dolls.

"Do what I say!" He yelled the ugliest words as Mary gagged from his pumps. "I'll slice your fucking throat, bitch!"

I never heard those words put together like that before either. Mary cried for me to do what he said as she whined my name in fear. "Gigi." Her tears fell from her eyes in a steady stream. I can't believe she almost married that man.

One threw a brick at her face and dislocated her jaw when we barely escaped from his oncoming truck. One was inserting his fingers in the jitney on the way home from Kennywood Park with me in the back seat. Mary forced his hand away the whole ride, but when he threatened to kick us out of his car, Mary obliged so we could make it home.

Since I was adopted, men have been inappropriate around me in some shape or form. One of Mary's boyfriends, Mr. Neft, had conveniently moved with us, as many of her suitors had, and was just another druggie bum that didn't have a place to stay. He smelled like he leeched from women with his half-used bottles of girlie lotions wrapped in his ripped plastic grocery bags. Her choice of men was questionable, and I could sense their mistreating tendencies. My fists usually bawled tight when they came around, and I often disappeared into my room to avoid their beady eyes.

One day, I noticed a stream of blood sprayed up the tile on the shower wall while using the bathroom. I overheard a conversation Mary was having over the phone telling a friend, that she thought Mr. Neft was shooting up again.

He used to do some weird stuff. He used to conveniently drop his towel when the moment presented itself: coming out of the bathroom after a steamy, twenty-minute shower, leaving the bedroom after jumping on the mattress with Mary, or when he would sit directly across from me on her green couch with his legs cocked wide open. A white towel, no underwear, and an extra appendage that almost touched the floor. It was so big it looked like it had knots in it. I thought Mr. Neft was deformed and had three legs. I didn't even know what I was seeing. He exposed his private leg without shame, and I knew that mess was dead wrong. He would offer me expensive candies and dolls so that I wouldn't tell.

I should not have been exposed to Mary getting dogged out. On numerous occasions, I witnessed men rape her in different ways. Her body, her mind, and her wallet. It left a lasting impression on my brain growing up. It made me not like men. Every time one came around, he caused pain. It made me imagine being surrounded by acres of land as far as my eyes could see. Where the grass was greener than any field, and the skies were layered with white, pillowy clouds of sunshine and goodness. Pure happiness. On those acres of land were women happy in their days. There were no men allowed to hurt or abuse us. We lived in peace and pure harmony with no painful moments to stain the definition of trust or love.

The men Mary chose were good teachers. Hearing her attacks about them all being gay and loving their booty holes played with was a comedic skit. Her massage therapist stories ran on for minutes. She believed every man was a faggot on the down low. The word, unfamiliar to me at the time, was one I quickly learned. After a while, I started thinking that men weren't good and took on Mary's view of the opposite sex. That ruined my take on men. What I witnessed rang true in every case. She said all they cared about were their little dicks that they didn't even know how to use.

Cycles created patterns. From Mary's perverted fly-by-night boyfriends, to being called a hoe by my classmates growing up, I just wanted to die. The kids made it seem like my birthmark was a disease. That created a pattern of insecurity. It was made fun of. The children would point at my birthmark and make horrible comments about me having cooties. No one wanted to touch anything I had just placed my hands on. They made me feel different. I was different. I felt it in my bones.

My shape set me apart from everyone else. Daily, I was bullied by the ugly girls in school, especially by Raven. Her and her plump friend, LaQuanda, picked on my height and preyed on me for my thickness. They called me names like muscle lady because of my short, hippy body. Raven and LaQuanda were mean to me because I was a quiet girl. They believed I was the weakest link, but I knew I was much stronger than that.

I was an easy target, or so they thought, until I stood up for myself and hammered a boy with my fists that made him lose an eye one recess. It shocked the school and no one believed I had it in me.

"Watch the quiet bitches," Mary would tell me during her words to live by moments of learning. "Move like a quiet bitch and no one will see you coming." Her words didn't carry much weight considering she failed to live by them herself. They were mostly 'do what I say, not as I do' warnings.

The boy in school failed to heed my warnings. He didn't see my fists tumbling over his face like Supergirl. He freaked out when he noticed his eyeball hanging from his socket. He had to learn how to keep his dirty hands to himself. It kept Raven and her ankle-biter follower, LaQuanda, off my back and onto another pitiful victim. They always thought they were the plug to school gossip and knew everything that happened inside of the jailhouse indoctrination box. That's what the building reminded me of, a preschool for prison. They locked us inside once the school day began. No one could get in or out without being buzzed at the front desk. Get in line over here. Stand up straight and be quiet. Don't breathe unless you raise your hand.

Girls hated that my hair was silkier, envied that I was prettier, and jealous of my light skin. My clothes fit incredibly close. The boys would pop my bra strap, cop a feel when I walked down the hallway, and catcall stupid stuff like, "I bet that is onion good." It made me want to cry. I thought standing up for myself would earn me respect. The coochie calls were not the kind of attention I wanted. No one took the time to get to know me. I liked football and heard the songs on the radio, too. Now everyone was afraid to get close to me, thinking I would beat them down on site. Elementary school sucked.

By the age of eleven, we bounced from D.C. to Texas by the time I started middle school. In Houston, I met some of Mary's family members. While living there, we suffered through a lot. While evacuating from a hurricane, a flying brick flew through the car window and hit my face, dislocating my jaw in two places.

Months later, a serial rapist ravaged the city, and violated our neighbor three doors down. Her dog, Dolly, was frantically scraping at our front door that night. Mary thought she wanted to play, but it was too dark outside. She darted back and forth and jumped up and down on Mary's legs numerous times to get us both to come out. It wasn't until the police swarmed our apartment complex asking questions that we realized Dolly was seeking our help to save her master. In her statement, she said thank God the police came because he was attempting to stick her in her booty hole, but his penis was too big to fit. She said he tried numerous times, but her hole was too tight and wouldn't insert.

After we moved from that area, Mary found a dead body in another neighbor's apartment. His lover had committed suicide. He left a letter saying goodbye and sorry for giving him the AIDS virus. The lover perished in the same apartment when he set the studio on fire after his results.

The glow of the flames was bright as it cracked near my bedroom window. Mary thought I was taking a shower in the middle of the night before she realized it was the building across the walkway engulfed in flames. I wet the bed for a brief period, afraid to walk past my window, fearing being set ablaze.

That was a horrible time for me. The trauma I endured there as a young child. The visions that are pressed deep in my memory. The thoughts of dragging spirits that live there back with me terrorized my well-being and kept me from visiting anything with the name Texas behind it to this day.

There were men that moved in with us that would flat-out grab my coochie and smell their fingers right after. One was caught licking my face and groping me in the middle of the night. Mary was too busy chasing checks when she should have been the checking the men, she had around me. She tried to make things better for us, but all it did was brew frustration. I would hear her vent about signing up for more than she bargained for. Mary fussed about how much money I was costing. She made it sound like I was a burden. She complained that the adoption agency stopped sending money because her tax information indicated she was earning fifty cents too much an hour. The extra money placed her into the "no-help zone." Mary was tired of struggling. She just wanted better for us, and being responsible for me, came with extra costs as I continued to get wider at the hips, chest, and backside.

CHAPTER 4
Mr. Willy Green

In the summer of '86, we returned to Pittsburgh and moved in with Mary's mother, Ghi. She was a lovely woman. Very private in her ways, she oozed Pittsburgh class. Neighbors didn't come over to be nebby; Ghi knew how niggerish they were in their sociable folly. They craved her German Chocolate cakes. The moistness in every bite caused the yearly uptick in visitors to her address every holiday season. Everyone knew it; her residence on Vann Road was recognized city-wide for her baked goods.

I was twelve when we moved to Bel Mar Gardens. The area, though nestled high in the hills of East Liberty, was a well-known community throughout the city. Its closely built units are known for their spacious but affordable brownstones. Families grandfathered their money into a timeshare they never owned—the monthly rent designed to assist low-income families in getting ahead financially.

Mary started dating again and eventually hooked up with Mr. Willy on a whim. Everybody in the neighborhood knew him. Since her mother lived on the same street, it was easy to see his daily patterns and run into him occasionally. From his morning rushes with coffee to the grass-parked drunken stupors at night, Mr. Willy was a real character.

Being nice to all the kids was his thing. That is what he hid behind. He was nice. We would talk about him in the neighborhood, though. Everyone knew he liked to flash his body. We started calling him Naked Man because his nakedness was always in the window. He willingly exposed himself regularly; his blinds and drapes always drawn open. Mr. Willy was ready for action.

One time, he noticed me watching. I was standing there with my mouth wide open. I couldn't believe how big his third leg looked. What is it with men? Why do they expose that retarded looking thing all the time? What's so special about it? The damn thing looked like a baseball bat. It was long, fat at the head, and stiffly made of meaty wood.

After a while, he didn't even care. One night, he had candles burning like he was making a video. He walked back and forth across the window, stroking his arms and greasing them with baby oil. More than a few times, he would grip his penis and stroke it until it got hard. That night, he even placed his hands on the window and looked directly down at me, jerking his meat, and spewing cum on the glass. It sprayed like spilled milk. I stood there mesmerized by his stroke and enamored with the sheen of his skin reflecting off the candlelight and oozing semen. As time went on, Mary started dating Mr. Willy. He must have caught her looking when he was making another one of his Naked Man window videos in the midnight hour.

I was sixteen when we moved in with Mr. Willy. My neighborhood friends from Bel Mar roasted me for weeks, asking if he walked around the house nude, if he closed the door while he peed, and does he put porno-roids in my lunch box. When we moved with Mr. Willy, I didn't know what to feel. One side of me was at ease, while the other was anxious. I knew we had a secure roof and didn't have to worry about food and necessities. Mr. Willy looked like a man that took care of his home. On the other hand, the butterflies in my stomach made me nervous. His mischievous eyes lurked around every corner, and he smiled like a Cheshire cat with every grin.

"Hey, Gianna," he greeted when he passed by me daily.

The situation between us started with his soft comments. Mr. Willy tried to play it off as innocent, but the stench of weirdo escaped from his lips like pedophilic trash. He commented on how nice my outfits looked before I went to school, asking me to show off my choices to ensure they looked fly. They were the clothes he purchased for his sister that she didn't like. I was grateful for them; I even hugged him for thinking of me.

Then, he started buying shirts and jeans, fitted ones at that. As I thanked him, he grabbed me around the waist and pressed his lips against my cheek. He told Mary he knew where to get stuff for girls built like me and that it wasn't a big deal. He talked about his sister having the same issue and jumped at the opportunity to take me where she shopped.

Mr. Willy paid attention to the condition of my clothes and offered to assist. Mary didn't have the money to spend on name-brand jeans and tennis shoes, and Mr. Willy knew that. He used that to his advantage.

In the stores, he would have me model outfits to make sure the clothes fit me right. Pointing out jeans that puffed my coochie print too much, how inappropriate they were, and too grown. Instead, telling me to try on stretch jeans that hugged every nook and cranny of my backside. Mary disagreed because of how they gripped my figure; Mr. Willy defended his choice in what the kids were wearing, and he didn't want me to be left out or ridiculed.

That shut Mary up. She agreed because the clothes she rendered for me were patterned pieces out of a sewing catalog and had nothing better to back it up with.

I twirled and spun. My body was on display for Mr. Willy's perverted pleasures. I was proving my worth again. Even bending over to make sure the seams didn't rip.

Mary continued to scroll through her new cell phone Mr. Willy had just purchased and was more interested in switching between the five cameras to take a selfie for her screensaver. Vogue!

Her lip service pissed me off that day. She didn't even look up to notice my position, my face down and my booty up, proving to Mr. Willy how the seams going up the crack of my behind weren't overstretching. He made it sound innocent like he meant no harm, but I was familiar with how men talked.

They stress certain words to see if we look up. I learned quite a few things watching how men moved with Mary. Mr. Willy knew Mary wasn't paying attention and shifted accordingly. I was watching him watching her, seeing if she was looking out for me. Mr. Willy learned our patterns and was available for every one of them, which opened the door to his access to me. I was cared for but didn't feel safe—not anymore. I prayed he didn't try anything crazy and force himself on me. Mr. Willy was too fine to lose an eye.

Mr. Willy had always been a little creepy, but his generosity wore me down along with his kindness. He picked up trendy binders for me to show off at school. Mr. Willy made sure the snacks I liked were in the pantry. He purchased boosted jogging suits while he was at the barbershop. He made me feel like a tenderoni. Mr. Willy made me feel like he was courting me to be his girlfriend. It was weird. All I had to do was be cute, look fly, and act shy. That was the easy part.

Then came the trinkets at Christmas. One year, Mr. Willy gave me a heart-shaped necklace with matching earrings. They looked expensive, unlike the 10-karat gold jewelry downtown on 5th Avenue or the gold store in East Liberty. I thought he was being nice since he didn't have a daughter to shower his money on.

"They match your birthmark," he said as he feathered a soft hand stroke across my chest when he placed it around my neck in front of Mary.

His touch sent shockwaves to my privates that morning. I felt like a princess and a homewrecker. I didn't know how to react. Mary looked at me with jealousy; I could see the hurt in her eyes. She just lit her joint and watched him put it on. Naked Man had finally touched me with his creepy hands. Skin to skin. My panties became drenched. I was afraid to walk away in fear of them both hearing my thighs slosh. My knob was pounding like a stubbed toe. I didn't understand that either—the weirdness of it all introduced me to feelings of hunger for the first time.

His intentions were mere tools to make me feel comfortable. Mr. Willy shared things with me as a father figure should have. He thought it was the right thing to do, considering the situation, advising on stuff from a man's point of view. He told stories about how men that give bullshit gifts are not serious about you in the long run. Mr. Willy would give Mary stuff like pounds of weed and leather coats.

Mr. Willy said how shacking up with a man is a terrible idea and how they'll be getting everything for free without any legal commitment. It was funny how he threw Mary under the bus on the low, secretly referring to her in his statements. Almost like he was saying, I was better than her and was worth better, more meaningful gifts.

He emphasized wearing shorts under my dresses so boys couldn't see my panties. Not showing my teeth to every boy I meet. He had a saying for everything. I constantly reminded him that I wasn't a little girl anymore.

"I know. You look like a grown woman, but you're not one yet." His response made me giggle, but I knew it wouldn't be long once he said that. It was as if he was patiently waiting for the right time to make his move.

Mr. Willy wasn't going to rush anything. He had the world of Mary and Gianna at his fingertips. We lived under one roof. It was like I was a piece of fruit sweetening on a vine in Mr. Willy's Garden of Lustful Expectations.

He focused heavily on how I should be treated by a man, too.

"You don't even know what you have yet. Girls like you should never go broke," he said every time he slipped me a fifty-dollar bill, one time, smacking my ass for confirmation.

Mr. Willy said men would do anything for girls shaped like me and how important it was that I chose wisely. He would test me to see how far he could take it, squeezing behind me in the hallway to pick up some imaginary piece of nothing, casually brushing across my breasts, and acting like it was a mistake.

"Sorry, Gi. Are you cold?" He questioned why my nipples poked him like rubber darts. I knew what he was doing. Mr. Willy played with the air conditioner most of the time. He changed the temperature of the thermostat to make it chilly. It kept the house from reeking of weed. It kept him from breaking out in sweats hotter than Mary's private summers. Mr. Willy had an issue with spirits. Not the scary kind, but with alcohol. He didn't drink the hard stuff a lot, but he loved beer. Drinking a keg under the table, if dared, and usually finishing with a shot of tequila to call it quits.

He started telling funny little jokes to see how far he could go. Mr. Willy figured we were all smoking weed together anyway—sometimes rolling a thin thread of opium to heighten the buzz, and no one thought that was inappropriate at all. Neither did Mary. We didn't do it often, but it inched Mr. Willy in further once we started.

The longer we lived there, the more comfortable we became. How we dressed around each other, how we spoke to one another, and it was easier for Mr. Willy to create different scenarios. He watched my titties bounce when I ran down the basement steps or zipped from the bathroom to my bedroom because I forgot to grab a towel and told him to turn his head.

Passing my driving permit test was everything. It meant one step closer to freedom and away from Mr. Willy's creepy ass. He eagerly jumped at the opportunity to teach me how to drive. He only wanted to go so he could test-drive my thick thighs. The first time startled me. He claimed his hand landed there thinking he was touching the gear shift for demonstration. He kept his hand there with caution and looked at me in waiting, eager for me to buck his touch to say no, but my body desired for him to touch me. My plan was to use his ass to get out quicker. So, I played a woman's game and offered what he wanted. My thighs squirmed from his touch, sprung open, and welcomed the nasty bastard to explore my untapped well.

"Touch me, Mr. Willy." I licked my fingers and placed them on my sweet box, and then his lips.

"T-touch you?" he stuttered as his lips automatically kissed their tips.

"Yes, touch me right here." I lifted my body and pulled my shorts down to my ankles and removed my feet from the panty holes. "That's what you want, right?" I took his fingers and placed them over my throbbing bump.

"Oh," he sighed in pleasure as he ran his fingertip over my slick mound of wet joy. "Girl."

He stroked my bump with pressure. Mr. Willy asked me to show him what makes me cum, questioning me if I knew what partner masturbation was. He wanted to get me off with his hands and fingers only. He told me to thrust my pelvis meat up against his hand and grind. I took his other hand to spread my lips, controlling his hand work—slower than faster. I held onto the steering wheel, jerking my body while he got me off.

"Oh, Mr. Willy," I called out in pleasure.

He made me feel loved, blurring the parenting lines with sexual demonstrations. Mr. Willy was gentle, teaching me the game and how it played out in its purest perversion.

"Can we go to Highland Park, Mr. Willy?" I asked, signaling to Mr. Willy I was game for another session. I wore a ruffled skirt and the panties he bought for me one practice drive.

"Oh, I love it when you say my name, girl," he confessed as he quivered in his response.

The minute we pulled from the house, he placed his hand on my thigh and began to massage my succulent body.

"You're so soft. Just like a cushion."

Every inch he went, he looked to see if it was okay. Each stroke moved closer to my puffed-up box throbbing uncontrollably, waiting for him to press his fingertips right underneath my drenched panties and feel my pulsing knob. It was like we both couldn't wait to touch each other.

"Niggas will want something in return when they give out their money but you ain't got to do shit if you don't wanna do it," he spoke passionately. He slid me a fresh blade for the demonstration on that drive. "Slice his fucking jugular if the nigga acts like he doesn't *understand the word no*," he rambled on about the young girls getting raped that summer. "You're still a virgin, right?"

"Mr. Willy! That's nasty!"

"Well, are you?" he asked as he twiddled my pouch while I drove. "Don't be out here giving this good stuff away. Make a nigga work hard for this." He started saying the nastiest things about the teenage victims, talking about how grown they dressed, and that's what probably encouraged it. "I'm the only motherfucker that you better be entertaining. I'll do that sweet box right, little girl. Ain't none of these raggedy bums out here putting a roof over you and your mama's head but me!" He flicked his finger erratically against my clit to prove his point and feel me pound against his fingers.

Maybe my hormones were more mature for my age than they should have been. I have always had this appetite to touch on myself. I would do it in the tub when I listened to Mary and Mr. Neft jumping on the bed. I even tried to grind on Mary's knee when I was little to see if she would catch onto me humping on it before pushing me off her. Numerous times, I lay on the couch with Mary watching television, and she asked if we could tickle our legs.

At first, she would do it to soothe me at night when I was younger. She wanted me to feel comfortable in my new life, my new home, and with her love. Her touch was motherly and showed a lot of affection. She would take her fingertips and lightly stroke my body until I fell asleep. Her touch eased my anxieties. They tingled as she softly feathered up and down my legs. One time, she accidentally feathered over my private parts as she fell asleep.

But, once I turned sixteen, and she was still asking me if I wanted to do it, it became sexual to me. I wanted to press against her privates like I did when I climbed on top of my stuffed dog and masturbated.

We would lie opposite each other so our feet and legs could be tickled by one another. It was sensual because, at times, as she would stroke my legs her fingers would brush across my secret area.

I would do it to Mary to see how she would respond to my touch; sometimes squirming my foot or leg up against her privates on the sly. Once, her hisses escalated as she took the heel of my foot and rubbed over herself. Her private was moist. Forgetting she was with me after smoking some light purple weed with Mr. Willy, she moved her panties over to expose herself. Mary was high. She didn't realize what she was doing; her eyes closed to her sin. She pulled me up to her and started gyrating her body against mine. Me, climbing on top of her and rubbing my pussy against her pussy. I couldn't believe we were pressing against each other. Mary's face turned to the side the whole time she moved in her shame and controlling my hips as she moved, feeling the pressure of my body against hers. Her whispers were quiet; her guilt released its cry.

"Oh. Ah. Oh, Gianna," she panted. "Wait, let it roll first."

My vagina pounded in pleasure from pent-up frustrations. I wanted to rub against Mary for a long time. I would watch her ass bounce when she walked. Her touch was my fist introduction to feeling aroused by a tempestuous woman. Mary had some hidden demons she didn't know existed.

Neither did I.

On the way to Highland Park, Mr. Willy said that men would probably kill to taste my sweetness.

"My sweetness? What's that?"

"The stuff that comes out after your first time. How gooey it is. Your nectar. The jelly that slides from your kitty-kat after you lose your virginity," he revealed as he circled outside my wet, throbbing canal and pulled his hands out from underneath my panties to taste it. He started jerking, animating his crackhead twitches for humor like my taste was addictive. "You didn't answer my question, Gianna."

"What question was that?" I asked innocently.

"Are you still a virgin?"

"Yes, why?" Playing dumb was something that came easy for me. I didn't know much about being with men; I just knew how to get their attention and tell them what they wanted to hear. I didn't have to do cartwheels, and batting my eyes submissively usually hooked them instantly. My body did all the talking for me like a beautiful love song.

"Can I taste you with my mouth?" Mr. Willy asked like it would be an honor to be my first.

CHAPTER 5
Parental Discretion Advised

The teacher was now the student. Making a nigga work hard for this was a motto I vowed to live by. The more I teased, the more I received; and just when a nigga thought he's going to get the grand prize of all prizes— I re-nigged. Made men go crazy and willing to do whatever to get back to that intimate space once more. Wallets started flying out, atm cards were swiped. Mr. Willy was working hard, too. The only thing I gave Mr. Willy was my pussy to suck to keep his desperate ass hanging on. Sixteen was an interesting year for me. A lot of things were changing on the inside. Desires grew more. The hunger for intimacy grew with it. I was yearning for something I wasn't receiving, and had no clue to what it was.

As handsome as Mr. Willy was, it wasn't hard to get over how wrong it was. His hair was Puerto Rican curly. He smelled manly. His breath didn't stink. Mr. Willy was fine. He vibed with the teenagers in the neighborhood because he was young at heart. His adolescent character kept him close to our age group—even though the bastard was in his early forties.

To look at Mr. Willy, he easily passed for an early twenty-year old. His skin was bright and hydrated. He had a few of the ingrown hair craters on his left cheek, but they weren't that noticeable. Mr. Willy worked out three days a week and ran the neighborhood with his dogs. He bumped the music we listened to, usually hearing the boom of his Grand Am speakers' way before he swerved the bend entering Vann Road. His base and treble causing Ghi to flip him the bird when he zoomed by.

"Niggers," she usually called ignorance, or anyone displaying its action, what it was.

Mr. Willy knew the lingo we spoke. Pursuing a career in education kept him abreast of the young adult crowd. The hip scene. What's crackin'? His weekly barber appointments at three o'clock at Walt's Barber Shop kept his fades crispy. Mr. Willy never wolfed. He listened to the latest gossip amongst the athletes and men such as him. Getting the 411 on the phattest asses in town and who was fucking them, was normal conversation. He drove the phat rides, his urban wear never disappointed, his kicks were always the top brands in shoe industry, and Mr. Willy was just fresh.

Mr. Willy played with that power and knew when to proceed forward and fall back. He was gentle when he inched his way across the boundaries to secure his spot, showing me how to open my lips and correctly expose my nodule. He would lean the seats back and hold his head up from his elbow, instructing me on pressure and how important it was for me to be vocal in how it felt.

"Moan if it feels good," he would say.

"Mmmmmm."

His other hand focused on fingerplay, stroking my pussy lips and knob with his middle finger at a soft tempo, letting the excitement of his manipulations slick the way. The pressure he applied to it, ordering me to open my lips more, and thrusting my pussy against his hand.

So, one drive we parked behind the grill stations along the Reservoir and chilled. We drank Champale and rolled a gar as we watched the runners go by from behind the trees. We talked about graduation and what I wanted to do with my future.

"This," I acted on my excited passions and started kissing Mr. Willy forcefully where we climbed into the back seat and I rode his face.

I learned how to straddle that afternoon. He pulled my pelvis down against his mouth and told me to grind. When he flickered his tongue, I exploded like fireworks. He also taught me how to get off by rubbing up and down his shaft that drive, too. The grind intimacy was crazy. Our energy was unlike anything I had ever experienced. The unity in our hip movements released a different energy. Focused. Slow, hard pressure. I wildly drew from its euphoric drug like a junkie. Mr. Willy was zoned out.

"You're too young to know about that," he confessed as he caressed my thighs smothering his oxygen from between my legs. "I wished you were a little older. You know I'd take good care of you, Gianna."

Mr. Willy paid Mary 's way to nursing school so we could play around more. We would do on the nights Mary had clinical practice. I didn't know I had that kind of power. That's when I knew Mr. Willy could make shit happen. He could help me get away from them both, using his monetary resources.

My orgasms were so powerful with him. I wanted that feeling all the time. Mr. Willy had turned me out, licking my pussy three times a week or more had me careless about where it happened. I didn't care if someone saw us. I was familiar with grinding on things to get mine. I knew how to move my body to stimulate the release of pleasure from my hips. Grinding on Mr. Willy was intense. As he moved his body with me, his dick got harder and harder. It pressed against my pussy and made me cum faster and faster. He *never* penetrated fully, not even with his fingers all the way. Only the tips teased my lusting holes.

"Let me put the head in," he whispered as he rubbed his dome up against my clit and hole. The juices from my pussy eagerly awaited his entry; but his penis was way too big, and his digits measured the same. Not wanting to break my hymen, he wanted to make sure I was ready. "The first time we go all the way should be special…not in the back of my truck." He discussed getting a hotel room downtown and making everything perfect for me. "No pressure. Whenever you're comfortable. I have to ease you down on this dick, girl. It's a lot to handle. Ask your mama."

"You feel how wet my pussy is. It is ready," I tempted him to put it all the way in as my pussy dripped on his pulsing head. "I already know about Mary. We've done a few things."

My words shocked him and made him take pause. Mr. Willy realized he was a part of a sicker circle, one that hid their illnesses behind a thicker veil of Freudian silk.

"I would never hurt you like that. This dick is big. I want it to feel good to you," he would whisper before he gently flipped me over and slurped my orgasm from my juicy walls.

Mr. Willy needed to protect where he lived, his reputation with the school board, and his freedom. In a demented way, he thought what we were doing was okay because we never went *there*.

To be honest, I flirted with him. I wore tighter clothes, modeled a little sexier, and did things to give him a peek when Mary wasn't paying attention: flashing one nipple, rubbing my pussy print along the seam that ran down the middle of my tight jeans, and teasing him with my tongue when we ate dinner together. I knew how good I looked. I knew I made his stuff hard. It was practice for me to learn myself and the art of being attractive to an older man.

I learned how to move more secretly. Ducking and dodging people that knew us kept it exciting. Giggling at neighbors that noticed us coming out of stores they knew I was too young to be in. It taught me how to be slippery in my movements. I had to be messing with six guys at the same time, outside of Mr. Willy. The bus routes made it easy to do. I had seven niggas eating my pussy in Pittsburgh while in high school: two at Allderdice, one in Point Breeze, one on the Northside, and two in Bel Mar.

I lost my virginity at seventeen to a big-dick classmate named Brandon. Everyone knew how big his stuff was and other girls warned me not to let him pop my cherry, but I did.

There was lots of jelly when Brandon broke me. He slurped every gross drop. He shook in convulsions, too, and said it gave him power. I only did it because I was tired of my friends talking about how fun it was, and I wanted it to be ready for Mr. Willy. I wanted it to feel good when we got together. I didn't want to be embarrassed, not with him. Mr. Willy was a pleaser, and I didn't want to disappoint with anything that might gross him out.

I would sneak down into the basement and help him wash the dogs. We would sometimes play in the water, and Mr. Willy would suck my nipples. He would often masturbate my clit with the water hose until my nodule made my insides shake. The stream of water that flowed effortlessly into his dog's face and onto the puddling floor made memories that my mind will never forget.

Men would show themselves to me or make it attractive to try new things with them. I never told Mary anything. I was walking around with money in my pocket and didn't care. I was experiencing things that I had never experienced before. After a while, I got used to the attention. I liked getting my pussy slobbed down. I was sleeping with a few guys, but not Mr. Willy. That's what gave me power over him to get exactly what I needed.

On my eighteenth birthday, Mr. Willy introduced me to a remote device to wear in my undergarments. He controlled it to the restaurant and at random times throughout dinner. That was one of his gifts to me, even though it was really for him. Mary wondered why

I jumped around at the table so much that night. She thought I was excited about eating lobster for the first time. She complained about a buzzing noise and asked numerous times if anyone else had heard it.

"See, that sound right there!"

Mr. Willy politely told her the sound was probably another earthquake she heard vibrating in her ear and could detect it. The asshole in Mr. Willy was creeping out of him as the remote buzzed three more times as he smiled at me.

"You didn't hear that?" Mary called out again.

Earthquakes was something Mary swore she could hear; saying her ears started closing and a sharp-belled hum began drowning out every sound around it.

"Ouch! Did you just kick me?" Mr. Willy shouted from across the table.

"Sorry, Mr. Willy." I tucked my chin and apologized; soon cutting my big, brown eyes at him for dangling his upper hand of our deceit.

The things Mr. Willy showed me over the years helped me. The things he gave me took me away from how poor we were and how my body was a precious commodity. It made me feel special and that I could use my unique figure to get whatever I wanted.

Sometimes, Mr. Willy would invite his boys over for card night. They played everything from Tonk to Spades. I hated when they would visit. Mr. Willy turned into this asshole I had never noticed before. Unashamed of the hunger beating in their eyes, his friends would make gestures when Mary turned her back. Laughing at Mr. Willy's digs on her burnt fried chicken and soupy potato salad. What a bunch of assholes. I hated how they made fun of Mary. No matter how blind she was to shit, including him and I, she was still a woman that deserved respect. I was tired of Mr. Willy's slick comments and how he shamed her in front of other people, including me. But once I glanced down at my outfit in all its splendor, I didn't give a fuck.

When the bets were settled at the end of the night, Mr. Willy would ask me to go around and collect his winnings. I hated it when they flashed their twenties at me, fanning their sweaty foreheads from the brown liquor. Their whole bodies leaned sideways in their chairs in disbelief at the width of my hips and my figure. They shook their heads at the roundness of my butt; once overhearing them making a wager to see who could get me first. Mr. Willy made it painfully clear that if anybody was going to get it first, he was.

"If anybody's going to get that ass, it's going to be me! All the money I spent up in here?! Her ass is mine!" He flashed his gun and threatened to kill anybody who tried otherwise.

At that moment, I was scared for Brandon. I figured if I didn't hang out with him or wear his varsity jacket, Mr. Willy would never know. I didn't want Brandon to die because he had taken my virginity. My consciousness buzzed for days. Over the weekend, my brain talked to me frantically in yes and no responses.

My mind played different scenarios of Mr. Willy killing Brandon: running him over with his truck at the bus stop, shooting him in the back as he ran across Chadwick Field, or even drowning his mouth with the hose in the basement as his German Shepherds mauled the flesh from his bared bones. All for taking the sweet nectar Mr. Willy thought he had ownership of and did not, but I still couldn't chance it. I broke up with Brandon that following Monday and never talked to him again.

What Mr. Willy said that night stuck with me for a long time, and once I learned the game of men, I used it to my advantage.

CHAPTER 6
Oh, So You Grown Now?

I was finally an adult and could venture out into grown territory. After dancing at clubs and private parties for under a year, I wasn't even nineteen and out here. No one knew anything.

After graduating from the Dice, I hid myself behind the beauty academy. No matter how bad it got, I could pick up my clippers and shears and make a quick buck to get by. That sold me when the representatives from the campus came through for career day. Mary instilled this without realizing it. Her hustle game was an art, and she had a library of skilled trades.

It was the perfect cover-up. Not only was it convenient because they both were located "dahntahn," as Pittsburghers would say it, but it also gave me a chance to acquire a taste for the finer things. It was a way to support myself and dine at upscale restaurants on a man's dime, and it exposed me to a different circle of people. People with money. Money with connections. Connections that would take me the fuck away from Pittsburgh.

After night classes, I started dancing at Controversy, a well-known strip club. I twirled and spun for their perverted pleasures also. I slid up and down the pole in upside-down positions. I did cartwheels. I sprung muscles doing splits. My ass jiggled when I motioned my legs to waddle from side to side at my feet. I often turned and smiled back at the audience with my eyes, tucking my chin closer to my chest to appear shy. My sumptuous strut hypnotized the crowd as I bent over and spread my ass. I would snap my neck back and tickle my ass crack with my hair before exiting the stage.

The frequent visits of familiar faces from Bel Mar made me feel recognized. It made me feel like they only came into the strip club to see me, making it more comfortable to dance nastier for them. We cracked jokes while I blubbered my titties in Boomie's face, with his light-skinned, freckle-faced ass. They talked about my body as I walked the room and couldn't believe it was me spinning around the pole while I twerked my hips. I could hear their comments about how juicy my pussy looked as I approached the stage. They flashed their money like desperate gamblers waiting for me to snatch their sleazy offerings.

I felt popular, famous even. Famous enough to know when a dollar is an insult for the shit I did on stage. Black men were stingy in their tips, wanting me to do the most for little or no money. Mr. Gill stopped into the club a few times but didn't recognize me as a grown-up. He just wanted to smoke in peace. The lux suites were perfect for hot boxing. They were small, every vent could be closed, and the smoke filled the space quickly. Mr. Gill wanted me to roll up his weed, put my four-inch heels on, smoke with him and dance. It didn't dawn on him that it was me until his sixth visit before he noticed something that caught his attention. Maybe it was when my eyes smiled back at him with innocence, or that he noticed my peculiar birthmark.

"Gianna, is that you?"

And when the club closed because of the exploited underage females, I started dancing for Wild Thingz Entertainment for some serious money. Piddle, the fat boy I had stolen all his shirts from back at the foster home, was gunned down the last night it remained open. There were twenty-three bullets lodged in his stomach and back fat. The one bullet stuck in his spine was the one that took him out. Rest in peace, Piddle-Widdle-in-the-Middle.

My twenties introduced me to wilder engagements, where escorting took over. Even when the wormy older men would pant and sweat on top of me in the deluxe, one hundred square-foot rooms, I would be far away. Far away from what was happening at the time. Thirty minutes seemed to drag on for hours.

Sometimes I stared at the pile of money on the chair and beside me while my back squeaked on the floor, or up against the mirrored wall. As they turned me over to fuck me doggy style, I counted the tens and ones in my head and questioned how long they would be before I could get up from my bruised kneecaps. Usually told to shut up before I was flipped again to drink the sweaty drops of fornication as it dripped from their lips and forehead when they pumped on top of me. I stared so far away into space they would slap me to bring me out of my haze.

Before long, I started liking it. I played with different ways to please, using pain as a form of sexual intimacy. The white men drank that freaky shit like hot tequila with lime juice; they were no longer in control and welcomed the burn of submission as it ruled under my dominatrix supervision. They loved the spankings, being tied-up, fucked with beads in their asses, verbally abused and being physically tortured. I got off on it, too. Making them feel all the pain that was aching inside of my lost soul gave me an outlet to release other frustrations. My John's paid the price for every man that used by innocence as their playground. It gave me a sense of empowerment I could not explain.

Then came the threesomes with men and women. I'll never forget the first time I sexually coached a married couple. I was too scared to get involved because it was my client's wife, Rochelle Abaka. She was a notorious barber and had a name for herself in the Burgh. She would do fade and technique classes during hair clinics at beauty school. Rochelle was bad. Her crispy cuts were shaded to perfection. The ombre illusion was a skill few barbers knew how to achieve, and Rochelle mastered its smoky effect. She contracted with the Steelers and cut most of the players. Everyone who got the Rombre Cut knew where it originated from and who faded it the best, Rochelle.

Everyone also knew Rochelle liked to fade bodies. She was a master at that, too. Her hyper-nympho sex drive was something George was attracted to, and it opened the door to the swing community. To George's surprise, his new wife was frequent to this world and knew some affluent movers and shakers. Maybe her sex drive was something he thought he could match. But six months in, George was worn out, dried up, and tired.

She messed around with a few defensive players and licked their wives' pussies on the side. Rochelle just liked to fuck. George was a pay master. He had to pay women to master his game. George paid Rochelle to piss *everybody* off. He knew marrying Rochelle would make them leave his life alone. That was something George had to accept if he wanted their marriage to work. He had a choice to accept how Rochelle rolled, or pay her a lump sum so she could move the fuck on. She often teetered between both sexes. George was just ignorant of the memos, didn't care, or wanted to anger the people who thought they could run his out-of-control lifestyle.

George was dating the blackest bitch in the city, and it ruffled more than a few feathers in his circle. It pissed his mother off, his constituents, and his best friend. Their names were in everybody's mouth—especially since George was Polish and bumped elbows with the Sunseri family. It didn't look so good that George married a Mulignan for a wife.

Everyone knew Rochelle was fucking around; George did, too. Rochelle had a private suite in her shop for VIP members. The whole while, eating pussy in a specially made barber chair with stirrups.

She stood at average height, and her complexion was motherland Nubian. Her skin glowed like burnished brass. Her ass was plump, small, but tight. Slender and muscular, she just looked like she didn't take any shit. Rochelle cut foolishness off at the knees in one swift stroke—just like a Polish or any Italian would do. That's one of the things I couldn't understand about them not liking her. She was one of them, respect to respect, but her skin color made them uncomfortable. They judged her and called her everything from a thief to a nigger.

Her husband, George, wanted to rent me for the evening to cater to her. I knew she wanted me by the way she watched me dance the nights he would bring her in. He told me he believes she's more into women and not him anymore. He shared how he walked in on her masturbating to lesbian porn more than once and her scissoring the maid on the kitchen bench. George wanted to make sure he was reading the right signals. I don't know what bigger signal he needs, but scissoring the maid is a big, red flag.

George was acting desperate. He acted like Rochelle was the only African walking these Pittsburgh streets. Her birthday was coming up, and he wanted to give her something he knew she would enjoy…me.

George paid top dollar for dances and private rooms when he brought Rochelle in. She never said much. She played with my ass constantly and loved watching it wiggle around, saying it looked like a red bowl of gelatin wobbling in real life.

Rochelle asked if we could kiss; it was a line I didn't want to cross, but we could not ignore the sexual tension building between us. I said no over a hundred times and seriously considered once they offered me five racks to do it. I needed the money badly. I had to get away from Mr. Willy and his wormy ways. Mary was expecting us to tickle our legs at least twice a month. Moving out had become my number one priority. Five-thousand dollars meant I could get a place and out from under them both. Their perversions were becoming a regular occurrence, and my peace of mind was everything.

I told George I could coach them. I could assist them and show them what to do. Join in here and there to excite the experience. I learned quite a few things in my journey. I learned about my body and what gets me off. I offered to bathe them, walk around naked, and rub on her clit while he ate her out...shit like that.

"No, there needs to be some pussy eating and clit grinding going on. Understood?" George handed me another rack just to be sure that I did.

The night started interestingly. George was a little nervous. He wanted to perform well, pulling out all the stops: a penthouse suite overlooking the Three Rivers, champagne, strawberries, a private chef, and even hired a videographer to memorize the evening. He even had a few pills to keep the party going strong to satisfy her—days if he had to.

Money was nothing to George. He had car washes all over the city, two restaurants, three laundromats, and two strip clubs—one dahntahn, and one in North Hills. George wanted to please Rochelle in every way he could. His close friends heard the gossip and ragged on him continuously; saying God blessed his bank account because his dick account balance was worth zero. His dick size lacked more than a few inches and his money made up for his deficiency in the penis department. George was a choosey lover, and he didn't want Pittsburgh to know about his whittle problem.

George's gift was oral satisfaction. That was perfect for me. His penis was frustrating to fuck; slipping out and trying to perform positions his dick was not equipped to handle or execute. I was familiar with what it could and couldn't do. George's dick was a plug of sorts, easily tolerated anally. It barely popped the entryway and felt good when grinding on the pillows underneath to climax.

His best position was doggy style, his penis at maximum capacity and full extension. He had only fucked Rochelle for ten minutes before his bird legs gave in. George was ready to change positions. He had caught a Charlie horse in the middle of his stroke. His switch was immediate and all Rochelle had awaited. My sweet fragrance tickled her nostrils while George turned Rochelle into the missionary position.

In the middle of poking her, George was in his own little world and counting his pumps. As he thumped along, he looked in the mirror at himself, then at me. As I stood over Rochelle massaging her breasts, my pussy was straddling near her face.

"I wanna see," Rochelle spoke softly in mid-thump.

George's arms danced wildly from Rochelle's pump-backs. His reflection was muddy in focus. He wasn't paying attention to his actions at all.

"See what?" I asked as I looked down at her and tweaked her nipples.

"I wanna see how fast you nut in my mouth." She turned her head sideways and inched closer to the inside of my thighs. Her nose brushed against my pussy lips, and she kissed them softly.

"Mm, why you wanna eat it so bad?" I widened my stance to give her more headroom and began riding the bridge of her fat nose. "Sss."

Rochelle then inched a little further and released the tip of her tongue. I pressed my pussy lips against her mouth, looked down, and sat on her warm lips that puffed up to mine.

"Ah."

George and I watched as she got fucked from both ends when we looked in the mirror again. The videographer recorded the slurps of my pussy in high definition. He slow-motioned the bounce of my ass covering Rochelle's face.

I felt like we were in a competition, George, and I; he was pumping, and I was grinding. We were humping faster to see who would nut first. Rochelle was satisfying both our needs at once and George noticed her clench down on my thighs to eat my pussy more hungrily.

"Naw, bitch!" George yelled as he pumped harder.

"Sit that pussy down on my face," she ordered as she grabbed my ass and placed my pussy oval on top of her entire mouth.

"Oh," I called out.

From clit to the hole, Rochelle playfully lit her flicks. Her tongue moved with suctions of pressure, dipping her tongue into my hot, wet canal as I pumped back and forth. I was grinding on her puffy lips and opened my labia for her to ignite my orgasm. In quickened paces I rode her tongue and exploded into her mouth. George was frustrated that the pills quit working and sat and watched Rochelle fuck me with a dildo, scissor more orgasms from my hips, and made me nut all night long.

CHAPTER 7
Forbidden Tastes

Rochelle and I started kicking it after that night. For months we hung out at different night spots and shopped around the city. Art galleries became our thing. She was more of a renaissance collector; I liked anything eye-catching and weird. We ventured into fashion houses and created styles for each other like two girls playing dress up. She played the retro-lesbo with linen pants, silk crop tops, and penny loafers; I was the whore planked in leather wear and red lipstick. Rochelle developed a niche for styling that she didn't know she had. She bought me things as a gesture for helping her see the light at the end of the tunnel.

"I want to be with you, Gianna," Rochelle declared to me one Sunday brunch. "I feel like I can be faithful to you. You supply all my needs, baby."

She shared her relationship recipes, how excitement dies on the menu with traditional marriages, and how freedom from its confinements was detrimental to her escaping George. By the end of her lessons, I had a closet full of her combinations. We'd do a movie or two, workout at the gym, travel to surrounding cities just to get away, and even have afternoon rendezvous at art studios painting and sipping wine. While George was at the club popping G-Strings, his wife was priming me like Mr. Willy—using gifts and shopping sprees to pull me in. She knew who George was and couldn't care less. Rochelle knew George was getting his little ass dick sucked on the regular.

"I know George hunches on the girls," Rochelle claimed; and he was. I was one of them. "Let's be real, you probably are, too."

Because most of the girls had cocaine habits, the money they made dancing and sucking dick circled right back into George's hands. Eighths went down like sugar cubes, and George had the best grain of smack. It kept the girls wired all night—some dancing for twenty-four hours or more. They left the stage looking like zombies as the sun cracked over the horizon. The bags of money they would get escorted out with was unbelievable.

I didn't care about any of that. Neither did Rochelle. She was tired of George and her sex addiction with no decent prospects, not until she fucked me. Rochelle had slept with the whole city and had run out of people to screw. She needed another circle to party with, was curious about the money I made, and wanted details about the gigs. Rochelle was looking for a way out of her marriage and couldn't without a good backup plan. She was at the point where she didn't care how. Not that the barber industry didn't produce hundred-dollar bills for her, but she'd had enough of showing barbers how to be professional. They were just a bunch of raggedy backyard counselors that knew how to cut hair. She was frustrated with reminding her team not to play gangsta music when children and the elderly were in the shop. Rochelle felt like a mother babysitting grown-ass adults on the job.

I told her escorting wasn't bad. It had its ups and downs. Rochelle was a kept woman and didn't have to work, but she had to beg George for money all the time. Not that her reputation as a barber wasn't lucrative, but George's money was longer. It made her feel like a child whenever she had to ask for money, and she didn't like that. It made her feel like she was begging, or worse, having to suck his uncircumcised dick to get a stack. She said it was like eating chitterlings, and Rochelle hated pork.

"Take me with you, Red!" Rochelle pleaded by grabbing me close in good cheer. "Please."

Rochelle only married George because of his connections. She liked him because he was good to her and her family. Rochelle loved how quick he was to accept her swing lifestyle. Rochelle also knew she got underneath a lot of people's skin in his circle, and it would only be a matter of time before they started their shit. Rochelle was anxious to know how it worked in my world. It wasn't that different from hers; we both didn't perform any services for free. So, she asked if she could be my plus one for my next private gig. Rochelle said she didn't want a cut of the money; she just wanted another piece of me.

"Come on, you gotta take me! He'll just have to get in where he fits in," she teased, making it clear how badly she wanted to come along and eat me out for aesthetics. "His dick will stay hard, watching me turn you out. That night with George was nothing. Wait until I have you all to myself."

So, one night Rochelle went with me to the North Side where I met up with another client, LaDell Starling. LaDell traveled the world with his sports agency, 69-Stars: Peru, Japan, Hawaii, and even Africa.

LaDell, standing just shy of seven feet, was slender and muscular. His physique was sculpted and refined. Strands of prominent muscle carved out by years of overseas basketball and all-night fuck sessions. God created everything from the hardness of his chest to the curvature of his oblique muscles that connected down into the V-shape of his groin.

Word on the street was there was no word. Nobody talked. Not about him. LaDell's pockets ran baby deep back then, especially for a man his age. He kept his sex life as private as possible and paid a pretty penny to keep it that way. He was a prominent baller that came back to Pittsburgh after his career-ending ankle injury. Living the high life of a not-that-close-but-close NBA celebrity, he had his choice of women. He was twenty-six, handsome, dressed real flashily, stood six feet-nine inches tall, drove a phat-ass Lincoln truck, and owned two condos: one here and one in Florida.

His dick game was intense, and whenever he called, I picked up. I went to the dick. I came *hard* on the dick. Though pretentious on the court, his sexual pangs of hunger were for tight lips. LaDell hated mouthy females and had gag orders from here to Australia. He said the quiet ones were hard to come by, and he had to make sure of it. This was perfect for Rochelle, if she was caught outside the marriage without her husband knowing, even though they do swing, she would be left with nothing.

"What does she look like?" LaDell asked in the rudest curiosity.

I knew what LaDell liked.

He liked fat asses and deep pussies.

He liked anybody that liked him.

He wore the most intoxicating colognes.

LaDell fucked as an art and he gambled.

In fact, that's how we hooked up...a ghetto-ass bet in the middle of a gentleman's club. One night, at a private party, there were some name droppers who knew people that knew people. To make a long story short, LaDell and I placed a bet that my Steelers were going to hammer the Cowboys. Our season sucked in 2016, four wins to five losses, and it was our time to shine again. But the cowgirls was a group of competitors that didn't back down so easy. "If my Steelers win, you have to take me out on a date," I slammed my twenty onto the marble counter.

"And if my Cowboys win, you have fuck me all night until the sun comes up." LaDell slammed his twenty down to stake his claim on the pussy. He brushed off a few females that night until he circled around to me.

"Oh really? You think your dick can hang with all this ass? You don't know me, sir."

"Naw, you pretty, red motherfucker. You don't know *me*." LaDell was the only man I ever allowed speak to me that way. It was the way he sweetened his voice like syrup whenever he said it. His baritone dropped and his dick got hard as a rock.

We wagered our money and waited for the battle to end. Every game was a fight to the finish between the two rivals; and when they beat us 35 to 30, I had to make good on my trash-talking—and did; bouncing back against his nine-inch dick as we watched the sun come up behind the trees.

"Don't be bringing no jiggaboos with you. I want my dick to stay hard," LaDell expressed.

The reference itself was offsetting, considering Rochelle is a chocolate goddess that is eloquent in every way. Her tiny frame towers in confidence. Never disrespecting herself and firm in her purpose—she wears the scars of life fiercely. Her hair, back then, was reminiscent of the Afro era: black, shiny, and full of power. Her lips full and cherry-like. Her thighs rubbed together from her muscle mass and synchronized her hips with each sweet step. They created that perfect space for the tiniest ray of sunshine to permeate through.

See, LaDell's Diabetes sometimes kept his blood flow weak, thus the need for the women he slept with to stay quiet in case it happened. Limp dick labels traveled fast in the sports community and had LaDell's life on public display. Few overseas ball players were in the Burgh, and the ones that played had clout. If that information leaked out, LaDell would lose his dick status for sure—*and that was everything to him*. It gave him special passes that weak lovers wished to acclaim.

The thing was, LaDell wasn't shit. Even LaDell knew he wasn't shit, making promises to me, and every woman he lured, just to get the secrets. LaDell flashed his money at thirsty hoes. He hinted at fancy cars, extravagant places to shop, and far-away trips. LaDell knew that made my eyes big—sweet-talking me right out of my panties. Half the time I didn't bother wearing any, knowing they'd be flying across the room as soon as I walked through the door.

I would do the nastiest shit with him, allowing him to fuck me in the ass to prove how raw I was sexually. Then, LaDell would re-nig on his promises after his dick got wet.

"Don't worry. I got you." Those were LaDell's favorite words.

"I'll make it up to you next time." Were usually the others.

LaDell used his status like any other athlete or client before him. LaDell lured me into his world with empty promises. He usually dumped one thousand dollars on the counter and the number to Uber with it.

At times, LaDell was a cold bastard. He said slick shit under his breath to anger me like I was the reason why people didn't know who he was. It wasn't like they were highlighting him on Sports World for a triple-double shot with two seconds left in the game or anything. Nobody knew about his African shoe commercial over here. Nobody cared about his Italian watch deal with Kisarra. That was international shit that we didn't patronize.

His rudeness pissed me off at restaurants when people didn't recognize him. The waitresses that did recognize LaDell were probably fucking him. Hell, LaDell was running a close second to Rochelle in the 'fuck the city' department. I'm surprised they never bumped into one another in that scene. Often, when we hung out at the outlet malls and he was making up for his last broken promise, he hurried me to the side when fans *did* ask for his little funky ass autograph.

"Move over, girl."

Then, after an all-day shopping spree, we dined at the most bougie eateries. At dinner, LaDell bought rounds of bourbon shots for the bar to loosen up the sticks everyone apparently had stuck in their cracks, according to him. And once the smoothness of the spirit settled in, he softened up like a fluffy teddy bear. He loved when we snuggled up close after a hot and intimate love-making session.

"I love the way your body smells," he chanted often; and as he got lost in the aroma of my pheromones, could get talked into anything.

"I need a new purse."

"Um, hm. I got you."

"I want to go to Punta Cana."

"I'll get tickets."

When he sipped the woodsy elixir, he no longer stereotyped a rude boy fishing for social attention or complements, but a smooth operator that was ready to dick me down. LaDell got fancier with his words, while creative in his love making. He had to be. Willing to go the extra mile for bragging rights after, the wrong position, or person, could be detrimental to his fuck game.

He didn't like me being on top because the blood flow stopped when resting on his back to fuck. He said that it was the damage in his arteries from his condition. LaDell stayed on top because it kept the circulation flowing, sometimes all night and into the morning, as birds chirped to awaken the new day. We were good for that. The first time we fucked until daybreak, LaDell couldn't believe I hung with him like that.

"Woman, the sun is up! Are those fucking birds?" he questioned as his hips continued moving. His leg muscles puffed up from the work he had put in. His veins were at total capacity. One more pump and they would have burst from underneath his skin. LaDell nutted multiple times in his little, white hand rag as he would stand before his big, metal fan to cool the sweat from his body. He made a few moves here and there with some upside-down fancies. Most times, it was me in the inverted position while he stood. Most times, he held me around my waist to secure me from slipping out from his coconut-oiled grip.

In India, LaDell studied practices to dominate his skill level during his stay. He learned how to make women orgasm from any position. He paid a lot to understand it, and I, practicing with him, was instructed in its fine art. I was ready to test what I had learned through him, with Rochelle.

The way it squirted in LaDell's face was proof enough to him that he knew what he was doing. I would never verbally admit to it, but he thought it was my orgasm spraying in his face. LaDell was too dumb to realize he was receiving golden showers and that his ten-thousand-dollar investment would have better results if Mr. Willy taught him.

LaDell and I never kissed; that was too personal for him. We just sucked, fucked, and sweat; heavily breathing the whole time. Luckily, we only had the blood flow issue once. That's how I learned about the gag contract between him and other women. LaDell whipped out this wordy piece of paper and asked me to read it and sign accordingly.

Before Rochelle and I arrived at his condo, I could tell he was anxious. I could hear it in his voice over the phone. I hadn't seen him in close to a year, and he was eager to get it on since he was back home. LaDell wanted to get the preliminaries out of the way so it wouldn't interrupt the night. LaDell arranged for the doorman to hand us some papers that needed to be signed before we were allowed up.

"Girl, is he for real?" Rochelle questioned as she read the information and laughed.

The spring in his pants awaited satisfaction, but he tried to be classy with it. LaDell didn't want to look like the asshole he was in front of guests. Whether he realized it or not, he already had with the limp dick contract.

When he came around the corner to greet us, I noticed the weight drop immediately. He tried to layer his clothing to conceal the loss underneath, but it was noticeable. His shoulders were less broad. He was checking his stance to make sure everything looked copacetic. He was probably questioning himself if I noticed the difference.

LaDell's frame looked skeleton-esque. His cheekbones extended beyond the edge of his face. Even the skin under his eye sockets was no longer plump and supple, but gaunt and disheartening. Maybe his thyroid was hyperactive, and he didn't know. I was blown away by how frail he looked. Fuck it, I'm saying it—he looked sick.

CHAPTER 8
Yeah, Bump Men

After Rochelle and I left disappointed, we decided to hang out downtown on the Three Rivers. We walked along the bank and watched the boats go by. Some boats had music blasting across the water as people celebrated another Steelers victory.

At first, it wasn't noticeable. When Rochelle would come into the club with George, I was ignorant of the flowers, the gifts, the compliments, and the hugs. Rochelle was entertaining the moment. Clients do that to show their appreciation, that's not uncommon. I would hang with them outside the club to make extra money; that's part of the industry and is a vast network. Hell, she's even sat in my chair at the school a time or two—George, too.

But when I felt the deep stir inside of me when she reached for my hand, it energized me. Her touch made my clit pound hard. That's what made her so tempting. Her approach was soft. Her delicate swoon of affection caught my attention. She made me curious. The tickles inside of my palm were her way of exciting my body and letting me know how badly she wanted to fuck. I knew what it meant.

The way she touched me when I danced for her and George, Rochelle was into it, really into it. I could tell she was intrigued on an intimate level. We talked about her life and she asked me about mine.

She shared how she grew up in Crawford Roberts, the most dangerous neighborhood in the Hill District, and built her life from the ruins of those violent streets.

"Barbering saved my life," she said with humility. "That's how I met George."

As we talked about what led us both here, she asked if I was young when it first happened. I was transparent with Rochelle and shared one of my first real experiences with a female.

"I was fourteen, for crying out loud."

I remembered the day like it was yesterday. It was on the couch in the basement. My best friend asked if she could try something and told me to pull down my panties and open my legs.

"And the next thing I knew, she climbed on top of me and was grinding." I hit the gar and passed it to Rochelle.

Rochelle shared her experience and how tender hers was. "She masturbated me on the 20 Owl train that ran after midnight in Philly. I moved there for three years after I graduated from barber school." Rochelle starts describing how the women in Philly were bold and how she linked up with some random chick after a rap concert. "The tunnels were dark; only an old couple was back there with us. She kissed my neck, and when she slid her tongue into my ear, she started circling my clit until I came on her fingers." She rubbed her digits together for dramatics, took the gar, and inhaled a long draw of the Rasta leaves.

"I've heard about you and how good you are to the people you entertain," I started. "They call you a Sugar Mama out here in these streets."

"Really?" Rochelle questioned. "I don't know about all that. I like spoiling who I'm with. If I'm happy, everybody is happy," she voiced.

I gestured for the two of us to sit down and chill on a bench facing the water and away from everyone.

"I'm not that much different than you are. I like spoiling the person I'm with, too. I just haven't found the right person," I told her.

"Whenever I share things with people, it's like they start judging me," she voiced. "Everybody thinks I'm not supposed to be anyone other than George's wife and Chelle the Barber."

Then, she shared how she wanted people to see Rochelle, the woman, in her freeness. Free to be who she wanted to be and freedom from George. She asked more detailed questions about what my first timer and I did in the basement.

"We were trying to be quiet. Hell, Mary thought we were down there listening to music."

"So, you came while she was grinding on you or eating you out?"

"Grinding. She tried to eat me out, but I didn't like her scratchy tongue. I just pulled her panties down and pulled her up to me."

"Damn, Gianna! You have been a freak for a minute."

"Yeah, I guess so," I replied, and at that moment, I realized my demons had run deeper. Mary deeper. I was too embarrassed to mention that sleaze. "I used to masturbate a lot." Words spilled from my mouth like a confession bucket.

"I masturbate thinking about you," Rochelle confessed. "A lot."

There was a cool breeze that sifted through the air that night. It caused her nipples to swell from underneath her shirt. Her thin, cotton tee failed to hide any sexual urgencies. As she talked about her disappointment in George to LaDell, she mentioned how badly she still wanted to do me. Feeling flushed on the inside, I wanted to touch her, grab her, and slob her down. I held back since we were in public. I could have played with my pussy right there in front of her while she watched. Knowing it was the weed that made me feel that way. It always did. At that moment, I understood Mary and why she had no fear. The weed gave her the courage to do what her emotions felt. I wanted to reach over and taste Rochelle's lips, both of them. The moment was perfect. The atmosphere evoked a scripted pornographic movie ready for action.

"Has he always been that rude? I mean, signing papers at the door?" She started complaining about LaDell's immature action. "It just looked like he played you. Why do you tolerate that?" Rochelle asked while she eyeballed my every move. "It was obvious he didn't cherish your goodies," she leaned in and whispered.

"That's just how it is. I'd be a fool to think LaDell keeps his dick in his pants until he gets back home to me," I explained.

"That's too bad. By the looks of it, he doesn't keep it in there for long. He didn't look so good. When did you say you fucked him last?" Rochelle questioned.

"Over a year ago. Don't worry, I'm negative, if that's what you're thinking. You know how George is. We get tested every month. He doesn't play about that. Even though some of the girls look worn out, we're clean."

"I forgot about that." Rochelle paused for a second before she continued. "You're a good woman, girl. He doesn't know what's in front of him. Men are such fuck ups," she added.

"I know it. He's young."

"You are, too. That's no excuse. Because you know a bitch like me would come along and make you forget about men like him," she confirmed with confidence.

"Chelle, you crazy!"

"I'm dead serious."

"I might end up and like it." I laughed, but on the inside, I was seriously contemplating how true her statement was. Knowing I *would* probably love it, end up turned out, and give up dick forever.

"I'd make sure of it," she said under her breath. "Hey, I need to stop by my house for a minute once we leave here. I need to take care of something I've been putting off for a while. Would you mind?" Rochelle asked me sweetly as the gar was smoked to the eye.

"Sure. Sorry about tonight, though. LaDell would have been a great first time."

"Don't worry. It will be," Rochelle confirmed before we travelled to our next destination.

After a ten-minute ride through the plush hillside of the city, we pulled up to a house that sat off the side of a secluded neighborhood and one George had to clue she owned. It looked like her old residence prior to marrying him and the one she failed to sell.

The red brick and stucco fortress sat high atop Mount Washington and hosted a four-hundred-and-fifty-foot drop not far from the Three Rivers. It nestled between the Monongahela brush and the mountains of Coal Hill. The view was spectacular. I could see clearly across the skyline and watched the fowl of the night take flight. They flew in unison, creating different patterns of beauty and breaking free into the wind. They circled swiftly high in the atmosphere, gawking at their tireless fleet. Spinning in a whimsical flair, I noticed the green plain of grass in its vastness and how the lunar glow of exquisiteness extended beyond the pasture. Its magnificence of how the moon blazed white in its glory along on the crest. The beauty of God's haven was right here. The stillness ushered peace and tranquility as it illuminated the sky and reflected from the dewy grass like an oil painting.

"Wow, this is beautiful up here, Rochelle." Its perfection mesmerized me. The moon hung amidst the blue dusk of skin that rotated for its night shift.

"Follow me."

Rochelle gave me a quick tour of her hidden treasure as we walked inside. Eclectic in its culture's design, African headpieces graced the entry. Linen cloth upholstered her finest seats in front of the window. The gold panes electrified the awaiting sunrise at dawn. She disappeared into a room and called me back to where she was.

"Check this out," she said while placing a DVD into the player. "I haven't been here in months," she disclosed as she told me to sit in the chair beside her nightstand.

The velvety smoothness of the seat made me feel warm and fuzzy all over. The center bump in the cushion was new; it kissed my lips as I sat. As I moved my body around to relax, the rolling hill of beads massaged my clit in comfort.

"Oh."

Rochelle reiterated how exotic the video was. I agreed. I watched the Latina's pornos plenty of times, mentally disappearing from my suitors. The perfectly bodied actress was a treat to watch with her sexy moans, fat ass, and juicy pussy lips that got devoured by the other female actress. Watching her made me nut faster while with them. Rub, lick. Rub, lick.

Then, Rochelle asked me if I was warm because she was feeling a little stuffy. I told her yes.

"It will cool down in a second," Rochelle confirmed. "I need to open these windows to get a fresh breeze," she shares as she moves throughout the house.

There was an instant drop in the temperature. I felt the capillaries in my breasts tighten. My nipples started rising from underneath my bra. Rochelle was pulling a Mr. Willy move. Turning the air on in the dead of fall was a nipple popper. Indian Summers were common in Pittsburgh and sudden spikes in the temperature were not uncommon. It caused two people to generate a different heat.

I felt like a young girl about to lose her virginity, both nervous and inexperienced. It wasn't my first time being with a woman, but this was different. It felt more intimate. She took the jacket from my hands before her next order.

"Stand up for a second."

I did.

Rochelle removed a pair of underwear I was partially sitting on.

"Sorry, let me get this up over here." She threw her underwear, and some other goodies, into a hamper, stuffed in the corner. "I'm going to..." she stretched her leg out to get between her pile and me. And as she bent over, her breasts intentionally brushed against my leg. "I'm just trying to find this toy," Rochelle rambled as she shuffled through the pile beside me.

"A toy?"

"Um-hm," she spoke; and as she rose, licked her lips with anticipation.

Her movements were slow. She paused at every section of my body to admire it. She gently touched my thighs as she continued exploring with her hungry stare.

"It's the toy I'm going to use to make you cum again. Your pussy is so sweet." Rochelle stopped and stared at me for a moment. She flicked the handheld machine to green and licked her lips.

I stared back at her with the doe in my eyes. The seductive moans behind us drowned out in a room full of faded silence and her buzzing toy. Rochelle looked at me and began breathing in erratic patterns of hesitation.

"I can't hold this any longer," she said as she stepped closer and rushed in to kiss me with every desire she had been holding inside. "I could eat your pussy out for days."

The taste of Kush and my sweet juices still lingered on her tongue. Rochelle had morphed into a fiend like Mr. Willy. Rochelle was cracked-out. Scratching on the corner and hunching over in the middle of the street.

I grabbed her face while her mouth had a hold of mine. The sound of wet tongue kissing echoed against the four walls. My desires responded to her naturally as I forwarded the lower part of my body and pressed against hers. She whispered dirty, nasty shit against my lips as we embraced one another.

"Your clit is juicy like a grape."

"Run your finger up my crack."

"Oh yes, suck on my cherry titties."

Rochelle wildly rotated her tongue in and out of my mouth. She placed the vibrator in between us and the low drums of the motor waved against our pussies in a crotchless hold. Before I knew it, I grabbed her ass and started grinding. My breasts, cupped in her hands, were warm supports as she leaned back to push her pussy against mine even harder.

"Ah! Ah! Ah!" she called out in her pumps.

I could feel the orgasm mounting underneath my skin. I knew I was going to cum fast. That had never happened before, not even with Mr. Willy.

Rochelle pushed the device from between us. She slid her hand down into my pants and touched my moist zone with passion. I put my fingers against her body. We moved in slow, exotic motions grinding against our hands, doing bunny hops to fasten the tingle. As my fingers slid across her labia, it wet my fingers and made her drip like molasses. She let out a helpless cry of disbelief. Rochelle took her fingers and stretched my panty material sideways to feel my lips. She tweaked my clit between her index and middle digits. Each touch sunk me deeper into her seduction as we undressed.

When she poked her fingers into my wet pussy, I gasped. I circled my fingers around her clit, too. I applied pressure and slid one of my fingers into her. Rochelle moaned as we finger fucked each other while the high screams of 'Donna Does Dallas' disappeared into the backdrop of our heavy lesbian rendezvous. She removed my pants. I pulled her shirt over her head. I leaned over and kissed her warm breasts as I stripped off her undergarments. We were both wet as hell. Her juices dripped from the tips of my fingers with delight.

"You taste delicious," I said as I smeared her secretions all over my lips. "Lick it."

"Mm, with pleasure," she whispered as she devoured both samples.

At that moment, I wanted to eat Rochelle the fuck out. I knew how it should feel. It required pressure and gentleness. Rochelle beat me to it and ordered me to lie down on the bed first. I did. She wanted to taste my sweet juices. I wanted her to. There was nowhere else for me to go. Rochelle longed to satisfy me, and I was too far gone to turn back.

She kneeled on the floor and separated my legs. Once she stroked her long, hot tongue over my pussy—that was it, and it was hooked. Fuck going to hell. I didn't care at that point. I just wanted to cum in her mouth. It felt too good not to enjoy. The intimacy was intoxicating. I didn't care about the consequences. It felt like I had been restricting myself sexually all my life. I knew that a man would never be able to satisfy me like this and make it feel as good as this did—no matter how big the dick was.

Rochelle moaned as she puckered her mouth against mine. It made me mutter with satisfaction. I'll never forget it. I could hear the saliva and pussy juices mixing like a lustful concoction. She went straight for my soul when she fucked me with her tongue while her lips latched onto my clitoris. She used them together in perfect unison. I couldn't believe how fucking good her head was. I loved how she moved her tongue in and out of me in sensual rhythms that rolled with every insertion.

"You like that, Gianna?" Rochelle questioned as she separated her mouth from my clit and slid her tongue in and out of my pussy without skipping a beat. She didn't even wait for my response before she went in again and placed her mouth back over my clit. She moved her head from side to side then, back, and forth; slowly, putting her tongue deeper into my canal of unsatisfied lust.

"Oh!" I called out.

I was speechless, reached down with mad energy, and grabbed Rochelle's natural curls forcefully. She crawled up my body, climbed on top of me, and we started to grind. Her soft, juicy meat moistened our clits as we slid against one another with pumps of pleasure. She stopped and looked down at me as if she was in total awe.

"This is how you taste. I love it," Rochelle stressed as she plunged her three-inch tongue down my throat and kissed me until we were pumping again. "I've wanted to do you for a long time, and my head game is about to rock your world." She panted hot bursts of air into my ear as she spoke, and spat my pussy juice back into my mouth.

I swallowed my sweetness in agreement. We were grinding the fuck out of one another. Then, Rochelle reached down between us and entered my opening with two of her fingers.

"Yes." I gasped for air as I pumped. "Your fingers feel like a dick."

"Wait until my strap-on fucks you." She hissed as she slipped another finger into my secret box. That's when I felt the burn when she pushed her way in slowly. She didn't want to cut me with her fingernails. Then, Rochelle slowly removed her fingers and placed all three of them into her mouth. I was so wet. The fragrance of sweet fruit filled the room. I was creaming everywhere. Before I knew it, Rochelle had slid back down between my thighs and printed her name on my nodule with her mouth.

The strokes of her tongue against my wet pussy aroused every part of my soul. While her mouth stayed fixed on my mini dick, she moved her head around, applying the pressure I needed to climax. In quick rotations, she reached under my ass and began thrusting me upwards against her mouth. She rocked my body, fluttering her tongue against my clit, and alternated her tongue in and out of my pussy hole until she could feel my orgasm pounding against her lips.

"Oh, yes, Rochelle!" I called her name out over and over. *Where am I? Am I in Wonderland? Is this happening?*

I squirted months of orgasmic tension right into Rochelle's mouth. She watched as I gasped for air, speaking strange obscenities, and rolled my eyes into the back of my head. Rochelle waited for my climax to turn over completely before she softly kissed my inner thighs, my stomach, and my trembling hands. She caressed my body as the tingling pulses subsided and my breathing slowed. As Rochelle stroked the outer rim of my pussy lips, she gently entered me again.

"Mmmmm." I immediately jerked with orgasmic convulsions when she rubbed her palm against my pelvic meat while her middle finger tickled my clit. It was unlike anything I had ever experienced. Thrusting her hand in fast strokes to make my mini dick swell again and beat with power.

Then, Rochelle climbed on top of me and extended my legs, stretching my legs in a V-shape to scissor against my pussy and ride. I was still releasing as our pussies stroked and pumped. Rochelle thrust against my lips with slow, controlled hip thrusts. The juiciness of our secretions smacked in desperation as orgasms rolled from our bodies like a broken dam racing down a flooded stream.

"Yes, bitch, this pussy is mine!" Rochelle started screaming.

I could feel her clitoris pounding against mine. I grabbed her ass and moved with her. Juice splashed everywhere: between our thighs, on the sheets, and against the headboard.

"Fuck George," Rochelle panted as she reached for her seven-inch-dick strap-on and flipped me to my stomach.

Men are worthless. All they bring is trauma to the table. I've witnessed it all my life. The gifts they bear only come with a dick in hand. I was irritated with their shit. They never made me feel like this. I always thought bigger was better, especially after living in Texas. Big dick only brought more significant problems and plenty of trips to the doctor.

Here it was, the lustful patterns of the flesh playing its repeat hit in heavy rotation. Too bad that a sin bared in haste is condemnation, but the freedom of acceptance is joyous, for its shortened satisfaction welcomes the foolish heart that bleeds it.

I tried to pretend like it wasn't in me. I pushed the magazines further into my school and the strip club lockers. Hiding my imperfection was becoming complicated at work. Erasing my digital track from web searches on the public computer took longer to cover. Looking at my coworker's undress after their set had me drooling when they lifted their legs to remove their shoes, and their pink pussies glistened from the dance sweat. I stared at beautiful women as they passed by me on the street, constantly comparing my ass to theirs. I quickly looked away when they caught me drooling. I denied its desire for a long time, but Mary started it, the escorting perfected it, and Rochelle confirmed it.

"Yeah. fuck men."

Tilling The Land

CHAPTER 9
Present Desires Awake Dead Pasts

But that was then, and this is now. Things are different. I'm in my mid-twenties, winging it as a couple with a forty-year-old cougar. After Rochelle decided to leave George, I bounced with her. She five-fingered a few stacks for our move and left signed divorce papers in its place.

Once we left Pittsburgh and moved to Bradenton, Florida in 2017, things changed here, too. It took us a few years to acclimate to this weird ass place. Our rendezvous became more immediate, like family. Not knowing anyone in this small town has us dependent like poor babies. Rochelle and I rely on each other for everything.

Rochelle almost takes on a motherly role that warms my soul. She kisses my forehead at night, and her caring gestures make me feel loved. Her girlish spirit also makes me forget she is fifteen years older than me. We call each other Boo Ma, not to speak our names in public; it takes us back to our teenage years when we snuck around with older men and created fake names.

Rochelle found a place to work while we went on a mini shopping spree one November and started staging windows at a bougie fashion house in Lakewood Ranch. Her personality allows her to move within different business circles. On my end, I work odd gigs to help pay for a place we never live. I started dancing at The Cheetah Club and doing various photo shoots for local ads, including promotional flyers for wannabe entertainers like Supa Stone still holding on to childhood rapper dreams.

Along with a side hustle of weed vapes here and there, we're getting by. Rochelle is gone setting up store windows most of the time and tells me how she wants to avoid opening a barber shop here. George would find her for sure. She is uncertain of his temperament and what he would do to her if he ever saw her. George hates a thief. The connections he has would only be a phone call away. All he needs is a blip on the radar.

No credit cards. No bank accounts. Burner phones. Cash only. Hats and sunglasses everywhere we go. No pictures. We can't post anything on social media. We get paid under the table. Work for three months and never show back up. Every angle is covered underground style. We are cautious in our movements and know the game.

Rochelle and I shift around like thieves in the night. Sneaking around with Mr. Willy helped me perfect how we finagle in these streets.

Rochelle suspects George has a bounty on her head for taking a hundred grand and one of his bricks from the bedroom safe. Rochelle's credit cards are unusable because they give a location, and she maxed out the limits before we left. That totaled twenty-five thousand from the big ones, and another three thousand from the other two. We were sitting on enough money to live comfortably for another year, but by the middle of year two, Rochelle had concerns. When we cut the brick, she knew the clock was ticking.

We vowed not to cut the cocaine unless it got worse, and it did. That's why working under the table was imperative to our plan. Cash only and at the time of purchase. No digital transfers. Money orders meant showing identification, and we couldn't do that either. If George put out a missing person's report and Rochelle's license number gets scanned, we'd be screwed.

Then in the beginning of year three, in 2020, a plandemic sweeps the globe and instantly changes millions of lives. Most die due to their poor life habits and the unforgiving attack it throws at the lungs by creating an overproduction of mucus.

Then, the gigs stop coming, the phone stops ringing, and everything suddenly comes to a screeching halt. Everyone is horrified by the fear that sweeps the planet. For two years, the world shut down. Businesses collapse. Basic supplies are non-existent. Limit two of any paper products, if any are left on the deserted shelves. Before long, we cut up rags to wipe our asses. We'd have folded months ago if it wasn't for Rochelle's weed hustle, the unemployment benefits, and PPP loans circulating in the community—especially paying twenty-four hundred dollars for a two-bedroom apartment in the projects.

Now, in 2023, there is a requirement to take the genetic-mutating death shot to keep your job in all hospitals and public businesses; its emergency authorization forces millions in line—including Rochelle.

"Think of this government's history. I'm not taking another vaccine of theirs. They may slide micrograms of that death shit in there. No thank you," I assert to Rochelle. "It's bad enough they're trying to inject the meat with that shit, too."

I begged her not to do it. All she had to do is read the information. But like the Black culture is known for not reading anything to gain knowledge, she stands in line out of fear of losing her job. The news fails to highlight the tens of thousands dropping dead to their feet days later from the mutated blood clots enlarging in their bloodstreams. The propaganda repeated lies over the radio and television daily. The fake physicians signed off on the toxic potion full of heavy metals, genetic codes designed to decompose the human body rapidly, three strains of HIV, and aborted fetuses to polish the concoction; all to create a new era of autistic mutants. Like your straw man's social security number, the booster-heavy immunization becomes the qualification to receive any state or federal assistance. The CDC's and doctor's Hippocratic Oath ooze with greed as they promote its experiment like so many pills pushed before it. Its feared dependence is the mandate for scheduled inoculations to enter schools, colleges, and becomes a requirement to process passports for international travel.

The world ends up vaccinated and afraid. We wear masks like the air is tainted, and it is, but the actual disease lies in the hearts of men that walk ignorantly in their false protections. Deep in their slumber, the lost sheep proclaim their false faith in God, giving the RNA modified potion more praise for its false-positive results. They believe their government is a friend, but the sparkle of fear keeps them in line, thinking they are protected from man-made death.

The vaxxed contaminate the atmosphere with their microscopic particles of flesh layered in spiked proteins. The masks now protect against their shedding skin that fogs the night. And to add insult to injury, inflation is on the back end of an economic collapse, the eviction mandate ends thirty days before to the holiday rape season of Christmas, and we're being kicked out of our apartment because Rochelle didn't sign the lease in time.

For a while, everything was tolerable. We made it through the senseless lies of the media. We're alive. We only need to sit outside and drink warm lemon water, the very opposite of what is told over the news. Now, I'm smoking weed, drinking yak, and eating a nympho's pussy seven days a week to earn my keep.

"My job is moving me to Jersey," Rochelle says before she pulls me close and kisses me. Her spaghetti sauce tingles my lips with garlic. "We move in a couple of days."

"Move?"

The thing is, I didn't want to move back up north—the severe depression of eating every thirty minutes to kill boredom. Closed-up in the house, gaining twenty pounds every winter. My legs and ass thicken to insulate my body from the cold. The sun, dead in the sky for eight months or more, spreads gloom and sadness in full glory.

Why would I want to go back to that? The truth is, I didn't want to be in a relationship with a woman. I didn't want to go to a state still on lockdown. Florida's governor ain't taking no shit and told everybody to "Fuck off!"

"Move back to my home in Pittsburgh if you ain't feeling Jersey. I don't want you out here swinging in the breeze," she adds in a hurry.

Pittsburgh? Mr. Willy would smell me the minute the flight landed. If I did take her offer, his Spidey senses could radar my location instantly. We have a weird connection like that. He always knows when I'm nearby. Maybe the taste of my pussy still lingers on his depraved tongue like a sealed coat of wax, loyal and ready to service for every meal

I don't know what I am going to do. Rochelle is leaving, and I don't have a place to stay. I feel abandoned again—no concrete stability. People are coming and going at will. I'm not one to shack up with man, but at this point, I may have to call one of my old customers and see if they'll be willing to take in a stray, maybe LaDell. I remember him boasting about a property he invested in near Sarasota and how he dips down here to get away when it's cold. Rochelle begs me to come and can't understand why I want to stay here and struggle. Her offer only takes my progressive steps backwards.

"I have a dream."

"A dream? Who are you, Martin Luther King Junior, now? You have a dream to do what? Go back to hoeing?" She angrily plops noodles into the boiling water.

"No, and don't throw that up in my face! Why would you say that?"

"What else you got? I'm just trying to figure out why you don't want to come with me."

"I want to have a family," I tell her.

"A family? Where is that coming from? What in the fuck does wanting a family have to do with anything that's going on right now?" she badgers me. "Bitch, we're just trying to stay alive! We need a place to live, and my job is helping. What else you got?"

"I just feel like I'm going in the wrong direction."

"With me?" she questions.

"With everything. I got caught up and let it go too far. You know I can't live like this," I add. "I've been living from pillar to post all my life. It's exhausting, Chelle. I don't even know who I am. I'm tagging on to everybody else's shit!"

"Now your morals are catching feelings suddenly?" she asks. "You ain't have no fucking morals this morning sucking my pussy."

"Neither did you, tramp! Tongue all up in my ass!" I bend over and demonstrate by dragging my middle finger in slow motion. "Don't act like you're any better than me, bitch! I want all the things you had. I feel incomplete. Security. A family. Things I've never experienced. People who have my back."

"Oh, so I ain't never had your back? How you think you got down here, hoe?"

"Hoe? Bitch, please! You left your husband, not me! All this shit I'm doing with you is not giving me the things I want," I stress.

"Neither is playing the fuck bag," Rochelle says under her breath and immediately stops, realizing her words cut through me by the sign of tears falling from my eyes.

"You have a lot of nerve. You were one of the biggest hoes in Pittsburgh! I deserve some fucking stability. You have no clue what I've been through!"

"I'm sorry. I didn't mean to say that. You don't know what *I've* been through." Rochelle stops to dry her hands. "All that family shit is overrated. So is being with a man. And kids? Fuck them, too. All they do is tear up your body, steal your youth, and tell you to kiss their ass after you've busted yours to give them everything you didn't have. I also thought it would give me everything I wanted, but it didn't. All it did was leave me in debt and give me gray pussy hairs!" She laughs. "Look, you sacrifice half of your life raising, and hopefully nurturing, your kids into productive citizens for eighteen years or more. Then, when you look up, you're forty-something years old and you don't know what the fuck to do with yourself," she says sarcastically as she reaches for her Rolodex sitting on top of the refrigerator to look up one of her connections to help me. "Good luck with that. I've been down that road already. I'm on some different shit and I want you with me."

"What are you talking about?"

"Three people, one union," Rochelle discloses.

I don't know what to say; but I'm positively certain that any state north of Florida is not an option, but her proposition tickles my ears and clit.

"Polygamy? You want that?"

"I do, but it doesn't matter anyway. I must separate from George. I can't do anything until I'm divorced."

Working in the fashion house helps Rochelle connect in new circles and bump a few elbows. Her street resume has even developed a few good relationships with a dentist, a decent bakery, and a local soy candle maker close by with tantalizing scents and lofty names, like Pussy Power, Jiz Juice, and Creamy Bondage. For someone trying to stay under George's radar, Rochelle's incognito cover sucks.

She connects me with a real estate associate who owns a salon with a living space attached to it on the second floor. She tells him of my situation, and I move in. No questions asked. His beady eyes lust over me like the others. He claims all he wants is for us to go and have a drink. I can do that. I'll probably forget about his ample stomach, his wide afro, and little wee hands with a few drinks.

I started working as a shampoo assistant in the downstairs salon to earn some extra money. Thank God the essential workers keep this place afloat. I began doing some light cut and styling work to help during the busy holiday season. One appointment, the owner allows me to perform a full service.

"Wow, where did you come from?" She slicked the sides of her hair with her hands and commends me on a job well done. Her words vibrate against her mask.

"Up north," I reply.

"I have been looking for someone to cut my hair for a minute since I moved here. Hello, I'm Dedrias." She extends her hand for me to shake.

I meet it with a fist pump. "You know, Covid and all," my words muffle from underneath mine.

Growing up as an only child can spark creativity. Mr. Neft helped with that. All the dolls he bribed me with ended up with different haircuts. Short-styled cuts, bobs, and spiked shags were just a few. Between beauty school and Rochelle teaching me fade techniques, I cut well. It's another skill set for me to survive.

Hair and ass. Good combination.

Working in a salon is pretty good. It's a blessing how all of this is piecing together. I could be at The Salvation Army, or worse, under a bridge. As I turn to grab my alcohol to cleanse her neck, she hands me a one-hundred-dollar bill.

"Oh wow! Thank you!" I'm shocked by the amount of her tip. "Thank you...um..." I try to piece her name together in my head and draw a blank.

"Dedrias." She lightheartedly laughs at my response.

"I'm so sorry. I'm not good with names," I state.

"That's okay. My name isn't common." She looks at her reflection in the mirror to bask in her hairstyle, and for a split second, her image in the mirror is glitchy and not there.

"But I'll remember your face forever."

"Mm, that's good to know. I know not to do anything illegal around you." Dedrias jokes; and appeases her statement by clapping her hands. "I don't think you understand. No one in this town can cut. Hey, I was wondering if I could set up a regular time?" she asks.

I tell her that I can, and Dedrias comes in weekly for months and sends referrals. Many of them I found to be her acquaintances. One is her close friend, Kim.

Kim is quite peculiar. Between her giddy personality and obscure facial features, she is someone not easily forgotten. It's funny how her lips pucker when she speaks. They cover her protruding teeth. Kim sucked on her thumb as a toddler, but the wide gap between her bucky gumline angled her teeth in a bunny-like shape instead of the normal protrusion. They are not significant in size. They force you to look down at her voluptuous breasts, for which she fails to wear a bra. Her nipples are always ice hard.

The perkiness in their shape is what mesmerizes me. Her size C-cup respectively melons their attraction as she floats around the salon like a fairy. When she tells stories and engages the women with her comedic spiels, her curly, blonde hair bounces with glee. Her ends reflect twinkles of light to energize her movements against her Florida-tanned skin. However, prissier than Dedrias' other associates, her sense of humor outshines them all. Her petite frame often mistakes her for a young girl with its attractive innocence.

Then, one evening, Dedrias' husband, Sean, comes in to pay. His presence is strong but humbling. He resembles a gentle giant with his meek temperance and slothful movements. Sean's soft and pleasant face warms the shop when he stops by. His cocoa-brown irises reflect in Dedrias' smile when he flashes his eyes at her. He stands close to seven feet and pulls his wallet out. He wants everyone to know he can pay for his wife's service by opening his thick billfold of crisp bills. Sean helps by sweeping up and removing the salon trash when Dedrias is the last client. I tell him the owner cleans up before the salon opens, and Sean says it's not a big deal and that he's used to it.

Sean catches me observing him in his strange chitter-chatter and we both play it off as nothing. Sean twitches his neck while conversing; usually mumbling to himself in response.

"He's always talking to himself, girl," Dedrias says. "Don't pay any attention to him."

Sean moves with care when he handles Dedrias. Sean caters to her needs as a butler would: he opens doors, he playfully replies 'yes, ma'am' to her questions, and he gracefully extends his hand for her to take as she steps down from my chair.

Dedrias turns to him and accepts his invitation, innocently revealing her submissive side. It's beautiful to watch. Sean is gentle with her. The choreography is so beautifully scripted, resembling the elegant arrangement of ballet, and Sean pays attention to her every interchange to assist her. Sean adores Dedrias, and he supports her every step. I can tell they love one another by how they move together as a unit, intimately absorbing one another's energy. I sometimes see the sweet wind of seduction pass between them. I envy that as I watch them engage within their sumptuous love language.

CHAPTER 10
A Warning Before Destruction

"It's going to be another scorcher here today in Florida. Highs will reach the mid-to-upper nineties, with a few afternoon thundershowers in some areas. It's hard to believe it's spring with these temperatures. Elaine, what's happening with the latest report on this pandemic?"

"Well, Dave, COVID numbers are dropping thanks to vaccine efficacy. Globally, more than five and a half billion people are vaccinated, with Africa being the least immunized, sparking the Pure Bloods campaign to another level." She turns her casting chair to another camera. "In local news, another woman is missing after she didn't return home from her trip to the Bahamas. Lynita Hayward adds another to the growing list of women missing from the Tampa Bay area. Here is the most recent photo of her." A picture of Lynita flashes onto the screen. Her skin is caramel complected. Her eyes are striking. Her smile is blazing white. Her beauty is stunning. My mind takes burst photos: the width of her nose, how angled and Chinese her eyes slant, and how her jawline is strong and squared to her ears that her bushy hair tries to hide. "Her family and local church desperately ask anyone with any information to come forward. Authorities are finding similar connections between the women that stretch beyond New York, Denver, and New Jersey. If anyone has any information on her whereabouts, Sarasota Police ask you to call Crime Stoppers at 1-800-222-TIPS." She turns and centers her chair back to Dave.

I ran over and place my hand over the screen and Lynita's face, praying for a safe return. The way this world is now, if she's missing, that's not good. Sarasota is only a hop and a jump from where we are, which worries me. The targets are random. Key West, Tallahassee, and far as bo-dunk Bristol have missing residents in the baffling case. The station warns that the recording we are about to listen to is disturbing and to please mute the volume if sensitive to sacrificial content.

Faint screams and sharp slashes.

Deep growls that scuffle between heavy, wet thumps.

And bells that ring every eight beats in the recording.

It loops twice before the segment dramatically exits with heavy music and fades into a commercial. As disturbing as it was, there was something about the bell that caught my attention. The waves crashing behind it. The sonic heaviness that silenced everything.

I decide to go to church instead of brunch with the landlord. I stop to straighten the flimsy, full-length mirror behind the front door to check my curves and smooth over my brick house stance—thirty-six, twenty-four, forty, all packed within a five-by-five frame. I observe how my black, wavy hair cascades over my bronzed shoulders and how the space between my neck and collarbone is one of the softest parts of me. My birthmark is beautiful. As I age, it perfects itself, sometimes changing to brighter hues of red and becoming more defined. My lips are popping. My teeth are white. Cheese!

Grabbing my purse and my bible, I bolt out the door. On the way, the pleasant surroundings of statuesque oak trees and grazing cattle along Mendoza Road usher in a calming spirit. There is an absolute stillness that sits well with my soul. The community of early risers' wave in their yards as I drive by.

As my muffler sputterers into a space a few yards from the front of the sanctuary, I shuffle some empty water bottles on the floor and reach for my heels. I sneak in before the whole church notices and two male ushers race to give me a program for today's service. I avoid any direct eye contact with either one of them, bowing my head, and sit in an empty seat in the back. The sound in the sanctuary resonates with my spirit. I raise my hands and join in with the men's choir as they sing Amazing Grace.

"Good morning, everyone. I am Pastor Thomas King, and welcome to God's House. I want to start service out with prayer," he begins, going into detail about Covid and members affected by the pandemic. He goes into a hymnal praising God for the unexpected and divine healing of members and the return of the missing women on the news. He asks God to guide him to deliver His Word in spirit and truth.

Pastor King dances across the pulpit like I imagine David had done. His suit is casket sharp. His hairline is boot black. His sermon is soul-shaking. He adorns himself with the finest gold and the rarest silks. He graces the stage with a psalmist's truth. Getting right with God is vital to me right now. That's one thing Mary implemented while in her care, the importance of faith.

I notice how Deacon Thomas drives a new Cadillac. I witness Ms. Baskin's gifted new roof by another member's roofing business. They are obedient in ways unknown to me or any light that Mary shed. Their lives are flourishing. Mine, on the other hand, is a mess. To take hand-me-downs from my female lover and to live in some multi-purpose, one space, one toilet, salon apartment is proof of that. Doing the same thing repeatedly, expecting different results, is crazy. To repeat craziness is insanity, at least, as Pastor King says.

"Keep your focus on God and your eyes on Jesus, and everything will turn out fine," he would say periodically throughout his sermons. He encourages anyone in need to seek the Lord. "God will never let you down!" he shouts with authority.

After coming to God's House for a few weeks, I meet new people, join a few groups, and volunteer my time in the outreach programs. I help feed the homeless and visit the sick and the shut-in. I try and stay as busy as possible, filling my schedule with God instead of a man or woman. Changing my mindset. I try hard—adding more and more to my plate trying to forget. I can't shake these feelings of how Rochelle pleases every part of me with her warm tongue. My body, so used to getting off a few times a day, is going through withdrawal—the shivery tingles from the lack of sex when I softly press my pussy against my hand. Wanting Rochelle to stimulate my genitals as my orgasm rolls from her dangerous love.

My smiles are fake to them. The "I'm blessed" responses are automated. Masturbating to porn every morning to relieve the frustration of not fucking is clouding my head.

CHAPTER 11
Pick Your Battles

"We all have our temptations and ungodly desires to battle with daily!" Pastor King declares to his eager congregation and snaps me out of my hazy thoughts. "But don't let those temptations turn into sin." His eyes focus only on me, hiding from his conviction. "I know it's hard. Sometimes those temptations are too much to fight. You must push through if you want victory!" He nods his head and surveys the crowd that listens to his proper instruction. "Rebuke the enemy!"

The organ player swiftly slides his fingers across the keyboard and heightens the pastor's declarations.

"And if you lose that battle, God still forgives—no matter what you have done. Turn to your neighbor and tell them, 'God will forgive you,'" Pastor King declares in a calmer tone.

We all turn to our neighbors and speak in agreement. There are shouts of joy all over the sanctuary. Coco, one of the other stylists in the salon, is to my left. He texts telling me he has my ticket for the art exhibition in Tampa tonight. He mentions this new controversial artist that struck his interest, one social media scroll.

Coco discovered them on the social site RIPPED. The anonymous creator is making quite a name in the mâché arena of the art and sculpture sector. His pop-up shows strangely last for one viewing night only. Attendees must arrive between 7:28 p.m. and 7:58 p.m. for the walkthrough. Viewers must be inside at this time. Only on-time attendees will be permitted. The exhibit begins at eight o'clock sharp.

"YO ASS NEED TO BE READY ON TIME." He texts in all caps. "Everything is time allotted. The show starts at eight and stops at 9:10. Don't drag your ass."

I immediately direct my attention back to the pastor.

"God's forgiveness also comes with some lessons," Pastor King pauses and focuses only on me. "And some of you like to learn things the hard way." The congregation laughs at his declaration. "Quit going back to the very thing that God is blocking! Pay attention! There's a reason!" He demonstrates stern gestures with his index finger at points directly at me. "Don't go!"

"You better say it, pastor!" First Lady King shouts. Her devil-red nails fan high into the air.

The church is on fire. The organ player plays a random rendition of his keyboard skills. Miss Anne, a client, is shaking her tambourine with fast, controlled wrist flicks. Coco frees his hand from his friend's and stands to his feet, waving his handkerchief as he shouts and professes his praise.

"There is always a warning before destruction, saints. Those who have ears to hear, let them hear. Lord, have your way," Pastor King professes his obedience by calming the room with waving gestures. "Shh."

Minutes later, there is total silence.

"I don't know whom I'm talking to, but the Spirit urges me to speak. Don't be fooled by how people look." Pastor King stands firm and looks out at us with gleaming eyes as we await his profession. "Remember these words I speak, beloved." He shakes his hands into the air before he adds more and blazes his stare at me once more. "They are not who they appear to be. They are wolves in sheep's clothing. Wait, they can hear you? Lord, I don't understand. Oh, glory!"

He shouts with a thousand tongues and falls to his knees.

"Don't be looking at the wrong stuff! Pay attention!" He seals his face down into his palms. "If your spirit is telling you something' ain't right—it ain't right!" he speaks once more as he jumps to his feet and spins. His shoes shuffle across the floor. "Be mindful, saints. It could change the rest of your life as you know it."

Women start falling out. The organ player done passed out. The congregation starts shouting. Mad hallelujahs call out from the elders. I'm sweating. Coco's fanning. It's two o'clock, and we still need to complete the communion part. It may be four o'clock before we get out of here. If the choir sings one more song, or if another person gives one more testimony, I'm dropping to the floor, too. And when we are released at three thirty, I stop by the corner convenience store to pick up some wine coolers for the ride later. Pulling into an empty spot, I notice two gentlemen walking out. One, being quite taller than the other, immediately catches my attention.

I step out of my car and am caught off guard at how fine this brother is. I realize the other man is Sean. He notices me and waves hello. Then, I glance back at the other gentleman, hypnotized by the Florida sun reflecting off his coal, black skin. It burns like hot oil, reflecting the flames of enchanting temptation. It even vaporizes like black steam. I watch how it moves from his flesh with the breeze. The glistening sheen of coconut oil, almost blinding me, is blocking any quick glances from its reflection.

Covering my face from the other gentleman's glow, I follow the frame of his jawline, where his tight beard trims against his face. In the corner of his mouth is a toothpick nestled securely between his full-defined lips. They look plump and soft like pillows.

I followed further, wowed by the dominating wideness of his shoulders. His neck muscles are thick and look like small mounds of hard chocolate. His chest is full and muscular. Each sinewed fiber fights for the front line. He commands attention from the taper of his waistline to the bowlegged sturdiness of his legs. His thighs are thick and hulkish. I figure there is nothing wrong with taking control of the situation, so I speak.

No one replies.

"Oh, so you can't speak now?" I say in a joking manner. "Black folks always act brand new when they hang around new people," I add. "Don't make me show my ass, Sean. You know I just got out of church!"

Ha! Go ahead, Gianna!" Sean responds with a laugh and smile. "Did it burn down when you walked through the door?" He starts laughing hysterically in his high-pitched gurgle, so distinct in its goofiness it could be branded and sold in a honking horn near you. Sean nudges the other gentleman for his attention. The other gentleman looks up quickly, then back down at whatever is in his hand. "I had a cookie in my mouth. How are you doing?"

"I'm well. How've you been?" I casually ask him.

"Good." Sean steps out from beside the other gentleman.

"You always eating," the other gentleman chimes in and laughs as he stays near the door and scratches a lottery ticket.

His pinky nail catches me by surprise. As he rubs the ticket profusely and flicks away any remnants, he raises his finger to his face and itches his nose. The animation in his movement is bionic.

I target the sexiness of his smile as he laughs. His teeth glisten like ivory tusks, shiny and prominent. I was not expecting to see the two hollow depressions sink deep into his cheekbones like craters. His laughter triggers their sweet, almost innocent, presence that illuminates like sunshine around him. It softens his hard exterior.

"You, too, nigga." Sean curls his lip into his cheek as he speaks.

"And?" The other gentleman looks up from the scratch-off he's doing and shifts his toothpick. "Keep it up," he says jokingly. "You've been trying me all day."

"Oh, wait. Let me finish," Sean mentions before his flatulence breaks the air.

"Really, man?" The gentleman pushes him away.

"Now I'm done, dear sir. Carry on." Sean laughs as he playfully motions his peace sign back at him.

I ask Sean how Dedrias is. He tells me she's been busy with her candle business and she's doing fine.

"She has to finish some big orders," he says. Sean tells me that she desperately needs her hair done and will call me soon.

The other gentleman curses flagrant obscenities probably because of his losing ticket and the lingering smell. Sean and I pass small talk back and forth, all while never breaking my concentration from the other gentleman's dominant, black frame. His skin almost crystallizes a bronzed overlay when he moves against the sun. It shifts in hexagonal patterns and reflects the rays of celestial light. His shirt is tucked tight and neat; his khaki pants, though not pressed, are clean and fastened by a thick leather belt. His boots are scuffed, but they tell the story of a man who gets down on his hands and knees and is no stranger to hard work. The other gentleman almost sounds embarrassed by Sean's actions. It wasn't a gangster move at all. He fans the air around him and grunts.

"Yo, you stink." He jokes as he puffs the imaginary cloud of air to push the smell away.

I see his breath blow through the gap between him and, strangely enough, a green cloud of funk.

"My shit stinks for sure," Sean responds. "So does yours," Sean's tone is arrogant like there is more truth in his statement.

"No doubt," the other gentleman responds as he attempts a recovery. "Don't get embarrassed out here in front of this pretty lady," his voice drops to a lower bass and carries a sprinkle of fact.

"Nigga, please. You got jokes." Sean replies. "I don't need *no* help in *that* department," he stresses while he grabs onto his crotch and eggs the other gentleman on, boldly taunting him with his gestures as he grips his nut sack like a thug. He aims his words like darts that stab below the belt. "No help needed."

And there it is.

The dick roast begins.

I assess their caveman talk with extreme cynicism.

Their dialogue is off-balance; sounding like they read from cue cards or script a grade-B movie. Sean's statements aggravate the other gentleman a bit; his eyes cut at Sean with nerve. They stop and look at each other. Then, they both turn and look at me, staring blankly. The two go back and forth like children arguing over who gets to go first or who's better at what. Then suddenly, they look at each other and double up in amusement. The man's laugh is deep and rolls like the first break of thunder in a slow-moving storm. His sense of humor is quick and disturbing—like unexpected rain droplets on a sunny, hot summer day.

"Neither do I. I can reach what I *need* to reach. Don't ever think you have one up on me," the other gentleman emphasizes—pounding his truth like a gavel. And there it is, referencing to his dick and what it can do. "You look like you don't have a clue in that department," he professes the cut-down. He is defining Sean's unfamiliarity with control. Trying to secure the upper hand, he goes into another comedic spiel comparing Sean's sexual capabilities to a thirteen-year-old boy with drawn-up balls. His comment exudes the aroma of sexual ridicule. He shames Sean right on the spot like a weak bitch.

Men talk about sex in one form or another—whether it's about their size, what they can do, or how many women they've had.

"Do I need to pull out some fun facts for you?" Sean instigates. "Do I?"

The other gentleman turns his head strangely, twisting his neck like a confused dog. His stare is intimidating. He pauses to assert the moment. "Don't show off. You know you'll have to deal with me later."

Sean then steps closer to his face and smiles devilishly. "Stop playing. You know what time it is," Sean states.

"Okay, remember that." The other gentleman then stands back with a buck and nods. He knew when to withdraw. "Hello," he turns and says to me. "We're not as crazy as this sounds. Sean's just always got some stupid stuff to say in front of people. He's forgetful at times."

His shifty conversation throws me off. I have never been around a man that initially radiates sexiness, confidence, humility, and a splash weirdness simultaneously. It's strange to be in its presence. Intriguing in its little way, his existence makes me take notice, mainly when those qualities are present in serial killers, savants, and crazy motherfuckers. I nod my head in agreement as I continue to scan his rock-hard arms.

I could care less about their weird conversation or craziness. I am too busy watching his swollen veins pump powerful bursts of life from his aorta. I see the pulse of blood pumping from his neck, down his arms, into his massive hands, and into each knobby fingertip.

Quickly shifting my eyes to the middle of his body, the meaty thump continues across his midsection and groin, where I can almost see the rim of his shaft suffocating against the crotch of his pants. As I glance at it again, his head looks strangled against his thigh and looks to be bending his enormous appendage. He shifts his hips a little to the left, shaking his leg a little; then back to the right, loosening the chokehold it has on his huge cock. I am mesmerized by the energy this brother is giving off. My eyes, now glued to the dimensions of his package, are stagnant.

"Up here, sweetness," he mumbles under his breath and softly snaps his fingers.

"Ooo," the sound unexpectedly escapes my lips.

Startled but trying to play it off, I lift my head to be met by his glaring sunglasses. The absorbed sunlight blinds me from looking at his glorious energy. I quickly turned my attention to Sean.

"Max, this is Gianna," Sean introduces us with hesitation.

"Hello," Max says as he reaches out.

"Hello," I reply as I look up, extend my hand to shake his, and then...POW!

A bolt of electricity shoots between us as we connect.

"Interesting." Max pauses, inhaling the current passing amid our hands and savoring its nuance like it breathes new life into every orifice of his soul. "Mm, nice to meet you, Gianna."

"You as well, Max, but you might want to work on shocking people," I say.

"Funny. Are you talking about the handshake or where your eyes were looking?" Max displays a wide yet welcoming grin that exposes the two hollow depressions on his face.

Before I could answer his question, Sean interrupts our engagement.

"Max just moved here from Jersey," he states.

"Oh, I have a close friend that just moved up there," I respond.

"What made them want to do that?" Max asks. "It's still cold as hell up there."

"Their job. So, what brings you down to Boringtown?" I inquire.

"*Boringtown?*" Max questions.

The colloquialism, well known to Bradenton locals, is one whose name precedes it. Nothing happens here except for the traditional functions that rape wallets throughout the year: the Manatee Fair, the Sarasota Arts Festival, and the Hispanic Latino Festival are in heavy rotation from January to December. There are no big-ticket concerts. The Rib Festival in Palmetto is the only time we see famous entertainers. The mall has three good stores. Snowbirds populate most of the residences in this town. It's where retirees retire, and young families with old money send their children to tennis school to raise them while they travel the globe. The forty-year-old rappers that still believe they have a shot at fame perform at The Hall, everybody sells five-dollar jewelry, and Bradenton is plain ho-hum. So boring, that it's a relatively safe environment to live in.

This city was perfect for Rochelle; too bad her job became her deciding factor to leave. George would never connect her to this dried-up place. Most urban residents here travel to their freak spots: Miami, Jacksonville, and Daytona. To eat and shit in the same town is taboo, and since Max had just moved here from another city, he was not familiar with the term or the weight it carries.

"It's just a name you'll come to know the longer you live here," I reply. "Better learn quick. These people will suck the life out of you."

"Oh." Max pauses. "Well, I got tired of the cold," he continues by referring the conversation to why he recently moved to Florida.

Sean checks his cell phone, which buzzes uncontrollably at his hip. "What in the hell do they want now? I ain't stopping at any more damn stores!"

"So, what do you do?" Max calmly asks as he towers over me, shading my face from the beaming sun rays behind him. His scent hovers the space around us—warm notes of patchouli and refreshing citrus dance wildly in the air, tickling my nose with satisfaction. I can almost see the focus of his interest staring through his sunglass lenses.

"She's Dedrias' hair stylist," Sean interrupts again.

"Oh." He looks down at my head and notices my black, wavy hair cascading over my shoulders. "Your hair is beautiful...," he speaks as he sees the shimmer of sunrays glistening from my silky locks. "... so is your tattoo."

Max watches me brush over my birthmark.

"Thank you," I speak softly, not addressing my birthmark at all. Subconsciously, memories of the head mother flash memories in my head for me to keep quiet about it and move on to something else.

His one eyebrow peeks above the frame of his orange-hued blockers. My hips extend wider than usual and beyond the edges. As my body flushes from the wired boundaries of his frames, Max starts smelling the air around us in tantric whiffs.

"Wow, what is that you have on?" Max asks.

"Church," I reply lightheartedly, and we laugh at my unexpected response.

"No, I'm serious. Your fragrance is intoxicating," Max says out of nowhere.

Max steps closer and inhales my scent like a junkie. He sniffs the air around me like a dog and leans down to smell my hair. For a split second, Max looks as if he wants to lift his leg to pee on me by the way he twists his hip to the side and elevates his foot off the ground. I notice my morphed body in the bottom right corner of his ariel view. My birthmark suddenly glows and reflects from his lenses.

"Come on, man. They're waiting on us!" Sean slides his cell phone back into the carrying case attached to his side and places the fresh six-pack of beer onto the backseat of his truck.

"Well, nice meeting you. Here, get my number," I say abruptly. I give zero fucks about the people waiting for him. I want to get acquainted and swing from his tree branch several times.

But as I approach the entrance, Max removes his frames and immediately reaches out to open the door for me. Just like Sean does for Dedrias. With grace. Chivalrous and deliberate. Then, POW! Our eyes lock, and another bolt of electricity shoots between us.

"Wow, that's twice in one day." Max looks down, entrancing me with the aqua-blue colors that flicker in his eyes. "That's crazy."

I reach into the sleeve of my wallet in an automatic gesture, never breaking my gaze from his, and pull out a business card. "If you're not too busy, give me a call. Maybe we can hang out or something," I say as I try to shake loose the static clinging to my fingers. "I'd like to get to know you."

Max takes the card and looks it over. "Nice pimp-move with the cards. I bet you give them to all the fellas, eh?" he asks as he scans the information. "Oh, so if I mess my hair up, you can fix it up?" he reiterates the slogan printed on the front.

"Well, first, you would have to grow some for me to fix," I respond.

He laughs under his breath while rubbing over his bald head. "You see what I got going on here." He continues to grace over his dome and grins as he pulls on his beard. "What if I just want a shampoo?"

"I do those as well. Best head you'll ever pay for."

He grunts at my response and turns the card to look at the information.

"Sir, you're going to have to close the door, please," the clerk calls out from behind the counter.

"Sorry."

"Come on, man!" Sean yells from the truck window, honking the horn with agitation. His mole is bothering him for some reason. He fiddles around with it, right between the groove in his neck and shoulder, bitching because he scratched too hard, and it starts bleeding down his chest.

"Okay!" Max scowls at Sean and then calmly turns his attention back to me. "I'll call you."

Some say a woman knows if she will sleep with a man within ten minutes of meeting him. I knew it the second my clit swelled, watching Max walk out of the store. Urging myself to go inside and not turn around, I keep the flirt game going and switch my ass to catch his eye. Something tempts me to turn around. I feel his eyes scanning my body. My legs fight to walk past the newspaper stands along the window, but I drop my keys in the closing door. Looking up as I grip the keys into my hand, my eyes blink in slow motion, and just as I suspect, Max stands there with his arms hanging over the passenger side door. He looks at me as he pulls the toothpick from his mouth and flashes his pearly whites.

CHAPTER 12
A Crack Underground Goes Unnoticed

"Close your fucking mouth. That smile is so fake. Gianna's going to think you're crazy as hell," Sean speaks as Max crouches into the truck.

"Shut up. Who do you think you're talking to?" Max reaches into the vehicle and thumps Sean's forehead. "Wow, that's the lady that does Dedrias' hair, huh?" Max hops into the front seat and slams the door. "She's cute."

"Yes, man. Nice ain't it?" Sean declares as he gulps his beer and places the cold bottle behind his neck to help stop the bleeding. "Want one?" He offers as he backs out of the parking space.

"Nah, I can wait until we get to the house." Max notices Sean in a contorted position. "What's wrong with you?"

"This fucking thing on the side of my neck! I swear I'm going to get it zapped!" Sean complains as he murmurs back at it, warning it of its last days. "It's bothering the fuck out of me for some reason." He then reaches down between his legs and adjusts his nut sack.

"Those bothering you, too?" Max asks, not forgetting Sean's ballsy innuendoes a few minutes back.

"Hell yeah!" Sean places the bottle between his thighs, alternating its cooling effect. "They've never bothered me at the same time. That's weird."

"Interesting, but seriously, do you know anything about her?" Max asks.

"Not much. I know she does hair. She started out as a shampoo girl. She's a little bougie, but she seems cool." Sean takes another quick swig of his long neck and then whips the steering wheel uncontrollably. Some remnants of his blood-stained fingernails stick to the leather as he turns. "Damn, that's good." He releases a loud belch and places the bottle back onto his neck.

"Yeah, I like her sense of humor. She's fine as hell, too," Max adds. "Do you see anybody come in for her?" Max sinks deeper into the seat to relieve his knees.

"No," Sean responds.

'What about a boyfriend?" Max fishes out information. "A girlfriend?"

"Man, I don't know." Sean presses the bottle firmly against his shoulder.

"You need to find out."

"Why? Mm, never mind. I know what that means," Sean says right before he takes another swallow. "Maybe she doesn't like dick," he stresses and concentrates on the road.

"Naw, she likes dick." Max cuts his eyes at Sean. "I caught her staring at mine. She might even eat a little pussy, too. Chicks that do hair got more freak in them than average," Max declares presumably.

"For your sake, you better hope so!" Sean playfully nudges Max and splatters a few drips.

"Did you see her ass? Gawd damn, that thang was hanging out on the sides and everything!" Max announces as he grunts and rubs his head in disbelief.

"Yeah, she does have a fatty. You know she probably got somebody waxing it already. That could get messy," Sean states as he looks at Max. "You have me in some shit sometimes."

"And?" Max replies with cockiness.

"*And* you be having me scrambling at the last minute," Sean stresses.

"There's just something about her. I can feel it." Max rubs over his beard and shakes his head. But could it be possible? Is the universe shifting for another caste? Are these the signs Max has been waiting for?

"You don't even know her, and you're already talking stupid. You say that about everybody."

Max notices how country people dress with their flip-flops and tank tops. One woman has the nerve to come out of the house in a bright pink hair bonnet and dimply thighs. One man is smoking a joint at the bus stop like recreational weed is legal. Max chuckles to himself as he remembers Gianna's statement. It does look boring here and ain't shit going on. Max knew from the selection of prospects that he wouldn't be in this town for long.

"I'll concentrate on her later. I have bigger issues." Max taps on his thighs as they drive past a homeless man pushing his grocery basket stuffed with tattered items.

"What?"

"I fucked up," Max states calmly.

"With what?" Sean pauses, looks at Max while shaking his head in deep thought, and bangs his hands onto the steering wheel. "Aw, come on, man. You serious?" Sean knows what Max is referring to exactly.

"I know." Max releases a deep sigh. "Just get it done."

"You need to tighten up," Sean reiterates. "This is what I mean. All this last-minute shit!"

"Don't tell me what I need to do!" Max quickly reaches over and slaps the remaining spit of beer out of Sean's mouth, banging the bottle against the window with beer spraying everywhere. "I done warned you already today! Quit trying me and do what the fuck I say! Do you need a fucking reminder in who the fuck I am?"

Sean sits in a silent rage, breathing heavily. The black cloud of anger snuffs from his nostrils as he wipes the spillage of beer from his face and shirt. Sean regains his composure and speaks. "I'm sorry. Forgive me. I'm just looking out for your best interest. Why weren't you more careful if you didn't want this to happen?"

"She was sweet. I couldn't help it," Max replies.

"You have to be more selective," Sean states in a lighter tone.

"It's hard to do that with this generation. You can't tell by kissing these women anymore."

"When is *your* ass gonna realize that? Ever thought about checking their panties in the dirty clothes hamper when you use the bathroom? Maybe finger fuck them first to find out before you make the wrong choices?" Sean's courage blurts out.

"You don't think I've tried that?!" Max unexpectedly hits Sean with three quick pops to his disrespectful mouth.

"Dammit, man!" Sean roars in anger and swings back at Max, letting go of the steering wheel and causes the truck to swerve to and fro from one side of the road to the other.

The two exchange a rotation of pounding licks and fight at lightning speed, hundreds of punches within the millisecond frame. Heads bang against the windows. Fingers bend in awkward positions. They curse at each other as they grapple. Beer bottles fly as arms swing between them from the front seat to the back seat, crossing from every angle. Flashes of light dart between their fist-a-cuffing blows before the sounds of honking horns stop them in mid-swings. Max takes control of the steering wheel and sneaks a few jabs into Sean's exposed ribcage while he wipes the beer from his eyes with his forearm.

"Umph!" Sean calls out in pain. He swerves to avoid another oncoming vehicle and punches Max's hand from the steering wheel before he regains control. Quickly whopping Max across his Cro-Magnon jawline, his beard expels bristles of curls upon impact. "I hate bringing new motherfuckers in that we got to feel out!" Sean asserts. "Stop doing that shit to me!"

"Know your place then!" Max scowls back with intensity as he plows another punch at Sean in retaliation.

"Ah! I do know my place! You're doing too fucking much! You need to tighten up on that shit for real. I don't care who you are. You're being reckless!"

Max then realizes he couldn't care less about his recklessness, but he knows what Sean says is true. "Chill out with that. I'm dead serious! You know what needs doing. Don't forget who the fuck I am."

"How can I forget?" Sean responds with sass. "I'm reminded every day."

Max pops him again and splits his bottom lip.

"Stop it!" Sean screams like a bitch and swings at Max.

"You stop it! Keep on with your slick mouth. You can disappear with the quickness. Maybe you do need to be reminded what can happen," Max stresses.

Sean's limbs freeze immediately. "No! I'm so sorry!" He pulls off to the side of the road, comes to a screeching halt, and shakes profusely. "Please, you don't have to remind me of that." Horrid flashes of darting spirits without faces flicker past visits. "No!" Sean repeats while clenching his teeth. His fears are getting the best of him and has his obligations making unfavorable decisions for him. "Please don't let her ass get you caught up," his voice is calm, downgrading the sparks of excitement surrounding them. "It angers me because of the work involved. Be mindful of me, *brother*."

"I am thinking of you. I'm thinking of all of us," Max pleads.

"Sometimes, I don't think you are. I don't know who you're looking for, but you can't fuck every chick you see trying to find her," Sean adds respectfully. "Besides, Dedrias says Gianna is into the church, maybe a holy roller. You heard her yourself."

"That means nothing to me."

Max thinks about the other women who claim to be holy rollers; they went to church, too. They were the biggest freaks. That was not a challenge to him at all. In fact, they were the easiest; making a nigga wait for a few weeks to see where your head was at before he knew where you lived. They mask their virtuous ways behind shirts that pop their cleavage, tempting *a nigga like him* to slide his tongue between their exposed titty cracks. The hypocrites of faith hold off, if they can, for whatever reasons. The test of wills usually takes three months before pussies get wet from his finger fucking in a dark corner of some dive-in bar to have a quick drink.

Then, Max thinks about how money changes their perspectives when the big fun comes into play. The jewelry. The weekend trips. Then, legs fly open, and religion goes out the window—especially when they can have everything forgiven. *Whatever that means*. Everything comes at a cost. Payment is due at some point.

Max knew the women who "believed" got lost in that respect. Gianna's beliefs didn't matter. What *would* be fucked up is if they find there is a blood relation down the line. It was possible, and talk shows highlighted it all the time. Gianna's marking intrigued Max. Many women get heart tattoos; but if it *is* her birthmark, that would be the kill shot to end this monotonous game.

CHAPTER 13
The Unlucky Imitation of Art

I hurry and pick up Rochelle from the airport since she decides to swing in for the weekend to check on me. She flew in to get a shot of life and I needed one, too. She says she misses lying next to me at night and pleads for me to reconsider Jersey. Coco's car is in the shop and needs to be picked up as well. My car can't handle this extra driving. Rochelle holds on to her half-rolled gar that she couldn't finish before the flight, and we hot-box four blunts before we arrive to the venue.

Luckily, we appreciate the fine arts. That's the creativity in us. The opera, plays, fashion shows, and tonight, we're exploring the new explosion of artists doing pop-up shows full of mysticism, disbelief, and dazzle.

"So, tonight's show is here?" I question as I creep through the dimly lit street lined with industrial warehouses and abandoned buildings.

"This has to be wrong," Coco voices. "As much as these tickets cost me, I know this ain't it!"

I follow the brick road that leads back to the sign that reads: LEAVE YOUR CAR HERE.

"What kind of mess is this?" Coco blurts out.

The street is faded and shady. It looks like we got played on the location.

"I should have known this was gonna be wild!" Rochelle shouts from the backseat as she exhales the last marijuana-packed cigar.

And just like that, the whole lot is lit up like someone just broke out of prison.

"Girl, this is too much!" Rochelle shouts.

"You must admit, it is different. Come on, let's go," Coco reassures us.

We stepped out of my car and noticed two people dressed in black standing under the bright lights highlighting the brick road. One flashes a large cue card that reads: LEAVE YOUR KEYS IN THE CAR. We walk a few feet before reaching the entrance door, and the two people dressed in black, jump into my car and zoom off. I just hope the bitch starts back up when it's time to go.

Upon entering, there is a young female serving shot glasses full of what smells like a concoction of fresh fruit.

"7:32. You made perfect timing." She stamps my ticket with a star. "There will be an announcement when to place these over your face." She tells me to get a mask from the bin before continuing.

"I thought this mask garbage was over," Coco complains as he waits for his stamp. He is asked to please step along and keep the line moving. In his rant, Coco twists his neck in ghetto circles of niggerdom.

Rochelle and I stand in confusion, blocking anyone from moving forward as we wait for the conclusion of whether the young lady is going to stamp Coco's ticket or not. The misunderstanding goes on for minutes. The LGBT agenda has Coco thinking his butterfly eyelashes and designer pumps pass for everything a female receives because he is a transsexual. He fusses about the disrespect in nice-nasty statements that upset the people waiting in line behind us.

"That was yummy." Rochelle tosses the empty cup to her right as the young woman stamps her ticket; not concentrating on Coco's altered-ego privileges, he continues to debate.

"7:43. You made perfect timing." She smiles wide at Rochelle, ignoring Coco's dramatic show. "Please continue," the girl says as she motions her hand toward the hallway ahead.

All around us are faint bell sounds. I've heard them before. Then, the heavy beat of a drum booms. One note vibration. Two-note vibrations. Three-note vibrations. It builds anticipation for whatever awaits us behind the thick, black curtains ahead. As we walk down the faintly lit hallway, there are random pieces of art on display encased within lighted glass boxes to guide the way.

"What's this?" I stop and look at the withered finger bound together by gold rings and thinly cut strips of blood-stained cloth. My eyes begin to play tricks on me. My vision is blurry. Worms ooze from the holes in the finger where the nail should be. Not sure if what I'm seeing is real. "You think they put something in that cup?" I look at Rochelle and Coco. Everything is moving in slow motion.

"Ooh!" Rochelle leans in to examine the piece more closely. "Look at how tight that mess is tied."

I, comparing the choked skin to Max's asphyxiated genitals, am shocked at the explosive puffiness of strangulated flesh. Coco points to another lighted box. Inside, a disfigured fetus is securely nestled among finely braided twigs. Its face is crushed in. The mash forced its dopey appearance to swell near the eyes and forehead more. There are thin stems of wood piercing its wrists to fasten the bondage to a latticed egg. Delicately wrapped in love, the baby is laid across a bed of flowers, highlighting the gutted genitalia and missing abdominal parts. Rochelle covers her mouth in disdain.

"Come on here. It's just art." Coco pulls her arm to carry on.

"This is not art. This is death," Rochelle adds. "Something's not right. I don't know about this."

Another piece hosts dangling crystals from a flowered planter high above a burning pool of crimson liquid. Each crystal is filled with a miniature doll inside.

We continue down the walkway until we reach the display area where here, it is still pitch black—except for the light shining above the individually veiled art. There are six large canvases covered in woven flax. One piece is ducked off in the corner by itself to make the exhibition view at seven. Everyone notices a flash of some sort darting in between the pieces, and some hesitate to examine the cold room.

As we enter, the lights above us start to flash. We huddle together like scared rabbits, and Rochelle and I jump as the mist touches her shoulder then mine. We cover our eyes, and when the lights stop blinking, the drumbeats stop. Out from behind the black void surrounding it appears a young woman dressed in a glowing, transparent gown. The sheerness showcases her nipples peaking at full display. Her pussy bush twinkles like fresh dew.

"Welcome to The Viewing." She spreads her arms across the display, and we applaud her phantom-like entrance.

Her voice is watered in its delivery.

Slowed down.

Her orchestrated octaves are in perfect pitch.

It hypnotizes the room with close attention.

"Tonight, is about a state of being. It is a reverent condition where time is the only player. This exhibit is not for the faint of heart or religious opinions. This viewing is for one night only. The art of Mastiqulation is a new, and upcoming medium in the art space. No pictures or videos are allowed. Mini baskets are coming around to collect your devices and will be returned when you exit."

We dump our devices into the zippy robotic baskets that stop at our feet.

"The masterpieces before you share a purposeful history. The women's stories have many dimensions. Please allow your mind to explore the beauty in death before you."

We're trying to wrap our heads around her flying in between the art pieces. She wisps around them, and then into the crowd. Blowing past, like a chilling spirit.

"Allow your senses to drown in the artful horror of their stories. Could it be fake? Is it real? Reality is only a dimension in your mind; it does not dictate the reverence of the universe. What is considered strange here is normal in another realm." She pauses as she looks out at the crowd.

We are amazed at how she floats in the air with no strings attached. Her breeze passes like a ghost. The softness of her smell is cold and metallic.

"Their journey has no time, but yours is limited. The exhibit will end at 9:10, so please move through the exhibit and exit swiftly. You may now place the masks onto your face," she states as she floats across the darkness of the room. Her voice disappears with her like shattered glass and the void absorbs her into its nothingness. Gasps fill the room in shock. Coco turns to me with surprised eyes. Rochelle covers her mouth in panic. As the lights above each canvas brighten like heated beams, the covers are lifted into the vaulted ceiling above.

The digital clock on the wall sounds an alarm at eight o'clock.

The artwork underneath is finally unveiled. I am taken aback by the odor of rotten meat and quickly place the mask over my nose and mouth. Coco and Rochelle do the same. The room is at a standstill as classical music begins playing. The grand piano keys strike with a soft vengeance. The stretched tuning of harmonic sequences damper in eloquence's doom.

"Whoa."

"What is that...jelly?" Someone whispers as they touch.

"Are those bite marks?" Another voice mutters.

"Where's the face?"

Gasps of disbelief filled the room. People ran out of the exhibit crying. Some analyze in small, circular groups around the pieces smoking cigarettes. I inhale the electricity zapping throughout the room. As we await our turn to take a closer look, I hear a man shout 'Jesus' from across the venue and sounds of vomit follow soon after.

"That smells terrible," Coco whispers back at us as he leans on my body to stay steady.

As we shift to the first piece, I can't believe people are into this kind of stuff. The gelatin mound resembles a glob of jelly with human eyes. Weird. It bobs around like a bouncy ball. The soft jelly stamps it leaves on the black floors soften the grossness of its composure when it lands. We can't even tell what the fuck it is. It just fell from the enclosure and started bouncing around. People move to the side to avoid the blob, pointing at the objects circulating inside its composition:

Bones.

Organs.

Digested chunks of green food.

The second piece shows a young woman. As she hangs, her small frame is pale and lifeless. From her face to her feet, her composure is crusty like paper mâché and has flipped-up slices of brick-laid skin winged in glory. The brittle dryness looks delicate to the touch, but is it? Nobody's skin can do that. Looks like she was sliced up, peeled back, and left out in the sun to dry. I touch the paper blades to see how sharp the edges are, and as I do, pieces of her dried skin break off and feather to the floor. Hues of blue-toned, abused flesh are underneath her nailbed. The orange-blue ring indicates healing in its presentation. Her feet are fitted with blocks of dried concrete and what look like candle wax socks puffing from the heavy encasement. I can't believe I just touched that. The creativity is disturbing, and that's what excites me. This dude is amazing how he fits her feet perfectly into each one. Each block was heavy enough to spin her effortlessly in the air. If the dude thinks like this, he needs to be off the streets. If it really happened, my God, what in the hell did she go through to end up like this?

"Coco." I grab onto his hand and squeeze tight, now leaning against him.

"Man," he whispers, trying not to awaken the demons he believes are hovering here.

The F-major key strikes our ears and the flashing lights sequence together for eight pulses and stops.

The third piece has her hands balled into a fist; silently, she fights from beneath her cloth enclosure. Her limbs are in a defensive pose, the hard cloth catching her in mid-jump by the way her arms are extended and high above her, maybe from a hill or something. Her one leg is stuck in a solid running pose like she was frozen in mid-action. The piece is confusing. It's hard to catch how intricate her support is, only because it is oddly strung together to hold her up. The only thing keeping her upright and in position is a thick rope hardened into a straight line through the center of her body like a spine. It enters at the heel, goes up the entire left side of her frame, and exits at the top of her head.

The fourth is posed gracefully. She is wrapped more securely in a rubber cocoon. Her arms were crossed on top of her chest. She is sealed within her canvas without a chance to escape. Wound together like a crazy jacket, her sealed casing squeezes her body tight. A skeletal frame locks her into place like a weight. Her face is peaceful as if she is content with her end. The flush in her cheeks is a rosy hue. Her eyes are Bambi-like and pure; her body is a mummified cask of suffocating material betwixt sealed skin and space. The numerous layers of latex and tar materials left the dust of its scorching heat marked under her eyes like dark circles.

"I'll be outside. This is too deep," Rochelle says as she leaves, using the wall to guide her toward the front. She signals for an escort to lead her out.

The classical music softly transitions to another calming sonata of piano keys in una corda, shifting the strings to hammer a sharper note and a softer sound.

"I just want to see the rest. This is amazing," I respond and direct my attention back to the pieces. I try to convince myself that this is not real. There is no possible way someone is getting away with murder in plain sight like this. Almost as if the artist was taunting their crime and dared anyone to contact the authorities.

Nah.

"This shit looks too real," Coco expresses and walks ahead to the other pieces.

"No wonder they asses won't allow cameras," I tease, and wouldn't you know it, some idiot's camera flashes bright.

Immediately a formed mist crystallizes in front of the woman, snatches the camera from the woman's hands, snatches her with it, and disappears into the crystallize void. Ten seconds. Quick and painless. Gasps fill the room and people begin scurrying toward the exit.

"They are so corny." Coco laughs at the optical illusion, clearly seen from the reflective eyeglass drilled into the wall. "I used that trick for a hair battle competition back in '95... Pbbsht!" He waves the flash of suspense off as a Halloween prop.

I study the fifth piece as she dangles from thin metal wires along the outside border of her whole arm shaft. Stretching from one hand to the other, she is labeled as "The Butterfly." The wire delicately loops into a line of golden rings sewn into her rawhide flesh. From one wrist, up her left arm, across the back of her neck into the top of her spine, down the right arm, and to her other wrist. She twirls freely. Her exhibition takes over a whole corner of the gallery so she may spin effortlessly. Her arms are overextended, and she softly whips through mid-air like a rice paper fan from China. The circulation is slow and steady. There is an option to slide the rings together and apart, almost like a shower curtain gliding across the shower rod. Her span mimics large butterfly wings as she opens and closes. The intricate impressions of feathers grace the sheet of material sewn to her back like wings that crinkle with her:

A flash of turquoise.

The death of ruby red.

Sapphire blues and emerald gems sparkle with brilliance when she flutters her arms in the shuffle. Beautiful misery whistles through each ring of her skin as she flaps and turns. It plays a cryptic chord of keys in a dark love song.

The sixth member has a darker meaning. She is nothing but half a shell. Nude on the front, the back and insides are gone—except for a few kept treasures: her tongue; her mammary glands that are inflamed puffs of hardened milk; and her fallopian tubes that are nothing but strung together sticks and stones for ovaries. Where her brain should be is a bag of nickels that hangs from the center of her skull like a chandelier. Her heart is a fake diamond. Her cut-out eyes have mink lashes twitching on the outside with a side lever to bat them for amusement. The mouth is a carved-out circle lined with overexaggerated red candle wax, posing for lipstick. The display is titled "Whore'derves, Anyone?" The name laughs at its title in shame. One onlooker stands behind it and his friend snap a picture, sticking his tongue through the hole in her mouth like a carnival picture board, and adjusts the lever to open and close the feathery-lashed eyes. On the outside, her pierced nostril, with see-through nasal canals, has a nose ring that shines like a star.

Her mutilated labial lip exposes itself to the elements and the crowd. Her pubic skin is carved into a rose. The labyrinth pattern of her flesh is beautiful in its cannibalistic irony. Red, puffed-up skin riddled with pain, almost beating from underneath, begs to be plucked from its dark, miserable garden. So, I rub my fingers over the bumpy mound, feeling the dampness of sandy residue between my digits. The maze of skin is prickly to the touch. It blossoms in its nightmarish beauty. Amazed at how freshly the sand crumbles from my fingers, I look up at her face cavity, which is only visible from one side. A shadow box of her throat is the window to her vacant soul. I spot grazed teeth marks along her stomach and inner thigh. A chunk of her side is also missing, including a rib, where the crocheted material intricately patterns itself underneath the missing bone structure from her throat, through her body, and exits from her vaginal canal. Sand sifts through her body like the grains of time were filtering her impurities into a gritty mound of sin below.

Oddly enough, the seventh piece is breathtaking. The creativity it takes to mentally visualize this kind of horror is astounding. The pressed composition tricks my eyes more. To think half of someone's body is perfectly normal on one side before they are...

"Fascinating, isn't it?" A male voice speaks from behind me.

"Yes, it is." I jump, startled by the deepness in their voice, and turn my head, only to find everyone around me engaged in conversation. "Wow." I stand here amazed at what I am viewing. The artist must be pretty messed up to develop these creations, especially this one. Nothing could be that horrible, whatever the artist is trying to convey. They fucking look sucked and smashed.

"Have you seen all the pieces?" His voice falls upon me like a plundering wall of waves.

"No, not yet." I reply as I walk up the steps to gain a full aerial view of the piece. "New Beginnings" is this exhibit's title. It doesn't fit what is portrayed. A new beginning to what?

One-half of the body is pressed between two glass slides for an experiment, smeared in blot to the borders. Back on the ground floor, the other half of the body is whole in posture, awaiting its part.

"Wow."

I walk back and forth in front of the piece, and suddenly a man's voice catches my eardrums like a bell that stands out amongst the crowd. He starts to mumble words I cannot understand. French, maybe Kreyol? I look at all the masked faces breathing through the stench. Some shield their eyes in horror. I feel the man move near my shoulder, masking who he is as he manipulates through the crowd. Whoever he is, his presence is heavy. A dark cloud. His shoes scrape across the floor, carrying with him some of the falling grains of sand and their grit. His hand softly brushes across the round peak of my ass as he walks by. The scent of hot bricks and patchouli profuse the air around me. I inhale its erotic infusion with delight. The elixir, warm in its breath, finishes like a citrusy ocean breeze at daybreak.

"I apologize. What about this one?" He steps closer and establishes his move. His nose heavily breathes warm expulses of air from his nostrils.

A concerto of E-flat notes complements a twinkling wave of playful keys into a chase of variations as the music shifts again.

"I don't know. It's making me feel a little uncomfortable," I reply, dropping hints for the unknown man to step back.

"What is?" he responds.

I am amazed at how life-like dried blood coagulates around the entry of the piece. The paint's vibrancy catches the twinkle of the lights above it to show the power and pressure of the compressed splash. The artist freezes the spray of red color that barely escapes the pressure of the floating plates in front of its back-spit.

"Two things," I reply. "I can't put my finger on which one is bothering me the most."

"Well, maybe if your eyes didn't get glued onto smashed private parts, you would figure it out," he responds prematurely.

"Excuse me?" I rotate my body to face the voice I've been talking to indirectly for the past few minutes, turning to see who this joker is, and discovering a bald head glistening underneath the tract lights above us like a beam from heaven. His head glows as he leans down from his stalking mist.

"You know you like looking at people's private parts on the sly," he responds with a slight laugh. "Hell, you were looking at my goods earlier."

"Max?!" I squeak softly, playfully hitting him on his rock-hard arm as he appears from the dimmed lighting. "You know that's how you get cut, right? Sliding up behind people mumbling shit," I say softly. "What are you doing here?"

"Same thing as you," he responds.

"You don't look like you're into art."

"What makes you say that? We just met this afternoon. You don't know me like that," he jokes.

"No, I don't know you, but art never flashed into my head," I respond.

"Why not?"

"You just look like you're into other things."

"Like what?"

"Weightlifting." I caress the arm closest to me. His skin starts firing off from my touch. I can feel the tingles fluttering underneath his dark, chocolatey skin. "Fixing things...maybe listening to a little bit of reggae? Your Aura is crazy," I rattle off.

"I do. I can. Maybe. Since you're putting it out there, you don't exactly look like you're into magical things," Max states.

"Magical?" I question.

"My Aura?" he stresses again.

"Yeah, it's crazy. You step on the scene, and people see you, but they don't see you." I walk over to the wall of showpieces, and he smoothly follows suit. As I step away, I stalk just enough for him to get an eyeful of my plump ass parts. "So, what do you think?" I ask as I stand in front of the canvas with burnt baby skeletons decorated with little yellow bows attached to the top of their skulls.

"Very interesting," Max states as he takes in the image of us both.

My ass is in his full view as I stand here, swaying my hips from side to side. My eyes pierce over the mask and twinkle back at him. His response warrants my flirtatious attempt.

"You don't think they are real, though?" I ask. "All of their heads are different."

"I don't think."

"What do you mean?" I question. "Like you don't think so, or period?"

"Of course, I think." Max pauses in his approach, noticing my agitated reply. "I knew to what you were referring. No, they're not real." He chuckles and shakes his head. "I just don't involve myself with bullshit," he contends. "I'm sorry."

Wait, what? Where did that come from? I don't even know what he's referring to now. His disjointed word choices fail to connect as I play them back in my head. Just that quick, he threw the whole conversation off with bullshit. Am I the bullshit he's referencing? Or was it my bullshit attempts to catch his eye? At this point, I'm looking around the room for Coco. I don't see Rochelle's afro anywhere puffed out amongst the crowd. I walk to number five and reshuffle her accordion movements as I play with the controller to regulate her fanning arm strokes.

At first, Max's approach was interesting in how he threw his voice to have me look around for it, but now, with his confusing responses, it's not impressive. How Dedrias references him in the salon, how arrogantly confident he is, how his dialogs are thought-provoking and engaging, and how sarcastically comedic he is—Max's persona fits her description perfectly. I always wondered why she talks about him the way she does. Max's name comes up at every visit. How he messes up every hookup she sets him up with, and how much he needs to get some business other than being in hers. She swoons at how fine he is. His presence immediately catches the room's attention without him having to say a single word—she's right about that. Her statements are dead-on descriptives. The way she brings him into play at every conversation, you would think she was fucking him.

"I get so passionate about art. It evokes so many emotions inside of me. I can't control how they come out," Max explains.

He walks back over to number two and motions to follow him. When he steps in front of the piece to take a closer look, he pauses; and then steps back to admire the exhibit in its sharpness.

"Her dried skin does look real, though," I say as I reach out to feel the paper blades of flesh.

Max also leans closer, staring dead into the piece's eyes that twinkle back against the lighting and at him. His stare is deliberate, taunting even. Then suddenly, the exhibit turns and scratches his forehead with precision, leaving its slice for remembrance. A chipped edge from the flipped raise of skin marks its victory as it, too, feathers to the floor in phyllo sheets.

"Hm," Max states as he smiles at the piece, pats his forehead, and steps back. He glances down at the flakes and scatters them with his feet. "Don't you think we should be asking each other how do these pieces make you *feel*?" He stresses in a softer tone, not recognizing my sudden disinterest. "I'm curious."

"Funny you would ask that," I state, looking for Coco again, and as I form my lips to tell him that I feel like it's time for me to exit left, Max's soothing tenor draws me into his voice and relaxes my tension when he touches my hand. "Well, it makes me feel afraid." His warm touch excites my nipples to pop from his electrifying caress.

"Afraid?" Max questions.

"Hell yeah, afraid," I reply. "Look at it. I mean, who would think of something this graphic?" I lean closer to him and whisper, "Motherfuckers disappearing from the room? What is happening in here?" I laugh under my breath. "My co-worker says it's a prop."

Max looks at the exhibit piece and nods his head. "What else does it arouse inside of you?"

"I'm a little fascinated by it. *Excited* may be a better word?" I question myself.

"Wow, that's a lot to feel over art." Max laughs.

"What about you? How does it make you feel?" I ask.

"I don't know." He steps back and looks at the display of women before of him. "Hopeless, threatened, maybe a little *defeated*?" Max questions his feelings.

"Defeated?"

His words take me by surprise, almost like he is stepping into their menagerie of desolation—his empathy ushers in his following declaration.

"Sadly, we may never know why," he adds.

"Why what?"

"Why an artist is a man that hates women. Maybe his mother, something she did." Max pauses. "It's obvious the artist feels a certain way about them." He animates with his arm circling the room. "Look, they're everywhere."

"Good point. No face or private parts?" I state.

"Yeah, that looks like a personal one to me. It's so detailed. It looks like some god-awful monster flew by and chunked the face off the exhibit's body," Max describes. "I love the way he makes everything appear. He's so talented. Look. You can almost hear the saw when you look closer." He pulls me to him and points out the razor indentations the artist exaggerates across her cheek and thigh. The scathed indentations are precise in formation.

I am slightly disturbed by his description and how the dead-on description facilitates the blade's action. I can almost hear the sharp buzz of the edge rapidly cutting into the exhibit's flesh as it carves.

"I mean, even though it's weird, it does make you think," Max adds.

"I thought you didn't think." I tease.

Max's eyes cut at me playfully. "Seriously. You're right. It makes you feel all the emotions you told me, but it also makes you think."

"About what?" I ask.

"Death."

Who wants to think about that?" I question his intelligence.

"Nobody does until it's dead in your face." He leans down further, hovers over me, and the sound of his tongue separating from the roof of his mouth echoes in my ear. It sounds creamy as he speaks. Max rubs his clothes against my body before he makes his following declaration. "We only get one ride through here, right?"

"Right." I move over another step.

"But what if death didn't have to happen for you to live forever?"

"But it does."

"In some form it does, I suppose. It depends on what you must do to pass over, right? It may be something else in another realm," Max emphasizes. "There may be a path to forever where death doesn't apply," he states calmly.

Now, he sounds delusional. Another woke brother spreading his blasphemous, black knowledge of the afterlife.

"I'm just saying. There's much more to this universe than we know or think. You believe a creator made all this, and we're it?" He demonstrates with his arms.

His statement makes me consider his position. The way his words sashay from his lips with eloquence is beautiful. Max is well-spoken. His careful choice of vocabulary absorbs into my eardrums like mesh.

"Not only that, but what if you didn't have to die to do it?" he asks in a light tone.

"But you do."

"Have you ever died and come back? You know anybody that has?" he playfully inquires.

"Jesus," I respond with authority.

"What did He say? Or are you going off what other people have told you? Where's your proof?" Max asks with a hint of sarcasm.

"I just know."

"Okay, so you can't even defend, let alone prove, who or what you believe in?"

I aim for a rebutted response but fail. Where's the Holy Spirit when you need Him to give the words and intercede? Max's statement has me perplexed.

"I can feel Him," I reveal.

Max raises his eyebrows in surprise. "Touché! To know is to feel is to believe?" he lightheartedly questions my answer, summing it up with a cherry on top. "You believe in a higher power, right?" he asks. "Church, the afterlife, and all its bells and whistles of gold-paved streets?"

"Yes, do you?"

"I do. Hey, you wanna get out of here?" Max asks out of nowhere.

"I'm not sure. I'm here with some friends, and I drove." I scan the room once more for Coco and Rochelle. I am still waiting to see her afro puff out in the crowd.

"I thought you said you wanted to hang out with me?"

"I do."

"Well, what's the problem?"

"Nothing." Slightly agitated in his delivery, I adjusted my mask. If nothing is said now, it will continue to happen. I must get this off my chest before this goes any further, if it goes any further. "You know, you can be rude at times," I reveal.

Max laughs under his breath. "Rude? That's just how I talk. Living in New York can make you sound hard. I apologize if I sound rude. I'm just to the point." He intermittently clears his throat to unclog the lies collaborating in his windpipe. "I was going to ask you to join me for a drink, that's all. I've had enough of this, haven't you?" Nodding in agreement, he says more. "There's a reggae spot nearby if you'd like to join me."

I look up at him and see the innocence in his boyish smile. It comes with an attractive invitation. I can see the sinister smirk of sin turning its lips at me. Not knowing whether to trust this unrelenting feeling in my gut, the smoothness in his voice swoons me instantly and makes me ignore any warning signs. It urges me to listen closely, but his smile distracts the red flags and quickly calms those fears. Images of me beating against glass to get my attention flash before my eyes. I see visions of me screaming at myself, banging profusely to snap out of my haze, jumping to wake up, and crying in failure because I ignored my gut and the visions, I see flashing in my head now.

And then suddenly, I fall into this freeing moment of unchartered territory: feeling girly, free, and spontaneous. Fuck it. I don't care what happens after this.

"Go home!" I contemplate his invitation repeatedly in my head as images flash again.

"You'll be fine," a breeze whispers past my ear in excited twinkles.

"His ass could be crazy!" My gut beats against my head.

He is fine though. Look at his shiny ass skin.

Find Rochelle and Coco, and leave!

I look at his dick right quick.

Mmm. This nigga thick.

Don't you want to see what it's like?

My heart flutters in palpitations as I stand here talking to myself like someone is whispering in my ear. I hear the pounding thumps of my intuition beat in my stomach and flash warnings in dispirited quails of defeat.

"Let me tell my friends," I blurt out as my mouth decides to speak.

"That was quick." Max releases a deep laugh. "I'm ready to go, too."

GERMINATION

CHAPTER 14
Gathering Minerals for Growth

"I've wanted to come here for a minute. The commercials are so funny," I share with Max as we enter Rodney's and sit at the bar.

Their Tampa location is lit, and a welcomed surprise. I knew they were opening another spot, but how convenient its location is close to the art venue. The weekly competitions in lunch and dinner specials knock Jerk Hut's numbers out of the box, according to Max. He casually mentions the radio and television commercials that play in heavy rotation.

"The one where the mom swats them out of the kitchen with her weed broom is hilarious! That's what made me want to check this place out," Max adds as he motions for the bartender to come over. "I wanted to see it for myself." He twirls his stool and points at the massive marijuana leaf on the back wall behind the stage. "That, and their rum punch. Two, please." Max places our order with the bartender.

"Mm, hm. Do you come here a lot?" I ask as I sway to the music pounding from the speaker box.

"Not really."

"You usually come here alone?"

"Well, aren't we nosey?" Max teases.

"I didn't mean it like that."

"It's cool. Sean, Dedrias, Kim, and I come here occasionally," he responds effortlessly. "I don't have many friends here."

"When did you come here?" I ask, and as I do, Max looks disorganized. Like I was asking a trick question he didn't know how to answer.

"Not too long ago," he responds in a blunt tone.

"I mean, I would have noticed you somewhere before. I never forget a face." I take more shots of his angles and movements with my eyes.

"I guess I wasn't paying much attention either. I know I haven't been here long, but I definitely would have noticed you. I don't forget faces either." Max photographs the dimensions of Gianna's frame from his eyes to his subconscious brain; they burst shots and capture her moves from the top of her head to the soles of her feet, and securely store them for memory. "How long you say you been doing my sister's hair?"

We laugh at his disbelief in not seeing me around town and at how his voice rises asking his question. I shake my head, not believing Rochelle missed this body—feels like we would make the perfect threesome.

The twerking of dancehall music interrupts our conversation. The quick, jerky guitar plucks take over my body. Bing-Bing, Bing, Bing-Bing, Bing. I start snapping my fingers to the quirky beat. Max bops in his seat. Lips poke out as we groove. Necks cluck like chickens as we bounce—another wave of laughter springs from our mouths as we dance in our chairs.

"That's my jam!" I poke my lips out again and jerk my shoulders in quick pops.

Bing-Bing, Bing, Bing-Bing, Bing.

"You're fun," Max admits. "Tell me more about you, Gianna." He wiggles his neck from side to side with the reggae beat.

"What would you like to know?"

"What you like...what you hate. Everything." Max's response is pleasing as he slowly winds his neck to the base of the rhythm.

"Well, I like art," I begin telling Max. "I love how it imitates life and freezes its emotion in time." I bring up the exhibit and how talented the artist is with his scary ass. All those dangling pieces of leather weirded me out. The smell. How well he evokes the darkest passions of man through fleshy, sculptured illusions. I mention how I I'm starting over after Covid, like everyone else. Revealing how abruptly my living situation changed and how music helps with my anxieties when I need to escape. I rattle on, wrestling with what to disclose, and tell Max that I volunteer for my church a dew times a month. I call off some other things at random.

Max can jump into the conversation whenever he gets good and ready. And as Max sits anticipating my next reveal, he studies my body and watches me run out of things to discuss. My mouth, now drier than a cotton ball from the nervousness, smacks the air with my dry lips and signals that I'm finished talking.

"Nice. I fart in the tub," Max adds, and his announcement catches me off guard.

"What?"

"That's my gift."

"Your gift?"

"Instant hot tub...," he pauses. "...with aromatherapy, thank you very much."

We both burst out laughing.

"I thought that was Sean's thing," I add.

"Don't act like you don't poot."

His adolescent word choice takes me back to foster times in Pittsburgh. It's right on time, too. He has a good sense of humor when he's not playing the stalker at the art show or displays rudeness in almost every response. He better be glad the words fart and poot still tickle me to the core—no matter how old I get.

"What else do you like to do?" Max asks, still chuckling at his comic relief. "Besides laugh at the word fart?"

"I like roller coasters."

"Thrill seeker, huh?" His voice heightens.

"Pretty much." My life is a roller coaster. I'm ready to get off and stroll through the park for a little while. Feed the animals. Eat a corndog. Stop and smell the roses...and then a flash of her flower-carved skin flickers in my head with its dark pattern of rubbery flesh. I visualize her soul panicking from the inside, calling out to anyone capable of detecting her plea.

"Do you have any brothers or sisters?" Max inquires.

"No," I reply. "Not that I know. Is Dedrias your only sibling?" I ask.

"I wish! We're not even sure. My father was something else," Max shares as he shakes his head from side to side. "Did you move here with anyone? A family member?"

"A girlfriend of mine. She's the friend that recently moved back to Jersey with her job."

"Oh. What about your mom? Are you close with her?"

"I'm adopted," I blurt out.

"Oh, I'm sorry," Max replies. Gianna makes her adoption sound shameful. She projects disappointment and sadness in her pitch as she lures him into her sob story. Max appreciates her not wasting any time with that major detail. He didn't have to dig very deep to discover an essential element to her story.

The rum punches are doing what they are known to do. Max sees her body opening to him. He dazzles with his dimples, and her eyes twinkle like stars. He could tell that just made her feel at ease by telling him. Max knows the stigma that rolls with unwanted children. He is familiar with it himself. He watches her shoulders rise and fall in a sigh; like she is relieved that she mentioned it when she did.

"Why drag it out? I don't know why people are embarrassed by that. I don't know who my real mother is, that's all." And little do I realize that *was* everything. My defense mechanism just kicked in. No wonder no one wants to stay in a serious relationship with me. Rochelle was right; I am a fuck bag. That's all I'm worth. Even my birth mother knew that. I must have been a reminder of her fucked up ways. Who wants to look that demon in the face all the time? The more I think about it, the quicker I fall off inside. How could she leave me alone in this world? The steel wall of shame blocks further questioning. He can probably sense my hesitation vibrating off my body like a pheromone. Wait, is he sniffing the air right now like a dog?

"You ever thought about looking for her?" Max questions while flaring his nostrils in quick, subtle pulses.

"Not really. There was never any interest." I don't think about her at all, not until now.

She loved me enough to ensure I wasn't left in a trash bag. I think back to the nights in the foster home where there was no actual image of her appearance, who she may be, or if she's alive now. The organization kept that information sealed until I turned eighteen. Not that it matters, but I couldn't care less about her. I don't know how she slept at night. Not knowing whether I ate, had a roof over my head, or how I was treated over the years. She never attempted to search for me after she got her shit together, if she got it together, and that still hurts.

"I can't believe no one has snatched you up," Max stresses. "You seem like you're such a beautiful person on the inside," Max's words seep into my soul with sincerity. He sounds genuinely interested in who I am—asking about things that are close and more personal to my heart. "I love how warm it is nine months out of the year here. I'm not too fond of cold weather. I gather you like the sun?" Max turns the subject like a page in a book.

"I do. That's one of the reasons why I moved to Florida. It gives me life."

"It certainly does," Max says tenderly. "What made you leave the Steel City?" Max flips another page.

The darkness of the winter months can drag on for what seems like decades. Day by day, depression sets in. The sky gets grayer, the slush gets older, and hope fades away with every disappointment and failure. Not only that, but Rochelle also had to get away from George and I was desperate to get from under my parental abusers.

"It was just time to get away from Pittsburgh. I had to if I wanted to live. Do you know you can shrivel up and die if you don't get enough Vitamin D?" I casually mention.

"Yes, I do. It's such an important part of our well-being. Without it, we wouldn't be sitting here talking to each other right now," Max implies.

CHAPTER 15
Breaking the Ice

"Ha!" A small laugh escapes my mouth.

Me now intrigued by the definition of his Vitamin D and whether we are talking about the sun or his dick. I tease him by dipping my pinky finger to taste my drink and then delicately between my lips.

"What's so funny?" Max asks.

"Your statement."

"What makes you laugh at it?"

"You're presuming your dick is the Vitamin D I take it?"

"It is," he announces confidently and starts chuckling himself.

"That's real funny!" I laugh along with him and guide the conversation in another direction. "You must be a thrill seeker, too."

"What makes you say that?" he asks.

"Anybody who willingly goes to the type of shit we were at earlier must be living on the edge," I conclude.

"Ha! I feel like I am. There are a lot of things going on in my family right now. Everybody needs me. I'm the only one they can count on." His words are heavy and carry the weight of the world. The pity in Max's voice is childlike and optimistic. "We take care of each other, no matter what. Sticking together is what we live by. Nothing else matters. Family over everything."

His powerful words beat against my aching heart. The sincerity in his tone seals it with the truth. Max just clicked the lock to my heart and threw away the key. At that moment, I fell in love with Max. That's the type of shit I need in my life. I don't care what Rochelle says.

"Yeah, family over everything," he repeats and throws his drink back like it was his last. Then Max starts talking more in depth about why he came to Florida. He talks about the importance of everyone in your circle doing their part when things need handling. Coming to Florida was something Max says he didn't want to do but did not have a choice in the matter. "It is too hot here! Man, I miss New York for real. The city has more life. It is slow in this boring town. Not much happens in this dry ass place." Max points out how backwards Bradenton is, asks me if I want another drink, and continues explaining his reason for living like a nomad for the past decade. His lips move at a blurred pace, and I only agree because I don't want to look lost or stupid.

"Yes, it is," I tell him. "I thought you were from Jersey?"

Thunder rumbles across the sky. Combustuous, rain-filled clouds release their built-up frustration on top of the metal shingles above us. They tap random responses in ding minor.

"I'm from a little bit of everywhere. I moved to New York for a few years before I moved there. I was making a couple of business moves that didn't work out," he shares.

Then, another roll of thunder booms across the sky as if God were bowling above the clouds. As the storm rolls in, we talk about my team having six super bowl rings, loving the vibe of nineties music, me stealing the toast of us hanging out, and how hungry we both are.

"After seeing that ungodly exhibition, I don't know how I could be," I say.

"It's only art. It looked that real to you?" Max insists as he skims over the menu, barely looking up to engage.

"It did. The artist is super good, or he's super psycho. The weird thing is one girl had eyes like the missing girl they showed on the news earlier today." I begin snapping my fingers to remember her name. "Lynita Hayward was it?"

It was creepy. My thoughts flash back to her piece. I swear her eyes moved as I rubbed over her exterior. Like she was calling out for help, I should have said something to someone. Then again, it could have been the potion we drank at the front door. Illusions. Coco was right.

"We're ready to order," Max interrupts and motions for the bartender to return. He starts scoping out everything in the room, pointing at the top corners of the establishment. He starts counting and stops at three.

"What are you counting?" I question as I sway to the reggae beat and slow wind my hips in gyration.

"COME NOW!" The reggae artist screams out from the speaker box.

I don't care what he's counting and only ask for the conversation to keep moving. I flip through my hair a few times to flirt a little more. Some strands land on the counter, and I brush them off.

"My fingers get caught sometimes."

"It's cool. Your hair is beautiful." Max reaches to touch it. "I'm scoping out the cameras in the room. See them there in the corners?"

Max points out the one above us in the bar area, the one by the front door, and the one on the wall leading to the outside cabañas. "Someone is always watching and listening," he adds. "I can't believe how beautiful your hair is," Max says while slowly massaging his hand into my scalp. He rubs his digits to the reggae boom. He manipulates my head with his badman juice.

"COME NOW!"

I think it's presumptuous of him to think it's okay to do what he's doing. Allowing him to run his fingers through my hair was unintentional. The palm of his hand almost covers the back of my skull like a supportive cup. His warm fingers move in a sexy reggae, massaging my scalp with tenderness and seduction.

His hand moves with my body, and begins to control the rock. Max pulls my head back in a soft motion—pulling the chair, with me in it, closer to him.

"Oh!"

He kisses my neck to calm the shock of his movement. Max is a giant, black magnet that draws me into his vibe. His vortex is like an inner force connecting us. This cocktail makes me feel good. The tingling in my legs signals the immediate response to his touch. It rushes the blood flow directly to my clit. Maybe I should stop drinking these rum punches to keep a clear head. His haze already clouds it. There is no telling what I'll do with him. I know I would fall in head first if I'm not careful.

We share things about ourselves as the night continues. Our likes, dislikes, and the deal-breaking peeves that make people hit the abort button in a relationship. We talk about the foods we like to eat. I mention my favorites: pasta, sushi, and occasionally a fried filet of grouper or red snapper with cheesy grits. I note anything that doesn't make my stomach turn when I look at it or softens to mush when it enters my mouth.

"You greedy," he says jokingly. "You eat just about everything then." Max jokes about my food confessions, and we laugh at his statement's accuracy...

The gluttony of the flesh is scandalous when greediness turns in its sin. When living in the foster home, I didn't know when my next meal would be. That's how nasty the head mother acted toward me. When I would eat, it was so much in one sitting that my back would hurt. She kept food from me when I didn't act right and made me sit at the table and watch the other kids enjoy their food. It was the cruelest way to break a child down. She tried to starve me as punishment. It just made me wiser. When everyone went to bed at night, I snuck into the kitchen and stuffed myself with the food I knew no one else would eat.

...Max clears his throat, and it snaps me out of my thoughts. He says he doesn't eat pork, hates spaghetti, and only drinks vintage Malbec at dinner. Max says that's the only way to enjoy chilled olives stuffed with blue cheese. The bitterness of the wine kills the funk of the curd that he loves so much. Max says he eats a lot of chicken and loves beans and rice. Then, Max casually mentions that he eats pussy, but not chitterlings.

"Oh, okay!" The words jump from my mouth in shock.

I did not expect the word pussy to play a part in our conversation so soon, but it doesn't surprise me. Men believe discussing sex the first time you get together is appropriate. I don't know what gives them that impression. Just because I want to does not mean right this second. I'm sure if it were up to Max, he would throw me above the bar counter and eat my sweet lips right now.

Max hungrily licks his lips and starts the small talk about getting to know someone. It builds from a library of questions asked in succession like it's supposed to expose the complex layers of someone's personality and character. All it does is scratch the bare surface of who they are. Discovering the core ingredients usually takes a minimum of three months. That's how long a man can keep his charades intact before the façade starts falling apart. It sounds like the same broken record on repeat. Max could have left the pussy eating out, but since we're opening to one another, that information is good to know for later.

"You date white girls?" I turn a different page in this story and throw an off-the-wall question into play.

Max stops rubbing my head and shifts his body. I may have to bow out if he does. There is no way to tell which hygienic or sexual habits he has picked up along the way, and I refuse to hunch on any animals again. Mr. Willy fucked me up with that one.

"I have," he admits with ease. "Why? Do you date them?"

"Ah, Touché," I lightheartedly respond. "I have, but for business purposes—not relationship-wise."

"Does it bother you that I have dated them?" Max asks.

"Not really. You can date who you wanna date. It's not like we're together," I assert with a soft passion. My response almost sounds sad that we're not.

Max pauses for a second to gather his words and wipes the sweat from his brow. "I thought you were about to tell me you were bowing out if I *did* date white women. Like, I picked up their weird bestiality habits or something. It's a touchy subject. I know how black women feel about that!" He laughs as he watches my face tighten up. "Oh, and just because I dated them doesn't mean I practice that shit. I don't fuck animals, baby girl."

He surprises me with his statement. It's almost like he was standing in my head as I thought it. How spot-on he is. We're in tune more than I realize.

"Oh," I speak softer as I sip more juicy punch.

"Tell me more about your experiences with them," he continues. "Mine is interesting. You go first."

I share an excerpt about stripping at Controversy a few years back, how famous the blue-eyed devils were for doing lines of cocaine before every set, how pairing up with them in private rooms helped to sell the jungle fever ambiance, and dancers know the white girls up the cash flow. Max begins rattling off about his mixed children and that he has some white baby mamas.

I drop details about George, how I met Rochelle, and everything that came with their situation. The confessions came so quickly that the story grew into a simmering pot of tea that I had spilled. Surprised at how the admissions drip from my lips with tempting luxury, I am relieved and take a deep breath. The weight of my past bears more than I admit.

No pictures, I couldn't talk to anyone unless Rochelle approved, and a pile of other shit that makes me feel like an insignificant child again. My transparency must be too much for Max to handle by how his eyes have widened and his raised eyebrows sit on his forehead. I done said too damn much. More cards are showing in my deck, and very few are, in his.

"Woman, please. That's nothing." he says with grace and humor. "A lot of women do that to pay for school. Is that why you did it?" he asks.

"Yes and no." My answer teeters on discretion.

"Elaborate." He gestures with his hands and turns his seat.

And once again, I start revealing things about my life.

"I went to beauty school, turned to stripping to pay for it, and it was a way to make enough money to get out from under Mr. Willy." Dancing allowed me to meet fatter-pocketed customers and clients—

usually the old, white men. That helped to get me on to the white girls and their strip game.

I share my feelings about white women also stealing our black men. The brothers that gravitate to them get the fat, sloppy ones that no white-collared man would be caught dead with. And if they do, it's only because his children will be cared for, he'll have a clean home, a hot meal every night, and knows his wife will gladly suck his dick after a stressful day at the office.

In the process, I fuss about a black man degrading his integrity and the purity of his bloodline when they mix our royal blood with their tyrannical craziness. When I say it, Max smiles.

"I'm not competing with no Becky doll for any man. Those white girls suck a dick for a grain of powder, and they can't be left alone in a room for five minutes before they're all over each other. If a brother wants that in his lifeline, that's his choice. I'm a big girl. I know when to bow out. I'm smart enough to recognize the signs when a man doesn't want me."

"You can't choose love, no matter what shade it's packaged in. It just happens. The color of love is a rainbow; its spectrum is wide. They're within that spectrum, too," he philosophies his statement.

It almost gets under my skin how he defends them. "I know that, and I believe that love is love; however, if I see one more brother hugged up with another white girl..." I begin.

"...if I see one more brother hugged up with another white girl," Max says like he has heard it a thousand times before. His hands animate his statement. "Blah, blah, blah."

Now he's creeping me out.

"Why does it upset you like that?" Max inquires.

I take another sip of my cocktail and respond as if walking on a thin sheet of ice. "I'm not upset, just tired. I'm tired of playing second fiddle to the Becky's in our culture. Don't they already have the universe behind them? What else could they possibly need? Do they have to take our men, too?" My voice rises with excitement.

"Black women can be difficult sometimes," he shares.

"We're difficult? I guess raising generations of your bastard children doesn't fall into that category?"

"Wait a minute, there's no need to get hyped up. You ain't raise none of my kids. I'm just saying. Black women can be a bit much. For example..." he points to our situation and chuckles. "...they get all extra when you're explaining how you feel and turn around and wonder why we don't share shit," he concludes to make his point.

"But the truth is, black women forgot one itsy, bitsy thing that makes us entertain white girls," he adds.

"Really? What's that?" I ask.

"Good credit. Most black men can't buy a stick of gum on credit. It's sad, child."

We burst out laughing again. Max goes into a poetic exhortation of comparisons between wants and needs and why different cultures value different things. He says that white women value credit and land while black women value materialistic stuff like blue crab parties and surgeries they must keep up with for the rest of their lives—both producing the most rotten, funkiest pussies on the planet. He reiterates how our culture always needs to look like we have but have nothing.

"The vision of presentation is but a lie, and those whose eyes are closed, will sleep in its ignorance forever," Max's arrogant truths spill from his pillowy lips in poetic messages.

"Who said that?" I ask.

"Some jailbird I had the pleasure of meeting in New York. He was quite versed in Latin Eros. Spending twenty years in the pen gives a man time to read," Max begins as he compares most black women to cartoon characters in paint. He curses social media for its fakeness in real-time, corroding the meaning of self-love.

Max grabs my hand and butters my skin as he speaks, professing how he wishes black women were less ashamed of their earthen beauty and how he wants nothing more than a real woman, one with stretch marks and all. Max then mentions how sick he is with platinum wigs, mink eyelashes, and fake fingernails.

"But seriously, that's real talk. You can't get close enough to kiss these females because their eyelashes tickle your face, and when their makeup rubs off, it causes pimples. It's terrible!"

"Too funny!" I reply.

"They bling out the exterior trying to cover up the ugliness on the inside," he affirms. "The shit is extra. I can't even get into women who look like that. I don't know who she is because she's head-to-toe with somebody else's stuff.
We need the white girls to go to the next level. They don't do that extra shit black women are known for doing. The white women don't act ghetto *and* you can touch their hair."

"Wait a minute! Don't do that. You don't need them; you choose them. On top of that, the black men that go to white girls, most black women .won't entertain they ass! Don't play yourself with that!" I laugh at his arrogance. "There are so many beautiful black women in this world, and the black man drags us back to the slave trade with their carousing of white women. Not all women who care about their appearance are clowns like you're painting them out to be," I add. "You ran your fingers through my hair a minute ago, and I'm not white. Our titty milk must be too chocolatey."

"Ha!" Max chuckles at my statement. "I like titty milk." Max thinks of how warm and sweet Gianna's must taste when he laughs.

"It just seems like the black queen is no longer the prize. They are," I add.

"How does it directly affect you, though? Not all the brothers find interest in white women. They're just there when black women aren't. We are not bitches to them. Maybe it's you."

I stop and think for a second. Not knowing whether to be offended by what Max said but more like, "is he for real?" Like he's degrading my worth without even knowing me. I wasn't taking offense to his last statement since it didn't apply, but it does make me think for a split second. Could it be me? It can't be. I'm the lady adorned with the features bitches die on tables for.

"Yes, it directly affects me—especially when the pickings are slim," I reply.

Max arrogantly laughs. "The pickings aren't slim; you're just traveling the wrong circles," he states.

"Do you see what I'm packing back here?" I smack on my ass for dramatics.

"You think that's what makes you stand out?" His comment is as is cold as ice. "Woman, please. Anybody can buy one of those. That's just how beautiful women, such as yourself, get caught up in *bullshit* they can't handle, thinking their bubble butts will save their asses."

"Really?" I immediately took offense to his outburst. Now, he's starting to piss me off.

"We know your game. You all aren't as smart as you think."

I cannot believe what is coming out of his mouth. The arrogance of it all. No wonder he's alone. If his sister only knew what it was on this side, she'd be embarrassed. I decided to do some ball-busting of my own.

"Mm, okay. Men are visual creatures, right?" I ask softly as I downgrade my passionate response to his audacious declarations.

"Yes, we are," Max agrees.

"We need to do so much to keep men interested, don't you agree?"

Max gestures with an approving nod.

"Between the cost of looking decent and attracting a man, we have to worry about some extra shit."

"Like what?" Max asks.

"We don't know whether we're competing with another woman or a man."

"Ouch," he responds with a flinch.

"Yeah, like, is the dildo for me to get done with when your junk quits, or am I slapping it on the wall for you to twerk back on? Which is it?"

We look at each other, and I shrug my shoulders. Max shakes his head as he lets out a small laugh.

"A woman like me has to factor in so many things," I begin.

"Like what? That last thing you said is big. Sticking a dildo to the wall?" His voice heightens.

"We don't have many black men left to choose from."

"I disagree. There's still a lot of us out here. Like I said, it just depends on the circles you're traveling in. You're sitting across from one right now," Max confidently states.

I laugh at his response, even intrigued by the cockiness in whom he's telling me he is. It sounds narcissistic to me.

"Not only that, the ones left may be on the down low or, even worse, in jail. Once you add white women to the mix, black women are straight losing," I release.

"Wow, that is a lot to contend with," his voice echoes assurance and understanding. He stops, eases further into the stool, and caresses my hand deeper. His body rests in our engagement. "You have your own flavor, though. Your vibe speaks for itself," his words flow effortlessly from his lips as he speaks. His tender assurance wisps past my earlobes in delicate flutters and beat-driven pronunciations.

"A lot of people never consider what the other person is dealing with," I say. "People fail to read the story before the chapter they stepped in on."

Max looks at me discernably. He nods in agreement with my statement. I sense he is engaged.

"*Everyone has a past,*" we say in unison as if joined by the vocal cords at the same time of inception. Our DNA strands scripted our words for this exact moment. Our connection intertwines intricate webbings of time, infusing our vibe beyond all existence. I feel his words. He feels my pain.

CHAPTER 16
Quick Decisions vs. Overthinking

Max could not understand why Gianna was as intriguing to him as she was. It could have been the initial shock that rushed through his veins when they first shook hands and again when they locked eyes. Since Gianna made it clear she was up for getting together, he was not about to let Sean's comment change his mind. Subconsciously, it did play a role.

He knew he would have to ease her into his world. He would have to make the obvious not so apparent. His questions required a simple yes or no response. No maybes. Max knew he needed to make her understand who he was without raising any suspicions and pushing her away. Those conversations were always the hardest. After a while, there were other questions asked. Questions that could not be answered with a simple yes or no. Once Max felt there was no need to clarify, the parachute would get pulled, and he wouldn't have to explain shit.

It was her first impression that sparked his curiosity. Not only was she fine, but Max thought Gianna was witty, sexy, and a little enthusiastic. He noticed something arousing about her right off the bat. Their meeting aligned with the stars at the precise moment of their encounter. Though brief, yet assured, their paths crossed within the universe, and destiny took the wheel. Max's flame lit, and his host cells swelled to capacity on site.

His body sensed her curiosity. Her aura danced around her like neon butterflies flickering pulses of excited energy. She felt familiar, and he didn't even know who she was yet. He could almost taste her essence when the wind blew through her hair, or the sweetness of her breath puffed through the breeze when she spoke. Max could see Gianna, and she said life, something he desperately needed to carry on in this realm.

All Max knew was that he had to go back now. There was no way around it. He knew he didn't have to spend his eternity alone. There is nothing pleasant about going through the casting. Every woman Max encountered needed to be for his purpose. It was imperative and more manageable if they were damaged. They were anxious to find something, or someone, to belong. They were easy to coax, and Max had everything they desired.

Max knew that his lineage would end with him if he didn't act fast. Too many within a cycle altered the sequence, and they emerged quicker, with more swiftness, and with an unrelenting fury that made the devil himself afraid.

Hell has no wrath like the Declotae. Max had dipped them once before and slid out of his punishment. Max was due to do his time. He knew the holes in the system and how to keep them at bay, but he realized his road eventually ended. Max knew it wasn't a matter of if, but when, his day would come. His assignment became something different once Gianna entered his world.

They wanted each other. Max could feel Gianna in his bones. They rattled and shook in her presence; the cartilage between them tingled with excitement, almost regenerating the genetically weaker knee to rebind its shortened meniscus.

How Gianna smiled with her eyes and touched him to accentuate her points was refreshing. She didn't act ghetto. Max could tell she had been exposed to men with money by the way she giggled at every joke he made. She kept up well with his shifty lingo and responses. Though Gianna never lashed out in ignorance, he could tell she was lost in his story. If she's as smart as she claimed, she'll get back on track. He knew she was curious when he caught her checking out his dick; that was all he needed to lure her in.

Dick and good conversation. Good combination.

Max knew how big his manhood grew and how to satisfy. He lusted to give every thrust her pussy needed to make her want him more.

Max knew Gianna was a different breed of red bone. He could sense it. Max didn't just want her. He wanted to fuck the shit out of her, sensing she could handle his enormous, and at times, vulgarly thick cock. By the way her hips widened horizontally to her sweet spot, which indicated her pussy went deep—leagues deep. Ocean depth. A big, wet void.

"Mm." Max thought as he watched Gianna squirm her pussy around in the seat, wishing his hand was underneath her meat to feel her warmth.

Gianna sparked an unrelenting fire deep inside of him that he didn't know still existed. Gianna looked like the kind of woman Max dated with sun-kissed skin, long hair, and a badass figure, but she was more superlative than that. Top shelf. Whether she realized it or not, women like her are still the prize. Her ass looked familiar—plump and round. It pays homage to her obvious Caribbean and African lineage that she was unaware existed. Gianna was exotic to him. Her mulatto skin bronzed without burning, and when she brushed her hair away from her shoulder, Max couldn't believe what he was seeing. He knew exactly who she was. Max knew his intuition wasn't misleading him. Tattoos don't change like that. It was like the gods had shined upon him and given him access to everything he needed.

Strong in her personality and beauty, Max recognized Gianna was a wounded spirit. He could feel her pain, hidden behind fitted wear and soft inuendoes.

He could smell the cautiousness in her speech. It reeked of darker addictions. She didn't want to give herself away by saying too much. A bone may have flown out her mouth, revealing herself too soon. She told the bare minimum and just enough to keep the conversation flowing.

There was always room for doubt when it came to holy rollers. How religious Gianna was, Max would see just how much. Nobody is that pure. Hell, she's already halfway through her second punch and let him touch her hair. With women, that's sensual...borderline sexual. Allowing a man to feel through it is a big deal and means she doesn't give a damn if it gets fucked up later. Max had heard her say at least five profanities since their first meeting, which didn't sound like she was sanctified. Max knew saved women weren't as committed to their faith as they broadcasted. He knew firsthand. Gianna certainly wasn't the first one. Women like her faked the funk. Acting all holyfied-in-church and getting fucked up the ass in private after numerous margaritas on Taco Tuesday. He figured out long ago that churchy women were the easiest to lure, and Max had everything he needed to reel them in—his big, black dick.

As he sat across from her, legs crossed, her toes pointed downward, his cock struggled not to stand at attention. He watched as she played in her hair and touched his fingers between her strands and spoke about things, he gave zero fucks about. He just wanted to know how she tasted. That's it. How creamy was she? Did it smell sweet? He noticed her guard come down the more she playfully touched his knee, the bad one at that, and at times gently rubbed. It's funny how she is attracted to the knee that collapses at will and the fragment of his plate where he needs surgery. The alcohol was shedding her inhibitions, his too, and she allowed his flirty fingers to lead the way.

CHAPTER 17
The Delicate Dance of Temptation: An Ode to Zero Fucks

"May I have this dance?" Max asks as he levitates from his stool.

"I would love to."

So, we dance.

Slow wind to the sexy reggae.

Bump and jerk to the dance hall.

Bloop, bloop.

I tell Max to play in my hair as we step.

We dance to our heart's beat all night.

Max has me in another zone.

His hips move hypnotically as he strokes my crown.

Max whisks me away to a gigantic two-story property to change cars.

His Aston Martin.

Top-down.

My hair blows in the wind and soaks up the dew from the misty after-rain.

We drive to Miami.

Classical music on blast.

I'm smoking.

Max is driving.

I can't tell him I'm not on his level now.

The conversation at Rodney's was deep enough.

It broke the ice between us.

I'm just a broke bitch.

Faking the funk.

Raggedy car.

A raggedy place to stay.

I have twenty dollars in my purse and three hundred in the bank.

I just make this shit look good.

"Wanna go to the Bahamas?"

Max stops at the road's intersection, looking at me for a decision.

"Are you serious?"

"Very. I mean, we're in Miami."

He shrugs his shoulders and taps on the steering wheel, waiting for my answer.

"I don't have a passport. I'm not vaxxed. Don't you have to show proof now?"

"That's an easy fix," he responds like he has everything on standby.

Max leans across my lap and opens the glove compartment full of passports with proof of COVID vaccinations.

Two red ones.

One white one.

Three black ones, all with different colored writing on the front.

He shuffles the selection and pulls out a gold booklet hidden under a billfold. Here's one. You two resemble. No one will know."

"Who is this?" I ask as I flip the worn, gritty pages.

"Passports that people lost while in my travels. I have no clue who they are," Max replies nonchalantly.

I look closer at the information stamped on the page.

Her name, which is hard to pronounce, also starts with a G.

Her hair color, black.

The automated smile in the photo.

The blank void in her eyes.

Where she traveled.

Argentina, June of 1944.

Korea, December of 1999.

Iceland, August of 2015.

"I don't have anything with me."

"You won't need anything. I got you."

'Fuck it, let's go," I respond without hesitation.

Max hits a left. "Let's go!"

We ride towards the dock.

He runs his fingers through my hair again, manipulating his want deep into my occipital.

Calming any fear, I may be having.

Sipping champagne.

Rubbing on my thigh.

Squeezing softly.

Feeling his need to touch.

The warm winds blow.

The delight of it.

I don't know him.

I feel like I do.

Deep in my soul.

From the moment we met, our destiny was written.

No matter what.

"You can make this whatever you want," Max whispers.
We sail upon rough waters and try to stand straight.
We're drunk.
We're laughing.
We're touching.
Dancing under the moonlight on the ship.
Being transparent.
Having truth moments.
Sharing funny stories.
Creating memories.
How sensitive my eyes are to the flash of the camera.
How high I look in most of the pictures.
Eyes shut.
Smiles wide and rehearsed.
His humungous hands are over my shoulders.
He is too big to fit into the picture frame.
His gothic ring blinds against the lights.
The photo looks like I am a million miles away.
His hold is makes me feel protected.
His towering dominance whispers French adages into my ear, melting
their fluidity into me.
Eating lobster and prawns at the Captain's Dinner.
Basking in Atlantis.
Gambling thousands away just for the hell of it.
Max doesn't care.
Neither do I.
Ain't my money.
My tan is popping.
My booty is Caribbean brown.
We're feeling the natives.
"Weed!"
Treating me to the finest pair of black and gold Versace sunglasses I've
never owned.
Gucci bikinis and sundresses by the pound.
Grandfather OG Kush by the pound.
He wants to eat this cake by the pound.
He's well on his way to getting all of me.
By showing me his world and the bounty within it.
The freedom.
Do what you want to do.
When you want to do it.

Answer to no one.
Playa-time.
Who gone check you, boo?
Traveling to Haiti.
He takes me to a remote property.
The mossy plains were covered in cotton.
Sugarcane.
Chickens are cackling.
In the back are sheds.
Boarded windows.
Piles of tree branches wrapped in yellow ribbons.
Vines are everywhere.
Guarded.
Intertwined.
Never resting.
Ready to attack from the root, if they needed to.
Sonic blasts of heavy silence.
Peaceful and Quiet.
It camouflages the deceit of the day.
It's there, but not there.
Glitchy.
"You'll find out about that later," his words envelope my ears as he
seals his hand to mine.
We travel to Jamaica and cliff jump in Negril.
Race with the bulls in Peru.
I have too much ass for all this running.
Going faster than I ever have.
I am running from the struggles of my life to stop and smell the roses
with him.
Moving at his pace, his race.
But it could end when he gets good and ready.
Any time is possible.

    Then, Max snatches me from the rushing crowd into a slender
cubby between the terra cotta buildings, where he kisses me
passionately and says that I'm the best time he's having outside of sex.
He repeatedly says how much he values me and understands my
hesitation. He tells me however long it takes he'll wait. He lifts me into
his arms and presses my body against the ruddy wall and we kiss
fervently. I melt into the chocolatey warmness of his soft lips. He slips
his cool tongue into my hot mouth. Instantly, we are sucked back into

the influx of raging bulls and the little red scarves cheering everyone on.
Max grabs hold of my hand, and we run faster.
I almost scrape my newly polished toes in our scurry.
He hoists me into the air as he charges alongside the herd.
He places me onto one bull.
Max hops onto another with magical ease.
He turns his neck and face to look at me.
His blur is cryptic.
His smile chatters with his stride.
No fucking way this is happening!
My ass slaps against the bull's spine.
My clit finds a grove to rub against as he charges faster.
The bull's racy blood gyrates against my clit with each angry tread.
"I'm cumming!" I call out in bestial release.
Max smiles as my orgasm streams down my leg and the bull's black sheath of hair.
It blows in the wind and lands on his lips.
"Fuck!" Max screams out.
Max thrashes his tongue to-and-fro to catch the spray of pussy gel.
Nothing matters except this.
I feel like I'm finally living, not just existing.
I am making my mark in the world.
With Max.
He and I.
Me and him.
Us.
Bae.
We are experiencing excitement without any demands or expectations.
As Max rides, his body glows with excited eyes.
My romantic warrior is in savior mode.
His is proud and strong.
Max saves his damsel from distress.
It makes me feel supreme.
Worthy.
Flossy.
Right now, the Head Bitch in Charge.
"You are everything I could have ever imagined," he whispers.
"I can't believe I'm doing this with you," I say as I clench his hand.
And as we jump from the plane together, Max is attached to me.

My shield.
I can spread my wings and fly.
Twirling.
We are falling into our forever.
Mesmerized by Max's grace and strength.
He kisses my hands mid-air and tucks them into his as he dives toward the ground.
We cut through the sky at lightning speed.
Frustration screams from my lungs.
Spit blubbers from my lips.
I watch my life flash before me in frames.
At the mercy of God.
Falling for Max.
We land in an open field.
My hair looks a mess as I stumble across the field to regain my legs.
We fly across oceans to savor authentic pasta.
He buys a custom pair of leather heels.
There are gondola rides through the city of Venice.
Roman bath houses.
Bathed by women dripped in gold.
Their second layer of skin.
Gold eye shadow.
Gold nails.
Gold, empty eyes.
They suck on my nipples and toes with their gold tongues.
One asks if she can taste my pussy lips.
She says my scent is unlike anything she has ever smelled.
Too sweet to go to waste.
Let her suck the pussy with her gold tongue.
Something sweet to give.
A teaser.
A pleaser.
A spreader.
A spitter.
Max watches my lips get licked by one gold demon, then two.
His chest rises and falls.
"Just let it happen, baby. Let both of their tongues get you off."
I call out Max's name as I nut in their mouths numerous times.
For days we graze on the tropical coast of Vietnam.
Picking random vegetables and goods as we creep down the waterway assembly line.

The Saigon Ben Thanh market.
Me.
Adopted.
Sexualized.
Abandoned.
Men issues.
Mary issues.
All the way over here in Gucci and shit.
I was getting tossed by some Golden Italians.
Running my fingers through the water.
Touching lily pads in their natural habitat.
With a man filling my head with his splendor.
Taking me far, far away.
Further, than I've ever been.
Revealing his weaknesses, too.
Showing me how quickly he can disappear.
Max displays his "Art of the Barter" skills.
Speaking that language, too.
Bagging free stuff at every stop.
If not, he threatens to move on.
I am not on his level.
I should move on.
I feel obligated to give it up.
Make up for my lack.
Using my abundance of ass as a bartering tool.
Traveling the globe isn't fun anymore.
I wonder if anyone cares where I am?
No cell phones.
I haven't seen a television since we left the States.
I'm waiting for the ball to drop, but before it can...
"I have to get back," Max blurts out.
"I guess we're done hanging out?" I question lightly.
"It's not you. It's me. Our lives are different and our versions of
hanging out are not the same."
Max relays the same reservations that I have.
"Hanging out is going to the movies or having a picnic in the park." I
laugh.
"We've been gone for weeks, and I have a job," I add.
Max gently lifts my face and looks deep into my eyes as we cruise the
waterway.
"I sense something else. What's on your mind?" Max inquires.

He dips his fingers into the water and moistens my feet once again.

"I'm waiting," he emphasizes as he presses between my toes.

His eyes reveal their soothing calmness.

Everything is beautiful.

This vibe, peaceful.

"I feel like you're spending a lot of money on me, and we haven't …," I begin.

"…We haven't what? Slept together?" Max interrupts.

"Yes," I confess.

"Is that normal for you?"

"Well, no, yes…not exactly," I stumble with my choice of words.

"Elaborate." Max gestures by squeezing my foot between both of his hands as he rubs. "Because I have some things of my own that I would like to share.

So, here I go again, releasing another excerpt of my story. I go deeper with Mr. Willy this time, sharing how obligated I feel to give some pussy to him. I learned that a man always wants something in return when spending his money, and Max stops me by gently placing his wet finger over my lips.

CHAPTER 18
The Lies We Tell

"Stop. Now, that's some bullshit. He was trying to control you with that. He wanted to justify his actions by making you think you were in control of how far it went. Dirty bastard." The discovery angers Max that this Mr. Willy had used one of the oldest diversions in the legendary playbook, the Book of Masteries. The This-That-and-the-Third Method was one that required time and patience. It only worked in stable living environments. He honestly wants to meet the slimeball and shake his hand, but instead consoles Gianna's misinformed guidance by massaging her ankle in tender presses. Max cups his hand into the flowing water and wets Gianna's desires with the trickling drops of exotic sunshine.

Max knew the more he was around Gianna, the more she needed his protection. She was out here without a guardian. There had yet to be anyone to fill that role. Gianna didn't know shit. Gianna had no clue who she was, and Max could sense that. He didn't want to scare her off by saying too much. Max would have sounded crazier than she already thought. If he shared everything now, he might as well push her off this narrow ass boat and let the piranhas eat her.

Max quickly abandoned that thought when Gianna's beauty ushered in an enlightening peace that he couldn't explain. He just wanted to hold her close and never let go. Gianna's presence offered so many things on so many levels. She allowed herself to be free with him, and that pleased Max. She was just talking and talking. Gianna was comfortable letting her frustrations out, which meant she trusted him with her feelings. That's big. He started feeling like the protector he was and smacked his hand for thinking crazy. He needs to be her knight in shining armor. Max loves how open Gianna is. She didn't second guess it. She went with her emotions and allowed her heart to show her the way. That made Max want to please her more. He could tell she was finally able to be the lady she was without covering her insecurities.

Max opened to Gianna organically and in pieces, allowing the universe to work its magic. It wasn't one specific thing that she did to him. Everything she could offer appealed to his heart and his loins.

Here is where Max wanted to be and where he needed to clarify his intentions.

"I'm serious about perusing you. I want us for eternity." His eyes dance, flashing their hypnotic gaze, and my submissiveness sinks further. They illuminate subtle neon blue and green hues that pulse an aurora wave of the night sky. They are truth pullers that instantly mesmerize me into his sensuous haze of comfort.

So, I tell him.

The foster home.

Tell him about my adopted mother and how poor we were.

I am still determining who I am and my origin.

The manipulation.

Dancing, private parties, and escorts.

About Rochelle.

The pussy eating.

Lost in a world full of nothing.

Damaged from the pain.

Scorned from lack of love.

A snapshot of my life.

Open and honest.

After that, Max may not be as interested.

Sometimes, I need to learn how to keep my fucking mouth shut.

I sound thirsty.

Easy.

Knocking my bucket over.

I'm only being honest.

I didn't know how to do that before.

Constantly changing into the person, they need me to be to please them.

No more hiding who I am.

I don't want to waste any more of my time or his.

No bullshit.

Showing my full deck of trauma at will.

"That's nothing," he comments. "Wait until you experience mine."

"That sounds interesting."

"It will be," he swoons with his voice as he places the warmest kiss upon my naïve lips.

CHAPTER 19
Confession Time

Max mentions that we needed to stop at one more destination before we returned home to Boringtown, if I didn't mind.

And with that, our travels take us back to Haiti, where he started his life long ago. It's beautiful here. The lush grounds are soft and inviting. We nest near the ocean bank on the northwest side of his family property. From it hosts a cliff with a thousand-foot drop that descends into the crystal blue waves below. Each crash pounds against the boulders along the sea wall in excitement. I can almost hear the haunting screams of women underneath the foam that sprays high into the air against their cries.

We look up into the night sky. Sagittarius is in the third cycle of the moon. The Big Dipper hangs over to the left. The stars are innumerable. They twinkle like diamonds against God's cerulean void of eternity.

"Stick close while we are here. The ground is not familiar to you yet. Try not to make any sudden moves." His explanation sounds creepy, and I'm anxious to know why. It excites me for some reason. His words express as if something is going to jump from the ocean and snatch me back with it. There is one command after another as he cautiously mentions the dos and don'ts.

Max graciously takes me on tour to show the DuBois Family Estate. The grand entrance is stunning. Each hint of gold is straight out of King Midas' Archive Collection. It reminds me of our travels to Italy. I look up at the ceiling, entranced by the height of its magnificence and grandeur. It looks like the gateway to Heaven. Glorious in its showcase, the tinkering sound of a tiny bell rings upon our entrance. The bamboo fan with its enormous, gold-dipped leaves whooshes through my hair in heavy circulations.

The sound hauntingly emulates the wind that rushed through the gold rings of number five's flesh. The holes in her skin hung on for dear life, some tearing from the tension and weight from the opening and closing of her shuffling arms.

Along the wall is a gold curio filled with antique dinnerware meticulously stacked and arranged. As we continue, I look to my right and notice an open space in the living room. Two couches covered in plastic face each other. Between them is a large, circular rug. I look past the seating arrangement and notice numerous gold mirrors. They remind me of the mirrors I used to sit in front of for hours, making funny faces, having haircut-dance shows with my dolls, and trying on different shades of lipstick I had borrowed from Mary's purse. I always chose red shades that I still pick today.

On each side of the mirrors are ceramic lion heads covered in what looks like flea market gold. They iridescently reflect the golden glow of the items close by. Some of it chipped off. Some of it speckled on the black marble floor like it had sprayed right from the lion's mouth. Hanging from their necks are gold beads. A gold shield and a gold machete are on the floor in the other corner. Everything is reflecting from the floor that disturbingly looks like a black hole. I step lightly; my mind, jumbled by its illusion, is hallucinating the view. Like one wrong step would plunge me into its darkness. I grab tight to Max's hand as he guides the way.

"The floor still fucks with me, and I've lived here half my life," he assures me of my steps. "Don't worry, you won't fall in."

The gold candles melting from their sconces blaze from a distance. We walked a little further, and I notice another break in the wall where there is a dining table seating eight. All the seats are gold. The place setting is gold. The wine glasses, the water goblets, the forks, the spoons, and the gravy bowl are all gold. The mirrors are gold here, too, but there is no image within the frame, only paint strokes of shimmering color blocking any ugly reflections. There are paintings of women draped in gold, golden statues, and a portrait of an older woman sitting in a gold rocking chair with a gold blanket over her lap. From there, he shows me the kitchen with its gold extras everywhere, from the blender to the toaster and fixtures. There's just gold all over the place. Everything shines at maximum capacity disrespectfully and the metallic overload burns my corneas out. I'm fucking blind at this point.

"Your eyes alright?" he jokes.

"Hell no." I laugh. "I'm blind!"

Max then takes me to his part of the house, where he casually discusses its addition a few years ago—dropping hints about the structure's necessity. He tells me how the concrete keeps the moistness from absorbing into the house, how that keeps mold from settling in, and why it had to be on the northwest side. Something about the horizon at night, when he could show me what he means, and how it doesn't come around often.

"I can't wait to show you! Wait until you see!"

The excitement in his voice is brought to you by a tour of his mancave entertainment center stockpiled with an 85" 4K flat screen television, a Blu-ray high-definition player, a turntable for the oldie but goodie records, a six-disc CD changer, web cameras, an AI touchscreen computer, and a humungous gold pendulum. There are surround sound speakers and security cameras nestled into the corners of the walls.

Everything on his dresser is lined up together, with the labels facing forward. French cologne, some almond oil hand lotion, and a few glass menagerie figurines are standing at attention. I notice a library of watches lined up near the edge.

"I take it you like watches." I run my hands over the different timepieces. There's a bulky watch, an antique stopwatch, and a display of other pieces to admire for name's sake alone.

"Yes, I do. Time is important to me," he mentions. "I try not to waste it. In some cases, once it's gone, you can never get it back."

"That's so true. Wouldn't it be nice to live forever so you wouldn't have to worry about it?" I ask.

Max twitches his neck and smiles. "Yes, it is."

"What's this?" The gadget, unfamiliar to me, is designed with circles and angles. The small, gold device is delicate and sturdy. Some sections have a shadow from the natural presence of the sun's daily routine. In this case, it's all black.

"A clepsydra," Max replies. "It's a clock that measures the tide of the ocean."

Max says that misleading people to gain access to their time can backfire, and how the importance of transparency is right from the start. No one wants to be left in the dark. Be upfront with people. Put out what you wish back. Give to get. Max claims he can wait, but his word choices project something different.

I turn to look at the grandeur of his bed. The royal plush of the material basks in wealth. "You must have had some military training." I notice the tautness of the corners with their pimped-out, sheikish accouterments. The tassels are draped in gold wires that spiral like curls.

"I have. My father and I weren't speaking because of it. I didn't get the chance to make it right with him before he passed," Max confesses.

He goes off into this spiel about how obligated he feels. I ask him about what, and Max starts explaining being tied to something that had nothing to do with him, how transparent things should be, and how there's no time to waste. He kisses my cheek before he continues.

"I need to share something with you, Gianna."

There is an unclear hesitation in his energy. And here comes the bomb. He's married with ten wives and shit, and he wants me to be part of his harem.

"It's important that you know exactly why you're here with me."

My heart pounds with excitement as I watch Max prepare words carefully through the shifts of his eyes and clench in his jawline.

"Do you have time for a story?" Max questions with his boyish smile.

"Where else am I going, Max?"

"I want you here with me forever. I love the way you make me feel."

Max is sucking me in with his openness and eager need of my presence.

"Tell me a story, Max. I'm dying to find out."

"Okay," he speaks as he takes a deep breath. "My full name is Trevallier Maximus Negus DuBois," he announces with his royal introduction before he quickly stomp-clamps three times, spreads his hands at his crotch, holds his head high and proud, then concludes his official presence.

"Wow, that was grand," I tease. "Trevallier?" I stumbled through the word to say correctly. "What's that?"

"My title. I am a world traveler, and my ancestors travel to distant lands and galaxies for eternity and beyond. I share my family's beginnings with you. I will also share our connection and why you are here now." Max bows his head and begins:

Max's father and mother being of West African descent by way of Espanola, settled on their piece of land secluded on the northernmost part of the island, the very one we're on.

As part of the Dominican and Haitian divide, his mother was betrothed to his father as an endowment when they united. After converting to Christianity from a cult his family belonged to, his father became a deacon in his mother's church.

"These are the reasons we are standing here, in this spot, right now," Max says nonchalantly.

"What?" It didn't make sense. "I don't understand. Can you run that back?" I respond like a young child to the way he throws his information at me slowly to remember at once.

"Yes, it is a lot. Let me break it down."

Max shares how his parents met in Haiti on a wellness mission. His mother, of Dominican descent, lived in the Americas, Florida at the time, and was eager to assist with distributing goods to the people after a torrential hurricane passed through one season.

The high-pressure block of Azores High impelled the anticyclonic circulation of destructive winds and torrential rains along the entire southern periphery. The Caribbean Sea inhaled a wall of water as the storm traveled across the seaboard. Smaller islands were swallowed beneath the ocean, while others flourished in commodities and wealth high above the dry tide.

His mother's church traveled back and forth to the impoverished island to help where needed. He describes how his father, a native and long sufferer of the stormy season, was a white magic healer and belonged to an ancestral line of Voodoo priests that settled in Haiti by way of France.

His father became enamored with his mother and was spiritually saved through the church's missions there. He tells me how smitten his father was with his mother. Max lightheartedly mentions how his mother and I resemble each other and that's what probably caught his father's attention, just like I caught his.

"Mm," I reply.

Once they married and decided to move back to America, they resided near a heavy community of their people, in Miami. Over Max's formative years, he, and his sister, Dedrias, became familiar with certain traditions and acclimated to both worlds.

His mother belonged to the Pentecostal side of the faith, which stemmed from Voodoo practices in its eastern foundation, but vowed never to practice that side of the religion's sinister traits. The tambourines, the long skirts, and the pictures of their minister in the front with candles all around him like a holy shrine were indicative signs of the cult in practice. Max fails to specify their other practices and rambles on about what they must do to satisfy their god.

Max boasts about both religions. The excitement in his voice is strange.

"One controls through traditional conformities of heaven and hell, while the other mystifies with magic and autonomy. One has consequences in the afterlife, while the other yields more instant

results in the here and now. They both carry rules of fearful engagement, each with a set of consequences if not followed to the letter," he concludes.

Max tells me that his father, and the word monogamy, would never be found in the same sentence. Community dick is what they called him, more like Slicky Ricky. He claims that his father couldn't keep his penis in his pants to save his life; he was too busy flaunting how big it was to the town floosies with the deepest pussies.

He slept around on his mother and introduced her to problems she didn't know existed. Max's father was good at giving out UTIs, which signaled a dirty dick. His father was good at giving the women in the congregation everything they weren't getting at home, and most left with door prizes they didn't ask to win. Gonorrhea, Syphilis, you name it; and if it was transmittable, chances were, Deacon Dubois was the culprit.

He was a nasty motherfucker. He ate pussy, licked ass, peed on women, did orgies, liked young girls, and fucked old bitches. The deacon serviced the women in the church, their town, and the world while on mission trips.

Max says his father sprinkled his diseases and his baby dust everywhere. Max then mentions, "There is no telling how many siblings Dedrias and I may have."

For some reason, that makes him uncomfortable.

And it is.

Max was thinking of how exponential that number could be as the fact of it spilled from his unsure lips. He had never thought of it until this very moment. Max remembers several warnings his mother gave his father, if he didn't change his ways. Max and Dedrias were afraid for their father but knew he was no good. If his father denied one more nappy-headed child, his mother said she would fuck him up in ways he couldn't imagine.

From the time they met one of their half-siblings near the end of the driveway when leaving for school one morning to the pull-ups of women at the grocery store—there were many women. Another time, his father stumbled in at four in the morning after a church conference with lipstick prints all over his collar. One time, Max was whipped for not erasing the messages from the same woman with a crying baby on the other end.

"The lashings alone kept me from interfering anymore," he continues.

Max recalls the stints in the backyard where his father bashed his forehead and left a dent, showing me the small scar that melts into his skin like silk. Even when told to go outside while the pastor's wife stopped by from the church. His father would grab him by the nuts to make him remember what to do and not forget.

When the pastor's wife stopped by often with her freshly baked cookies, Max knew what time it was. He says his father adored her treats.

"She always brought plenty of cookies for us to munch on while they disappeared into a back room for private prayer time." Max recalls how sleepy they would get after eating a few and waking up to walls banging and low moans calling out God's name.

Max mentions that Dedrias was too young to understand the fast-paced slapping noises coming from their parent's bedroom and mom not being there.

The pastor's wife always showed up thirty minutes after his mother left the house. His mother had choir practice, missionary meetings, and was never home gatherings, avoiding her dirty dicked husband. He says they didn't say a word. It wasn't their place.

So, Max fasts forwards his story.

One day, at adult church service, the pastor walks through the entire sanctuary talking about cheating spouses and points at his wife sitting in the first pew with her "'fake Christian ass,'" Max quotes word for word. He continues by saying the pastor questioned how his wife could be with children when the pastor couldn't produce any?

"God surely must be in the miracle-working business!" The pastor spread his arms high and praised the phenomenon; but the marvel was particularly spectacular—especially when the pastor was a female fighting transgender regrets and how she could no longer keep their lie hidden. She hated herself for what she did to be with her lesbian wife—filling the church pool of desire with blasphemy and hypocrisy.

The "she-pastor" is damned to preach about living deceptions within the faith. She horrified the congregation with her butchered chest by ripping her shirt open, buttons flew everywhere and revealed her scarred chest lined with keloids from her double mastectomy. The church was shocked to tears. Pastor lady-man was putting all their business out on Front Street when she pulled down her pants and revealed her surgically added penis that never healed properly. The dead, inverted vagina failed to stay hard without a cock ring. The mutilated abomination was infected and stunk. Puss was creaming from numerous incisions. Deacon DuBois had infected the wife, which spread to the she-pastor, with his unreported vaginosis. Max says his mother yelled strange Kreyol words that rang in magnificence, cursing the religion like a church on fire, the wife's stomach, and his father's diseased loins.

"Your seeds will blow away like dust in the wind, destroying your lineage! Your time of destruction starts now!" Max's mother laughed and heckled, pointing at the she-pastor's butchered flesh, and deformed fake man parts. Her beaming eyes glared at the she-pastor's wife with the hate of a thousand tongues.

"Ah!" Max's mother screamed and hacked like a demonic bird, running through the church, and spreading her curse like the flu.

Max says he watched his mother place a glass jar with eggshells and two plastic babies floating in it under the kitchen sink and warned he and Dedrias never to touch it.

"It will make your skin melt."

He references how she scared them with her words as he animates his hands like a witch. "She marked both of the babies in the jar."

Max shares how she carved a heart into the chest of one doll and cut two heads with the other. "I watched her cut that doll's head right down the middle before she put it in there. All I know is one baby was born with two heads."

Max says his mother drove his father away with her festivals of celibacy and garb wrapped to her eyelids, not wanting him to touch her. Why would she? With her husband's dick circling the city, she didn't want any of it. Too many fishy pussies, for starters, and there was no telling who had what.

Max mentions how his mother was tired of taking medicine. He says bottled antibiotics were always in the trash can; one day, her anger escalated, and she dumped every bottle on top of the bed she had ever kept. When Max walked by his parents' bedroom, he saw a mound of empty bottles; so many, he lost count after twenty. Soon after, the fire department showed up, dousing their parents' burning bed.

Max says that his mother would walk around the house chanting lullabies in her native tongue—once in the morning and once at night.

"One song for each baby," he adds. "It was so dark and cryptic. It scared the shit out of us both."

He tells me how the women in the church suspected his mother put roots on the pastor's wife as a lesson for all to see. Letting her adultery and his father's, blaze in its sinful delight. Max explains how the church shunned his entire family because of it, even though they had no proof, and wanted them removed from their church, town, and lives.

Then, he directs the conversation to how his mother taught him and Dedrias some spiritual stuff afterward. He stresses the tainted use of magic was originally meant for healing, contrary to what people believe and what his mother did out of hurt. The same goes for its power on the dark side; it manifests the same supremacy as its cursed counterpart.

"My mother wanted those babies to remind my father of his infidelities. She was devastated. Everything she tolerated to be with him," he voices. "People could tell my mother was into that. It was the way she stared through you. She watched your every move to learn about you. She watched you from when you entered the room until the time you left. The whole time tapping her toenail on the wooden floor below her."

CHAPTER 20
A Lesson in Kreyol

Max, now tapping his finger on the wall where he stands. "I'll never forget what she said that day, *'Se sa ou jwenn pou Fè sèks ak mari m.'*" Max mimics in his native tongue, Kreyol.

"What does that mean?"

"That's what you get for fucking around with my husband." Max pauses. "I'll never forget how she said it. It came from a place deep inside. She wanted to leave her roots in magic alone once she discovered Christianity. She told us that all the time."

Max reveals how his mother married for what she thought was stability. He states how life was less grand as the Americas promised. Even though his father had money, how he attained it, his mother was unsure.

"She had no clue what my father was into, not outside of his knowledge within the faith, his willingness to help, and his charm. My father flashed money everywhere. Once the gossip, the infidelities, and the extra babies started circling...it was too much." Max thought his mother didn't have a choice considering the situation his father put them all in.

Max says he heard what his mother told him the night before they left his father. She could no longer play in his *Jwet Lakou Dyab la* anymore.

"What does that mean?" I ask.

"His Devil's Playground."

After his parents divorced, Max starts talking about how his parents could no longer see eye-to-eye on how to raise their children. So, his mother kept him, and his sister in Miami, and his father returned to Haiti.

"My father was afraid of what she might do to him. He was unsure of all her gifts," Max adds, and rightfully so, for his mother to be terrified as well. "My father could have fucked her up just the same, but he was too busy sprinkling kids all over the place." He explains the battle he and his sister went through when his father fought for custody. "My mother thought that our lifestyle in Haiti had us in danger, but the *real* danger was her." Max claims that it was better than his mother portrayed.

When living with their dad, they had money, big homes, cars, and plenty of recognition. He claims they lived like the world didn't owe them anything. All they did was have fun and have huge parties. His family was considered privileged because of his dad's wealth.

"We had access to a lot of shit," Max mentions nonchalantly. "More than what *I* wanted."

Once the courts decided on joint custody, Max mentions that he and his sister traveled back and forth to satisfy the court order of shared parental obligations. For some reason, Max derails his story and starts rattling off random words as he fumbles around in his right pocket.

"Customs stopped Dedrias on every trip to verify she wasn't smuggling drugs. I hated it." The officers, usually slipping their hands under her skirt, defiling his sister in every way to check her viable canals for plastic bags.

"Open your hand," he orders me gently before releasing a gold coin.

As it falls in slow motion, it flips, reflects, and splats into my palm. The weight is solid and heavy.

I see the markings. "What is it?" I ask.

"An amulet."

It stuns my hand, and I immediately release it to watch it plummet to the floor. Max quickly bends down to pick it up. He looks at me and then down at his hand.

"That could have been me who got his head shot to smithereens during the war. My partner was standing right beside me," he says. "I had this coin with me the whole time. When that happened, I knew the power it possessed. I was able to slip through time and avoid those bullets. My father hated what my mother had exposed us to." He turns the amulet over a few times to look it over and blows it off. "See the red markings?" He points it out. "That's my father's blood seared into the metal." Max points to the eye in the center of the coin. "This represents the gateway to eternity." He rubs his thumb across the engraving. "This symbol right here?" He looks down at me like he's trying to make me understand more, "It represents the Power of the goddess Oya. It is rooted in her speed and ability to change things suddenly without interruption. Growth and harmony. Life itself."

My eyes are big and wide. I am amazed at the intricacy of the carvings and the story behind them. Max's demonstration fascinates me. The tone in his voice is gentle yet firm. Max instructs me on his divinity. Its folklore assures its legend as he skips over the amulet demonstration and refers to switching the two coins in his father's coffin.

"This is my father's amulet. I got rid of mine before he was buried. It was the only way. I didn't want the responsibility that came along with my amulet." He pauses and takes a deep breath. "Dedrias knows what I did. I had to."

Max confesses that when he switched the coins, it switched his fate. For decades he tried to complete his assignment but failed—that is, until now, right in front of his face, one of the missing pieces of his developing puzzle.

Max knew the consequences, switching the amulets, but his assignment was to find the babies his mother cursed. Max gave up too soon. He already secured one piece of his dynamic; but wanted out because he was tired of searching for the other. Max explains he must fulfill his father's job by bearing his father's coin from the switch.

He releases a heavy sigh before he continues.

"*Devwas* are attached to the amulets when given at our coronations." Max explains that he could never complete his father's devwa. The numbers are infinite; there is no end. It just goes on and on, and on and on…

"*Devwas*?" I ask.

"Sorry, assignments," he clarifies the translation of the word.

He shares that when he switched the amulets, that his father's coin was attached to the Declotae.

"My father had sold his soul to access his heart's darkest desires and needs: material wealth, eternity's time, women, traveling the universe, and supplying The Guff with its requirements. That's where the Declotae come in. The gift was a curse. Yes, he had it all: the land, the houses, all the *koko* a man could handle, and all the money anyone could ever imagine," Max explains.

"*Koko*? What's that?"

"Pussy." Max shifts his body and continues. "Everything your heart desires, but everything comes at a cost. People forget you must do some things to secure those riches and what fits that amulet's devwa or assignment. But after a while, that shit gets old," Max shares.

Decades-old, sometimes centuries, vanity goes from gluttony to murder. As the amulet passes along out of spite, Max realizes that he is trapped forever, just like his father. It all makes sense. His father's promiscuity, lusting after the flesh, and a humble flashiness are required to complete the task, whether he likes it or not. Max was his father all over again.

"I thought it would be the end, but it was only the beginning. I didn't know what that shit meant. How the Spring and Winter solstices are the only two times I could look for or even do it. My mother was afraid of what she caused with those babies. She didn't think about her own children and what it would do to them. She knew there would be reciprocity, a soul for a soul. That's how it stays replenished. It is only a matter of time. It's not *if* it will ever happen, but *when*," Max tells me. "This amulet carries special powers. That's why I can never be without it." Max jumps from one statement to another. "If I'm without a coin to slip through time, they come to retrieve me." He trembles as he speaks. "They fucking come out of nowhere! Like shadows from objects already in the room or even outside! They...they grab onto you and drag you back with them." He shakes as he grips the amulet tight.

Is he having an episode?

My head spins as I try to keep up. I'm fascinated by his descriptions. I want to know more. So, I ask some questions of my own.

"Dedrias knows you did what? What assignment?" I ask out of curiosity, skipping around, trying to make sense of his story myself.

"She knows that I switched amulets at our father's funeral."

Max's tale confuses me more. The severe tone he evokes. Vivid analogies he uses with such finite detail, his story goes into an endless circle. I can't latch on to where it's headed. The skin between my eyebrows wrinkles and Max sees how lost I am.

"Each male receives one at his eighth-year coronation." He demonstrates this by laying the gold coin flat in the palm of his hand. "A coronation is a big, fancy party where we get christened into accountability and manhood. The number eight represents completion, and by the eighth year, our bodies have produced all the sperm for our entire lifetime." He starts unbuttoning his shirt and steps out in front of me. "We're branded, too."

He whisks off his shirt in a frenzy. I'm horrified by the bubbled burn mark at the top of his spine. It blisters in redness; the scorched number eight is impressed into his skin like a branding, burnt and bubbled. The rich color of blood it exemplifies and, oddly enough, slowly circulates and pulses with his pain. Max quickly covers the mark in shame and relief.

"I switched my amulet with my father's. I fucked up and gave up too soon. I'm in this ongoing nightmare that never stops," he pauses. 'I thought putting my amulet in his coffin solved my problem. They wouldn't need to look for me any longer because I was 'dead.' Assignment complete. I wouldn't have to look for anybody." He articulates his fingers for presentation. "I took my father's amulet to make it look like he was still amongst the living, not me. But oh, somebody forgot to mention the private hell it takes to keep a dead man's purpose alive on this fucking side and complete their *devwa*! That was supposed to nix the curse null and void. *They* would be satisfied, and I would fucking be free! Always having to ensure I produce eight seeds in sequ...," Max stops and realizes he may have said too much. Max's words spill from his mouth like a bucket of sins. "The Declotae are coming for me. They want their pound of flesh, and they only care about *the time you do holding their precious ball of life*," he whines.

I stand shocked, cover my mouth in pity, and empathize with his agony.

"The Declotae? Who's that?" I ask. Good story, but it can't possibly be true. Sounds like a cartoon to me. This is some weird shit. Maybe he is having a PTSD episode from the war.

Max laughs to himself. He cannot believe he is confessing to Gianna like this. Max feels the weight of secrecy plundering from his chest.

"They are soul collectors," he responds while swallowing a small gulp of air. "They have this thing where they collect your coronation amulet when your bearer places it in your burial shroud. Supposedly, that was the ceremonial deal they agreed to; and they better fucking match up for you to regenerate before your soul gets tossed." That one he couldn't stop. The confession splashes from his tongue like a juicy peach. "But the nerve of that lie being passed down was unreal. Ceremonial deal? A motherfucker can't wrap no coin in his burial shroud if he's being tossed from a cliff and into the fucking sea!"

Yeah, he's having an episode.

More than ever, I want to get back to boring ass Bradenton. My heart pounds like it's about to burst from my ribcage. I feel the revulsion in his delivery. It feels more horrifying than burning in hell.

"Does Dedrias have one, too?" I try and stay calm.

"No. Only men are entitled to carry them. We are the protectors. Right here. Always in my right pocket," Max flips the coin, catches it, and reserves it in its respective place. Shaking his head as he recalls the time it was not. The sheer horror of being stuck there until someone else fucks up and that could last, gawd knows how long.

"Why there?" I ask.

Max goes into another educating minute about how his father broke him down. Max pauses and remembers what he suffered. He didn't have permission to folly in the back sheds. His father had it barricaded from the rest of the premises. For a good reason, Max did not know what lay underneath the brush pile and tossed a huge amount over the cliff to help clean it before his father added another chore to his roster. The brush would have fermented into ten pounds of coal, which formed about a hundred diamonds.

Instead, Max got punished for destroying precious materials. The time he went through it. Gregarious men sodomized Max for punishment. He couldn't believe his uncle and father were in line awaiting their turn. His father cried crocodile tears as he marched forward in the shitty ritual. There wasn't anything commemorable about it. How young Max was. How bloody and wide his asshole stretched after they finished. The ice baths he endured. His adolescent figure went into hypothermia numerous times as he healed. He wanted to duck his head under the water and die right then and there.

"It's just where it's supposed to go. It must always be here." Max pats his pocket for assurance, tapping it twice to confirm the rim for the circular shape. "Life is too short. We never have enough time to live it." Max scratches his beard and continues. "What would you sacrifice so you could enjoy life to the fullest, Gianna?" Max asks me out of the blue.

"Wow, that's heavy. I...ah...I never thought about sacrificing anything."

"*Would* you sacrifice anything to live forever?" Max asks.

"My Savior already did that for me," I say with assurance, but when it hits me, I add more. "I will live forever."

"How do you know that for sure? Don't you need to die to find out?" Max insists.

Something tells me he's the cynical joker he tries to be and delivers with a punch, but his statement has a hidden message. My fists tighten with beware intentions.

"Yes, you do have to die," I reply.

"Yeah, that makes a lot of sense. You only reap the benefits of the afterlife *after* your life is over," he replies with sarcasm, shakes his head, and twitches his neck to force out his following statement. "Time is the most precious thing we have. Think about it. I have all the time I need with this amulet." Max pauses in his admission and sighs. "You could share that time with me, Gianna."

Max looks deep into my eyes, and I lose myself in his proposition. They hypnotize me with poetic flashes of grandeur, stimulating my mind in gentle waves of wet deception. "I have something else I need to show you."

CHAPTER 21
WOW

Max takes my hand, leads me to the bed, and lifts me quickly. As Max places me on top, gets down on one knee, and speaks his want in the softness of his alluded words.

"You could be anywhere else, and you're here with me."

At this moment, he prowls with caution with his lips as he inches closer. Whispers of his sweet, molasses breath waft into my nasal cavities with velvety smoothness. Max puckers his lips against mine as his energy pulses an overlay of warmth onto my mouth. His mouth plumps with intent and moans the hunger of his deepest desires. They roll from his chest as he grabs my forearm and pulls me to the edge of the bed. Max wraps his arms around my calves with protection. His words are beautiful and envelope around my bleeding heart.

"You're so soft," he utters against my lips. "I love the way your skin smells."

Max wants to make me a part of his world and professes how much he needs my life force within it. He massages my feet in seductive manipulations that are slow and with purpose. His hands press my shoulders, rubbing his beard between my legs. He inhales and exhales in bitter relief. His fingers are between my toes; one hand is guiding me to stand, and one is running up and down my spine. It feels like he has three hands. Hell, maybe even four—shit, possibly five? How is he doing that? Did he turn into an octopus and grow extra arms? How is he holding me, squeezing my ass, rubbing my shoulders, and removing my garment?

Max tenderly touches my body and sends tingling sensations to every neuron wired inside. My secretions start flowing as Max gently squeezes the mound of soft tissue, desperate for more of his manly touch.

"Shit, this ass is phat." Max groans as he runs his middle finger between the separation of skin between my crack multiple times. Squeeze my ass. Rub on my hips, stretching his neck like a giraffe to kiss the back of my spine.

"Can I taste you?" Max whispers in heavy pleads. As he retracts his neck, he arches down to kiss my breasts. "You got my dick on swole," he boasts as he circles the tip of his tongue around my hard nipples. "You know you need me in your life, Gianna."

"Yes, I do," I declare. It is something I can't deny. I let out a small whimper of submission as his tongue flickers excite my body.

"It's everything you've been praying for." Max hoists my one leg into his arm and begins finger fucking me as he carries me across the room. Walking past the magnificent view as he speaks, he fingers, inserting his digit with each profession. Max milks the suction of pleasure escaping every haunting cry, heightening the spin in the room as we twirl. He wants his words to stick. Each declaration stressed like an old school ass beating—accentuating every word each time he inserts his thick finger. "Don't. Play. With. Me."

"Fuck no. I need you."

"Here is where we can turn back. You need to be sure."

He stops plunging, sucks on his middle digit, and shivers. Max pulls my pelvis close to his chest and places my clit on his nipple, pumping his muscle as a stimulant. As he steps up to his bed, he stops at the top step and begins pulsing his muscle against me harder and faster. We collapse back onto the bed. The fall is cosmic; it feels like we are falling from outer space—the ceiling shifts as we descend and opens itself to the night.

"I feel so good when I'm around you, Gianna."

He opens my legs and slides his tongue across my secret box. Max seductively licks my thigh as he begins a sensual rotation of his moistness. I circulate my hips in unison with his mouth. I press my pussy to his lips and feel the tingling sensation rising. My juices start flowing like a transparent river of sex waiting to release its water.

"This pussy-fruit is so juicy. It needs this hard dick inside of you," Max murmurs as his lips slurp my pussy juices.

Max yearns to plug my wet entry of satisfaction and please. He needs me to consider his proposal, if nothing else, desires me and only me now. As he eases his rock-hard muscle into my love canal, I can feel my walls breaking down, adjusting to the size of his manhood and accepting him into my dark, wet space.

"Gianna," he sighs as he enters slowly. He feels his way in, absorbing the juices that guide him. "Your pussy is so tight," he says as he savors each step until he reaches the top of my G-Spot. He stays here, feeling the vibration of his dick against my beating drum. We lock eyes and kiss passionately.

The trade of unspoken words are exchanged. We feel the immediate connection in a breath's turn. Max backs out slowly, not intentionally, as my secretions flood him. I immediately pull him closer to me with the mastered trick of Kegels. We both release deep exhortations of air as my pussy muscles suck his cock back into my wetness. The swollen head of his dick crowns against the pulsating walls of my love. His body moves . As Max strokes his love gracefully into me as we move as one spirit. We slide up and down in our soft pumps. With each deep thrust, I let out a small cry of pleasure. When I press my mouth against his hairy chest, his soft curls floss between my teeth. Max arches down and begins sucking my titties hungrily. Giving each one their turn, he clamps down for the sting and gently releases his sharp hold.

"My God, you're creaming." He groans.

As his dick swells inside me at an alarming rate, he penetrates deeper. The girth of his cock starts stuffing me; the burn from engorgement rips a tiny tear at my opening and uncomfortably stretches my walls. Suddenly, Max clenches my legs with his and locks me into position. My hair mats to the scalp as he moves. Sweat gathers in the pockets of flesh between us, and Max blows his breath in frequent grunts of power. He revs up like a warming engine as he exhales in winded pants. Max elevates off the mattress with his arms to strengthen a mastered stroke. His knuckles widen to secure his roguish dominance. Growling in his thrusts, I am taken away by his hip movements, throwing my head, arching my back, and moaning in pleasure.

His dick runs deep while his fuck strokes go on for hours. Max's concentration and focus magnify the growls echoing from his chest as his dark silhouette transforms into a solid black form. Max's shoulders widen when he looks down at me and thrusts his cock further into my pussy. But Max's face changes in illusions and his nostrils stretch to mimic an animal, a ram head with horns that angrily smiles back at me while he pumps. The intensity of kisses over my breasts as he morphs hides the terror of his shapeshift. Oh my God. The quickening taunt of his hips causes his shaft to penetrate past my cervix and into my uterus, making me push against his chest in quick heat.

"Wait!" I holler. "Wait! That's too much, Max!"

I push my fists against him harder. It makes him growl heavier, louder, as his thrusts penetrate deeper. "Oh my God! Stop Max! I can't breathe!" I shove at his chest that hovers over me like a smothering blanket. His pumps thrust faster as I punch away from the suction that his cock fails to dislodge from. "Max!" When I finally break free, tiny drops of blood stain the sheets when I sit up and check myself.

"Oh, my goodness! I'm so sorry. I don't know what happened just then. You pulled something out of me. I felt like a beast," he boasts in sorrows dripping in apologies. His penis deflates like a poked balloon.

Rubbing over his hairy chest, I console him with compassion, tell him I'm okay, and that the dick just got excited because of this good pussy. Max cradles me like a newborn showing his disdain for hurting me.

"You bring emotions out of me that I didn't know still existed," he confesses. "I love the passion you bring to the table. My body felt like it was fusing into yours. I can't explain it. It felt like my dick was entering your soul." He strokes my hair as he holds me close. 'You make me feel like I can do anything with you. I'm not afraid to jump in feet first. I need you, Gianna."

I release a sigh of relief. "That was too much dick, Max. It felt like you were busting through my chest. I felt like I couldn't breathe."

"I'm sorry, baby. I never want to hurt you in any way. I value you."

Max's words melt my heart, and I fall deeper into his spell. I playfully wrestle him over, kiss his chest, and rub my fingers across my pussy opening. Max awaits his offering of forgiveness. His mesmerizing eyes glaze over my body in fine detail. Max blinks in slow observance as I withdraw a smear of blood on the tip of my finger. Max softly takes my defiled hand and spreads the lustful glaze across his lips and mine. He rests during the hesitant exchange, but finalizes the action when he passionately places my fingers into his mouth. He sucks on my finger like a dick and slurps the sticky blood from my tips with fervor. This temptation is deeper than lust. His zone is crazy; his vibe is more cataclysmic than a vampire's desires. He places his finger inside my thighs and tastes me again. The need and want are committed. There are no boundaries to hold us now. The freak establishes itself on another level.

I carefully move back and forth over his eight-pack torso, kissing his chocolatey skin with care. His body is warm and robust, emitting devotion as he holds me. Max rocks my body while stroking my hair. The safety of his arms keeps me from rolling off his frame. Max then guides my hips against his stomach to get comfortable, feathering under my arm and along my ribcage in a tender sway. I lie here sideways and listen to his heartbeat. My juices fall onto his hardening manhood.

"Damn, you're wet," Max hisses as he softly moves his fingertips along my side, and down my thigh. He caresses with his fingertips with delicate shapes of affection: a heart, a diamond, and a squiggly line down my legs to my feet. "I'm sorry. I'll be gentle this time."

My jumping clit tingles from his apology. I turn over and move my hips in small circles, grinding my pussy against his deflated cock. It puffs up and hardens as I wind. Once his dick stiffens, Max shifts my position and straddles my legs. He lifts me by the hip and places me on the tip of his dick head. I feel his heartbeat pulse in powerful thumps. He slowly pushes his hips up and enters me, taking his time to insert his cock more carefully. The slosh is moist and juicy in his travel.

"Mm," we moan together.

When Max reaches the top of my canal, he rolls his stomach and the wave ripples to his meat log. It rolls inside me in a domino effect, grows instantly, and stuffs my walls. I grind in slow gyrations, applying pressure and pausing to expose my clitoris to his hard flesh. I am riding Max's dick strong. There is nowhere else for me to go.

"Oh...yes...wait, let me do this...right there...just like that, baby." I feel the rolling thunder of my orgasm pulsing off his dick.

"That shit is intense, girl. My ball is vibrating and everything." He smiles and starts fucking me slower to feel the thumping beat of my orgasmic release.

"Yasssssssss." I can hardly get the words out. I pant short, exacerbated bursts of my orgasm from my mouth. My lungs expand and contract quickly. Yes, this shit *is* intense.

"Sit on this dick. You need me in your life, motherfucker," he affirms as he drives his stiff rod deep into my love channel, slicking his meat with fetish intentions.

"Sss," I hiss in satisfaction.

His cavernous strokes go on for hours. The hypnotic gyration of his hips fuck a song of forbidden sex. The perfectly timed phallus insertions lock me into his rhythm when he looks deep into my eyes as he moves his body.

Then suddenly, Max grabs me, stands up from the bed, and lifts me across his shoulders. Bitch, I feel like I'm flying! My arms spread out to balance against the air as he flips me upside down until we are in a handstand 69 position. Max's arms wrap around my waist and suspend my legs in a V-shape, spreading my vaginal hole wide apart for him to slurp from. I feel like a gymnast doing a ten-star performance. From this angle, I swear he and LaDell were in the same instruction class. The way Max locks his arms in a complete circle to plant his elbows along my hips to secure my body, brings back vivid memories of my romps with Mr. Starling.

My wet, sloppy pussy is in Max's mouth as my open throat welcomes his thick, black cock. We twist our bodies across the room and against the walls, calling each other dirty names and exciting the freaks planted deep inside of us. He untangles his grasp and carries me to the bathroom to bend me over the sink. He sits on the floor, separates my legs, and opens the partition of voluptuous tissue staring him in the face.

"I'mma eats all this fat ass," he assures as he partakes.

Unexpectedly, Max darts his tongue in and out of the taboo space when rubs his face back and forth, and moans when giving his quick pokes.

"That's right nigga, taste them groceries," I growl. "You taste them pineapples and fried chicken."

"Sweet and spicy," he jokes before he inserts his tongue further into my asshole. "Are those red beans I taste?"

When the bastard said he would eat all my fat ass, he wasn't playing. I arch my back in compliance and watch my facial expressions in the mirror as he consumes me. A smile here. A sexy pose there. Even an 'ooh, this nigga tongue-dicking my booty' face once or twice while I point at his actions in the mirror, flicking my tongue in response. I begin winding my hips to the left and back to the right. That's when Max grabs my hips, takes control of my rhythm, guides me farther back against his mouth, and starts jabbing my asshole with his wet muscle of gratification.

"Ssss...ooo!" I breathe harder and beg him to stick his dick inside my candy box before I explode.

"You sure? I might turn into a beast again," he says hauntingly. Max gets up from the floor and pulls my hair from behind to help him stand.

"Don't pull too hard. You're gonna..."

Startled by his quick movement, I feel like a broken string of pearls that is snatched from my neck, collapsing to my feet by surprise. Max jerks my head forward and sideways, forcing me to see his body reflecting in the mirror. Snake-like in my adjustments, my spine should be popping; but instead, worms to his handwork controlling how his body stands. I move like a marionette puppet in my jangle and obey all his commands.

As he rises, his body glistens against the half-melted candles fading to burnt wicks in the background. The sweat cascades down his shoulder, nipples, and eight-pack stomach. His choreography is gracious. Max carefully handles my body as he stands to his feet.

"Excuse me? I'm gonna what?" He questions as he hunches over and devours my neck. Biting me numerous times and snapping the skin with his teeth. His tongue slips along the rim of my ear while pumping me slower. Teasing me with rhythmic motions and pounding me with heavy hip thrusts for the finish. He talks his shit, "Yeah, where you gonna get dick like this, *Gianna*?"

Max bends his entire body forward, pumping under the nook of my ass as he fucks me doggie style. He hooks underneath my arms and clench my shoulder blades. As my thighs bump the counter everything on it tumbles over. Max starts howling, making me burst out in laughter. Max howls like he is out of breath, but the bastard keeps going and can't help but laugh, too.

"Look at this! You got me howling?" His high pitch vibrates off my eardrum.

Though never faltering from any of his movements, Max rocks me forward and backward against his stick of meat, subtly turning our unexpected laughter into sighs of pleasure.

"I'll have you on those red-ass toes of yours, you know that, right?"

"And?"

"Oh, you trying to be hard?"

"I can handle you, Max. Your dick ain't shit," I provoke.

I think I struck a nerve or something. Max grabs my hair and starts pumping me harder. Doggie-style on warp drive. I guess he feels the need to prove me wrong. Then he starts yelling...

"Bang! Bang! Bang! Bang!"

My breathing elevates with each quick thrust. My throat is dry as hell. I turn the cold side of the faucet on and reach my hand out to cup what little water I can into my mouth. Most never make it. Puddles splash onto the counter as water plops from my palm with every forced hit. By the time the water reaches my mouth, only a drip remains.

"Oh, I ain't shit, hunh? It looks like you're the one who needs a break." He challenges my stamina, forcing me to put my toes to work. "Spread them legs and dance, bitch!" He slaps my ass with quick pops as he yells again. "Pow! Pow! Pow! Pow!"

And damn, it I'm twerking, booty-shaking, and crunk dancing all over his beast rod at the same damn time. My hair sticks to my eye as sweat showers from our bodies like a monsoon rainstorm. The sweet exchange of bodily fluids drenches our sex. Max's citrusy body essence perforates the room in our lustful exchange.

"Yeah, dance on this dick." Max pumps his hips while smacking my ass wildly. "Yasss, that ass is moving now, motherfucker!" He emulates how my ass shakes by forming an invisible barrier around it with his hands. His head wiggles to the motion of my booty as he animates the vibration.

I hoist one leg onto the bathroom counter, still twerking my ass off, and open my pussy to swallow his gigantic dick. "What nigga? You talking trash?" And as I spring my other knee onto the counter with urgency, Max stands at full erection and extends his arms to stretch. His knuckles scrape the textured ceiling and initiate a slow bleed.

I reach up and grab his hand, sucking the blood from his flesh with hunger. With his knuckles in my mouth, my springs start slow— moving to open my hips for wide rotations of my love. I maneuver around his dick, saturating his hot meat with juice, and wet his cock with sweet nothings of sin. Take the friction from sticky to slick as I glide up and down his shaft, massaging the dick with these secret grips. Max's hands find their way back to my waist and plump hips, softly caressing my thighs with his fingertips. As he feathers his strokes down the outside of my legs and calves, he quickly grabs my ankles and starts fucking me with quick pumps.

"Ah! Ah! Ah! Ah! Ah! Ah!" I call out.

My eyes focus on the task at hand. I whip my pussy meat against Max's cock in snap-holds. Stop and squeeze his shit in sections. Ride up and down the dick in blocks. I thrash my hips in hyperdrive against his solid frame, swinging my hair around savagely in wildebeest mode.

"Whoa, wait!" Max exclaims as his body jerks. He clenches my hips to postpone his climax.

"Wait? Nigga, are you done already? You need me to slow your nut down?" I reach down underneath the space left between us and reach for his balls in the palm of my wet hand. "Ooo, how does that feel, baby? You like your balls pulled, motherfucker? Do you?" I ask as I continue to move my body against his and try to feel for both testicles.

"Stop girl, wait! I only have one..." Max throws his head back as he stops my hip movement. "...nope, wait. You got me fucked up," he speaks in broken beats as he waits for his dick to stop swelling. Max slowly re-inserts the head of his cock and inches his way in, attempting to pause the climax seconds more if he can. "Let me do this."

I decide to show no mercy. I grab him with my leg muscles and bounce, holding his wrists from behind to stabilize my spring.

"Ah...Ooo...wa-wait...ooh... girl, wait now...FUCK!"

The force of his ejaculation quickly thrusts me forward and shoots his love cream all over my back and our reflection.

Thousands of his children slide down my spine and the bathroom mirror. As I regain my balance, Max brushes the hair away from my forehead and eyes. I look up, noticing the stars in his.

"Wow." The words fly from my mouth.

"Wow." Max swallows the ball of air caught in his throat before he speaks again. "*That's* what the fuck I'm talking about. I love you, Gianna."

And here reflects the blank stare we both have, gazing at each other in full adoration.

CHAPTER 22
Hunch Punch

"Nothing can change our destiny now. It's right here in front of us," Max says as he walks over to the twenty-jet shower and turns it on.

The powerful blasts beat in synchronized pulses against the cold, metallic tiles.

"Come here," he says as he pulls me close and passionately douses me with wet kisses—my hand, my wrist, up my arm, across my titties and my neck. "You can make this whatever you want, Gianna." Max empowers me with his words. "I have everything you want and need. With money, we can travel wherever we want when we want. Time would never be a factor. We could have everything," he temps me with the offering of his perfumed words.

"We can?" I ask with the purest of intentions.

His voice softens me like melting ice cream and confirms his post-fuck-haze of promises.

"I love you," Max says once more. "You're so sweet. Dance with me," he beckons.

My girlish tendencies spring from my dizzy eyes with joy. I laugh at his statement since the last time we stepped, led to a whirlwind trip around the globe—dancing under the stars in Milan, slow-dragging in Thailand under a full moon, and salsa twisting in the streets of Spain.

I take Max's hands, and we enter the jet-streamed box. The metallic square is slick. Steam quickly mists onto the sliding-glass doors. Max takes me into his arms as the water hits my skin with soft sprays. Our bodies are stuck together while his stomach beats against my cheek. We move as one, allowing energy to exchange between us. The water cleanses our sins and purifies us for more transgressions to follow. We feel connected on another level, knowing we have found our true love. To hold on and never let go. Max lifts me, holding me tighter, and rests his chin on my shoulder. He releases a sigh of relief as he gently lowers me onto the floor. I fall to my knees and submit to him. Max towers over me with hungry eyes as I unzip the desire beaming from his stare.

Max looks down at me with longing eyes.

I blow a warm breath onto his dick head.

He responds by making his cock jump.

"Put it in your mouth," Max speaks in quiet thunder.

I run my fingertips up and behind his calves and thighs, tickling his legs.

"Ooh shit, girl," he hisses.

I scoot closer, and the soft spray of water dances from my face. The heat from my mouth ricochets off the head of his dick when I open my mouth and hesitate.

"Open wider," Max orders.

I do.

He takes his shaft and runs it along the outer rim of my lips, tapping his sausage to demonstrate how stiff his meat is. His dick bounces from my lips like a trampoline.

"Yes," he moans.

Max inserts only the head. I pull his pulsing cock into my wet mouth with my cheeks, sliding my succulent tongue under the fat split of his dome and into the moist oasis of my love. I deep-throat his stiff, black beefcake down to the balls.

Wait, he only has one ball?

"Wait, baby, I only have…," Max begins, but stops because he no longer cares if Gianna notices his missing testicle flaw…

Max's dick throbs against Gianna's tongue as he moves around and shifts his groin away from her mouth to switch his movements—he doesn't have time for that long ass story right now, but Max knows Gianna will ask about it later, if she notices at all. Gianna was too busy sucking his dick super sloppy and probably didn't care. If she did, oh well. It didn't matter to Max because he was about to stick his fat dick back down her long throat.

…and as Max drives his cock into my throat, he starts pumping to redirect the blowjob away from the missing testicle. The sudden rapidity of semen fluid rushing through his cock-vein signals adrenaline rushing through his blood and his soon released ejaculation.

"FUCK!" he calls out.

I move my neck in circular motions and release him. A pop echoes his moans of pleasure that fill the enclosed space of the soundproof glass. His breathing is heavy. Sparks flash from Max's eyes; he is surprised at my depth to hold the length of his shaft. With my hands on his ass and my throat wide open, I quickly pull him towards me, savagely pumping his dick back down my throat.

"Ah! Ah! Ah! Ah!" He releases explosions of ecstasy.

My eyes tear up as the warm stream of damp sex drips from my mouth. The wetness of my throat bathes his dick in his semen. I move my head back and forth – up and down, licking and cradling his massive cock. I control every stroke. Blow jobbing the dick. Swallowing his nut. Making the dick feel wanted. Twisting movements unidentifiable to a rookie head giver, I manipulate my neck like a contortionist and turn my body underneath, facing away from him. As I twirl, he looks down at me in amazement as I sit and spin on his blowjob. Max moves to my rhythm, winding his hips, twisting with me, and pumping his pelvis against my lips in full engagement.

"What the fuck are you doing to me?! What trick is that!? Ah! Ah! FUCK, girl!" Max retracts the lodged meat, and I rest between his massive legs that surround me like a border of hot flesh.

My voice, taken by every breath, is too exhausted to respond. Max also gets down on both knees, facing me, and reaches between my inner thighs to feel the ecstasy dripping from my vagina.

"You are amazing," Max whispers. The tip of his tongue runs softly over the lining of my lips. He teases my pussy with his fingers at the same time, delicately exploring both holes. "I need you," he pleads. "Please say yes."

I open my legs wider and press my clit against his finger. While we kneel in front of one another, he kisses me tenderly as his tip slips along my flexible opening; his fingers massage the taught pussy skin in opposing directions. I pop like a hot firecracker. Without warning, he inserts his long, fat finger.

"Ah!" I call out. The depth of his digit quickens me and his swollen girth pulses against my pussy walls. My muscles squeeze his appendage as it enters, the water entering with it to wash away any chaffed skin left from his previous invasion.
The intimacy he shows.
The tender delicacy of my portion.
He is making love to me with his gifted hand stroke.
Gentle in the handle.
One-fingering the take.
His attention is focused on my satisfaction.
He retracts his finger and sucks the stickiness of my syrup.
How good it smells.
How sweet it tastes.

His eyes appear lost in a haze. Upon re-entering, Max moves his body into a sitting position and sits me on top of his legs, crossing behind him. My ankles locked Indian style, facing him. He holds me close around my ass as he moves, rocking in a slow and steady heat. His dick stiffens with every thrust.

"You are everything to me," he whispers.

"I am?" I gaze into his eyes.

"Yes, you are," Max says as his thigh movements slowly force his meat in further.

"Mm," we both moan.

I am lost in his eyes; his insertion takes my breath away.

He feels so fucking good. His dick fills my body and soul.

"I want to make love to you forever. We could have that." He kisses me softly as he rocks.

Escape my life and away from shitty Boringtown forever? To have his hardness fill the traumatic holes of my soul forever? Make love and fuck like this forever? Share his wealth? Maybe some children? Travel the world? The questions fly through my mind.

"All you have to do is say it," he whispers with each thrust. "Make this what we've both dreamed, we could have everything and *forever*." Max moves his hips in a wide rotation, then slowly pulls out.

"Don't stop," I plead. The water sprays through my hair like the wind.

"Don't you want me, Gianna?" Max looks over my body as he watches my breasts elevate and descend; he listens to the intensity of my breathing and awaits my answer.

The symphony of bells tingling around my clit, thighs, tongue, and head is rapturous.

Max pulls my pelvis close to him, grinding his body against mine.

He slowly warms my body as he re-enters.

Gentle.

Swollen.

Herculean.

Max plunges his stiff flesh into my wet pussy more...swelling and thumping.

He dangles me from his grip like a ragdoll as he fucks my soul.

Max gyrates his hips to obey his every command.

"Don't you want this, Gianna? Don't you want this dick in your life?"

Max seals his words with eight inches of his cock-strong pipe. He lifts me off his dick and teases, poking me with his head.

"You want this dick?"

"Oh yes," I moan.

Max slowly puts me back onto his shaft and talks his shit, telling me how très belle I am. His thirst to progress our infinite journey melts from his lips, and I faintly hear haunting whispers of women calling out as he speaks. Their cries murmur *"No!"* under his words.

"I can give you the *dick*." His hip movements hypnotize me with trickery, bouncing me from his thighs and pulling me down on his entire penis shaft. "Don't run from it. Take *all* this dick."

"Oh," my desires call out. "Sss." I chant as he fucks.

The head of his shaft throbs against my walls. My pussy tingles with every insertion. Max's dick bangs into my cervix as he places his other hand on my thigh and stretches my leg outward and his dick goes deeper. He gently rolls me to the floor and onto my back.

"You feel so good," I pant.

The focused sprays of water beat against my titties in a soft fire. Max is steady in his pumps. Never skipping a beat and only rotating when the space provides, his dick hits my clit and never dislocates from the stickiness of my vaginal walls. It feels like Max's dick grew an extra lump the way he presses his meat against my clit as we roll. When I see Max doing the mind-blowing trick, that's what his dick did. As Max strokes, the lump begins moving and massages my clit with every hip thrust he drives. The rabbit-like motions of his flesh roll like beads and heighten my sexual arousal.

"Oh my God!" I pant with his thrusts as I watch his dick form another massaging plug of skin and pushes it against my pussy clit. "Oh...Ah," more sighs of pleasure seep from my lips. Max is stuck inside my dripping lust as he glues his position to get on top.

Max reaches between the stuck layers of our damp skin, separating my labia to expose my pussy hole, lifting my leg to drive the home run. Max is everything I want and need. He suddenly starts counting his pumps, like George would do, as he pounds into me. Max's dick is unapologetic. He presses his body against mine and coils under my ass. Max locks into my everything.

The way our bodies respond to one another is explosive. So explosive that my orgasms are shaking the house, and the floors are moving, shifting, and vibrating simultaneously. The rumbling pleasure of my release splashes from my wet pussy, and the sweet juices of my ecstasy drip down his fat cock like corn syrup. Max stops pumping and allows the contractions to beat against his meat. As the creamy goodness gushes down his shaft, we are mesmerized by this feeling we share. Once the wave of volatile reactions subsides, Max takes my hands and places them over my head and begins fucking me. He slides in and out without delay.

"You're cumming all over me, Gianna," he whispers. His words hammer into my ear as he thrusts his hips with purpose.

We've fucked over twenty times and still want more. The hot sweat of sin licks the lips of engagement. As we spin in our body movements, Max takes hold of my hips and rocks me back and forth while I ride him. I'm fucking his head up with all this platinum pussy I'm thrashing, making each of his ejaculations more potent than the last.

The floor slicks our desires with fevered lusts. We slide across the wet steel as we maneuver our legs and flip-flop in our travel, gently banging against the metal wall behind us. Max is on top as we roll, then me, and the wetness of our plunder positions Max on his back when we stop.

I ride Max's hungry shaft with eager hips. I loop and bounce off his penis like a Trojan horse when I switch positions and fuck him backward. My ass slaps against his pelvis and stomach while slicking the dick in splashes. I twirl on the dick, slap his face—and it makes him pump harder. I bite his neck, and it makes him scream louder. Clamping his nipples makes him cum faster, and before we realize it, we've been fucking for four days straight without any breaks.

"AHHH!" Max releases his cries of satisfaction. "Yes, girl. Work that pussy. Ah, yes, ooh, ah, ah." Max's eyes roll helplessly into the back of their sockets. His eighty-five-inch wingspan clutches the posters of his bed at the foot. His lust cannot wait anymore, and the hardcore thrusts take control of his body. Max jerks in hyperdrive as we pump skin-to-skin in the doggy position again. Max uses the buoyancy of my moving ass to bounce from his final pumps of ecstasy.

"Gianna!" Max screams out as he releases his final orgasm into me, crying streams of tears that roll from his eyes, and then crashes fast asleep.

CHAPTER 23
Crushed Grapes

"Gianna...Gianna...," a voice softly chants my name over and over as I shift in my rising. The haunting voice whispers as I turn and watch its resonance escapes with the ocean breeze.

Delicate sounds chirp from the open French doors. The sweet melody of the morning sun prompts their melodious song. With a flutter and coo, the call and response of their sharp twitters awaken me. I'm so lost in Max's world now. How could I ever go back to mine?

There is a beating drum inside me that wants to stay. I've been here before, maybe from my imagination or in a dream. I carefully unravel Max's protection and step down from the bed. Walking across the cold floor, I check my reflection and notice Max's smack prints left on my ass and the bite marks along my shoulder and arm. I see three sucker bites on my neck when I pass the enormous mirror posing as a wall.

"No, he didn't." The marks usually told other men your hickey was marking his territory. I didn't think niggas still did that mess nowadays; but men are barbaric, and it's just their prehistoric language for control.

A pile of wet towels leads from the bathroom to the bed. The room smells like sweaty flesh and fermented red wine. Max turns in his sleep, sometimes jerking from the depth of it, once rolling to the edge and gripping the poster tight.

The crashing waves call out to me from the terrace. In their thunder, they shake the rock of land in substantial holding, sometimes splashing foams of tide high into the sky and spraying across my face with the passing breeze.

"Bonjour," Max speaks as he stretches his body into motion. "You ready for a few rounds?" he jokes, burping and farting in his body's awakening.

"Bonjour," I respond. My body turns and basks in the renewed rays of the day, stretching my nude exhibit for his eyes to adore.

"Ah, this dick got you speaking French now?" Max teases. "You're up early, sexy."

"The birds woke me up. It sounded like they were calling my name."

"They can do that." Max twitches his face and notices a look of disinterest upon mine. "What's on your mind?"

Max steps down and displays his massive, chocolatey frame. His height extends in weird positions as he stands to reach its peak. Max's dick hangs limp but damn near to the middle of his leg. It is flat and lifeless.

"Nothing." I watch his appendage flap from one leg to the other. The night plays over in my head as I watch him walk closer. "It leaves me speechless how beautiful this place is," I share as I gaze back at the vast glamour of the island that has held my attention for thirty minutes or more. The open valley surrounded by plush palm trees and tropical flowers in full bloom are a breathtaking display of God's colorful foliage.

Max walks behind me and holds me close. As he wraps his arms around me, the seagulls gawk in their splendor and flight. The warm Caribbean winds blow through my hair and refresh our exchange.

"That's the only thing that has you speechless?" His cock hardens against my back and awaits my reply.

"No." My girlish flirtation takes over instantly.

"Really, what's on your mind?"

"I was thinking, since we've had numerous days of fornication under our belts, let's say we go back home to our normal lives?"

"Go back home?" Max turns his neck in awkward positions before he continues. "This is my home, not Florida. You don't like it here?"

"I do, but…," I start to reply but begin reminiscing over my life back in Florida, and it makes me wonder. Is there anything of value to go back to? I think about how shitty the conditions are for me there. What *do* I have to go back to? There is no family, and I'm just out here alone.

"But what?" he questions. "We don't have to go back if you don't want."

From the extravagant lifestyle he lives, the sex, to the living forever thing, my head is spinning.

"Why? Are you asking me to stay here with you?" I question.

Max starts explaining why he does not want to mislead me. "You should know who I am before we move forward. This dick might be too much for you to handle on a regular basis."

"Ha!" I release a surprised laugh when Max says it. The nerve.

"Seriously, my life may be too much for you. You need to know some more things about me."

"Well, who are you? You hit me with so much at one time, and I'm just trying to process it all. I need time to think. I can't think clearly while I'm here. You've put so much on me; I can't think straight. I don't want to make any dickmitized decisions based on all this flamboyancy you're showing me."

I notice the bunched lines of skin that form between his eyes. His dimples sag in disappointment like tragedy faces.

"I just want to go home. I'm beginning to think that this may not be right for me to do right now."

"How can you say that? After everything I shared with you. The things we've done. The spit we've exchanged?" Max questions.

"That's exactly what I mean. You have me in this haze, and I don't want to make the wrong decision based on us fucking for four days. I just want to do the right thing."

"It is the right thing for you to do. What do you have to go back to, Gianna? You're right where you're supposed to be. Don't you see that yet?" Max questions as he looks out at the sun falling into its next position.

The clepsydra shadows its progressing gage.

"There is a connection between us, and when I noticed your heart, it confirmed that I had found you, too."

"Found me? Was I lost?"

"To me you were. Your birthmark was a sign, and I knew when I noticed it at the store..." Max discloses before I interrupt.

"...What about it? A sign for what?" I question as I look down at its delicate shape, now pulsing steadily.

"My devwa. You are the missing part of everything."

"The missing part of what? What are you talking about, Max? Say it already. I'm tired of the riddles."

The mark begins to circulate with glowing blood from the inside. Its illumination burns bright as it travels within its boundary. It pulls the unscarred flesh closest to it and tightens the skin around my marked heart.

Not recognizing how the day swiftly passes across the sky in what seems like seconds, time elapses in the backdrop without notice, quickening the horrid significance it steals. Our engagement moves in fast frames while our lips talk in hyperdrive. The sun's shadow fades with each fleeting second and word exchange. What feels like minutes of our conversation is hours passed.

"Let's go out to watch the sunset," he orders as he takes my hand. "I'll explain out here."

"No, I would like some real answers without the confusion. Your stories go in circles! What do you mean when you say I am the missing part?" My agitation grows, and I remove my hand from his hold.

"No." Max gently tugs at my wrist. "I want you to see this. It plays a huge part in what I am about to reveal," Max reiterates, gently pulling my hand, and we walk outside.

The view is breathtaking in the evening, just like Rochelle's. The land goes on forever and falls into the dusk of the night. The vast glow from the fading sun radiates the skyline in an orange and purple mist.

"Wow, this is amazing," I respond, immediately succumbing to its beauty, and away from Max's unclear story he hesitates to begin. I step in front of Max as the atmosphere welcomes us into the early cascade of night. My amazement is within its peace. His scent envelopes me like a plush blanket, breaking my stare.

"You like it?' he softly asks when he presses his body against mine.

"I love it, but I need answers, Max."

At first glance, the grass looks like it is covered with a vast field of illuminated cotton; but as we walk across the plain, a layered blanket of white butterflies detaches their wings and separates a path at our approach. They flutter with each step to follow, while the other layers stay in place. They redirect my attention with their grace and softness. The purity of their wing's glows around Max's dusky shadow that leads the way.

"Can I run through them?" I ask; then, I quickly run and skip through their ascension with glee before he can answer.

Max laughs as he watches me dance through their show. I do cartwheels. I spin in my pleasure, and as I do, the butterflies twirl and spin also, creating a delicate whirlwind around my body. Max stands engaged as he watches me turn into an innocent little girl before his eyes. The freeness in my steps. The giggles I release as they tickle my skin.

"Come on here," Max says as he lifts me into the air and continues. He chuckles as he carries me over his shoulder, and we tour the expansive block as Max explains everything we pass.

Each gold statue. The crashing sound of the ocean around us. The beauty in the sun is descending into the early slumber of the eight o'clock hour straight ahead. Max stops and releases me from his heightened view and place my feet on the dewy grass.

"I want to share my life with you, Gianna. Being with you brings me peace. I never expected our connection to be this deep. It fucks up my assignment. I didn't expect to fall in love with you. I can't do it. I need you to understand whom you are dealing with," Max stresses. "I'm exposing both of my worlds to you," he says as he rocks me like a baby. "You have me doubting everything. Now I must find it."

"What is it that you're doubting, Max? Find what? You're all over the place!"

"Well," he sighs in his hesitation.

"Say it."

Max squeezes me tighter and sighs. His arms lock together, and he kisses my ear with tenderness. "I care about you. The more I'm around you, the deeper I fall. Everything changes now, but…"

"No bullshit, Max. Say it!"

"Okay," Max hesitates and swallows a huge gulp of his fear before revealing his next declaration. "The two babies in the jar, cursed by my mother…," he begins.

"…Yea?" I interrupt in an unsure tone.

"You and Sean are those babies. You're the fraternal twins. You and Sean are brother and sister," he whispers and urges me to respond by squeezing my shoulders closer together. "You're my devwa," Max speaks in an eerie tone. "I'm supposed to get rid of you."

"Get rid of me? What do you mean by that? Kill me?" I quiver in my response.

"Yes, I am. You and Sean both."

It takes me a second to register what he says. It plays a broken record in my head, and when it hits me, my jaw drops.

"You play too many games, motherfucker! Let me go!" I twist and struggle to loosen his grip around my torso. "That's a lie! I want to go home!" I demand as I tussle to and fro.

"Don't do that." Max kisses my neck and squeezes tighter. "Relax. You can't go home right now. What goes on next is happening whether you want it to or not. Besides, everyone is waiting for you."

Max's tone is hair-raising and calm. It frightens me to a chilling level I cannot explain, and when I turn my head to look behind me, the view of the estate is gone and a humungous metal wall is moving in our direction as it screeches across the slick grass.

"Relax!? How in the fuck did that wall get there?! Ah!" I scream at the top of my lungs, twisting and turning in my skirmish movements to free myself from his strangling hold. "Who is waiting for me? Let me go, motherfucker!"

"If you look close, you might catch one looking back to see how much longer we're going to be."

"What!?" I scream in fear. Between the cold barrier and the cliff ahead, my heart starts pounding from my chest.

"Just look," Max tells me in a low voice as he ignores my fight. Max points at the line along the skyline where the sun is melting into the deep. He flashes delirious eyes at me and grins. "You can catch them when they peek back," he says as he lifts me off the ground and steps backward. "Ooh! There's one right there!" He points with excitement as the skyline snaps shut.

"Catch who peaking back?! No! Let me go! Wait, what are you doing, Max?" I question as I fight wildly to break free.

"I'm taking you somewhere far away from here. Where you've always wanted to go, Gianna. If you survive this, we can be together forever!" Max announces before he revs up and starts running across the vast lawn.

His bouldering legs wind his momentum and speed. Each pounding step rackets my bones. Max crouches lower, gaining whirlwind acceleration with a Tasmanian stride. My eyes cannot stay open. Max hurries faster, gaining the fluidity he needs to beat the metal barrier before it exiles his feet off the cliff ahead.

"What are you doing!?" I shriek in horror as he runs closer toward the edge. Max pins my arms to my sides. My capture is straight and narrow.

I look up at him as his dark eyes look down at me. Time slows as we race across the plain. The flash of the wind and trees zip by us at an accelerated pace, while Max smiles in slow motion within our traveling bubble. His mangled dimples, torn from the speed of his run, now show slits of skin exposing skeletal teeth. Distorted from my angled view, I move around in defiance, bashing my stuck-together legs against his knees. My head slams against his jawline to make him stop or stumble. To no avail, he maximizes his speed to reach the cliff's edge and jumps. We dart across the ocean like shooting stars. The cryptic howl of wind whistles past my ears and chatters my neck and teeth.

Then, Max released his grip and hangs me by the fore part of my arm and hand. I dangle like bird's prey, swinging freely across the dusky sky. He reaches forward with his other arm, extending his pinky fingernail, and slits the razor-thin sheet of existence to break the seal of the night. He lifts and separates the horizon; stepping over, he drops the wall of time behind him and disappears into the darkness of another realm.

FERMENTATION BEGINS WHEN THE SUGAR IS SWEETEST

CHAPTER 24
The Casting Call

I pass through the horizon's thinner entry as the setting sun descends upon my body. We join in unison, scissoring the dimensions of existence as we meet. The sun scorches my skin with five-thousand-degree flames as Max pulls me through its razor-thin compressor.

The molecular breakdown is immediate. My skull and bones pop and crack simultaneously, and crush into shattered blocks of calcium. My mouth stretches open as screams escape my deflated lungs. My body compresses and flattens to fit through the thin sheath. My eyelids peel away as I squeak through. Only exposing the ball and crushed calcium fragments around it. My eyes, now flat and square, watch as he turns and drags me through the finite entry below him. I slide through the thin sheet like wet steel. Max guides my assembly, leading my direction. He towers over the expansive space, his arms and legs magnified and super-powered as he navigates the journey.

I reinflate into a gelatinous mixture as I exit the entry. At immediate disposal, Max pulls on my arm, almost from its socket, as he stifles through the neon, sulfurous goop ahead of him. Max stomps and fights his way laterally. Snapping my arm with powerful yanks of urgency, he quickly pulls me through the sulfuric mixture with each drag. I attempt to breathe but inhale a suffocating amount of egg gelee. The gaseous mist chokes my throat in transit and burns what little sight I have left. I turn my head, noticing the tunnel we leave behind us as we march through its unrelenting stifle. The trail closes behind us, and the sweltering temperature of the jelly-like substance begins melting my skin away into its mixture. I notice a sheet of skin liquifying from my gelatinous blob and bones, attaching itself to his stride-ridden determination. My eyes see everything, so I will never forget.

From there, we soar high into the atmosphere, blazing a fire chain before disconnecting. This plane is darker and colder. It resembles an open warehouse packed with gloomier nooks and crannies. Haunting cries from beyond the black abyss call out from everywhere.

My body is a heap of gum and tattered bones linked together like a marionette. I am mounted and hung on a steel hook and it locks into my spinal cord for assured compliance. My arms are lifeless; they drop dead at my sides and blob like jelly. Max walks beside me, sliding the hook along the cold metal track, and making sure I catch the next clamp correctly. He leaves a radioactive trail of gigantic footprints on the floor that glows with his every step.

The hanger then zips me across a slick line, drags my gelatinous body speedily, and plunges my dense composure into a pool of boiling tar. The clamp sloshes back and forth in its gesture of coverage. Max observes my gummy facial expressions with each dip.

My face freezes in shock.

My chattering teeth clink in fear.

The slick tar falls away from the natural oils in my skin as the black emulsion of fire melts away any identifying indentations of my existence on my fingertips. My eyes, frantically twitching to and fro, feels like they will pop from my gummy sockets at any moment. My hair crystallizes like shattered glass into a sleek river of rubber. Max then removes my cubic sheet of skin from his leg, wiping the sweat and gelee off his mouth and face.

"I hate that part." He focuses on me and grins.

The terror in his smile makes me quiver. The hanger, dipping one last time, whisks me high into an open ceiling, strings me as I zip along the track, and dangles me like a latex cocoon. As I wiggle, my will to live fades. I struggle to breathe. The rubber, sealing any open orifices, makes it difficult to fight any longer. I start to suffocate, inhaling the rubbery seal. I diminish any hope of survival, thinking about what is coming next—the road to death travels straight to hell, just ahead. Then, I hear shattered screams from beyond the voided space, chains breaking, and their piercing shrieks of freedom ring with joy.

A forceful contraption hits me from behind, contorting my body, and arches me into a convex position. Anxious in my suffrage, my lungs suffocate more. My pelvic bone thrusts in an extended posture. My preparation is complete. I catch the reflection of the flying spirit hawking down the long corridor towards me. Her cries are loud. Her mouth opens wide, and her pointy teeth are hungry and sharp. Her tongue lashes against the metal borders confining her travel. She flutters and jerks as she flies at a chilling rate of speed. Her erratic movements reflect against the onyx wall behind me.

I quickly view her garment through the broken divisions of metal slate. Fragments of her incomplete structure mimic old movie glitches from the early twenties. The tattered hem of her dress dissipates a smoky silhouette as she travels through the tunnel. It sounds like tiny needles attached to her hem as they clank and spark along the corridor with her.

She exits swiftly.

Zipping by me once and snaps the seal of rubber over my mouth with her demonic, pointy teeth. I inhale a generous amount of oxygen in heavy panting. Soaring above the ceiling, she zips by my face again, piercing two small holes in my nostrils as her train passes. Screeching loud as she flies to the other end of the room, she darts by and bites the protruded mound of latex from my genital and exposes my clit from the encasement. The thousands of needles tickle behind her. They pierce tiny holes into my pelvic triangle of gummy, reforming flesh.

She punches by and saws away any pubic hairs left with extreme precision. Her shark-like assembly of teeth shifts and pulls to pluck them from their roots. She gnaws on my clit, rubbing her chin whiskers to stimulate my clitoris more. It leaves a linear groove into my inner thigh and gummy structure.

Once more, she passes, stopping to hover over my exposed genitalia to inspect it. Her tongue, now extracting from her transparent throat, titillates my sunken tissue, causing it to swell, beat, and throb—maximizing the rush of my immediate orgasm.

Max walks closer to my assembly and pushes her softly to the side. He pulls on the rest of the opening, and my legs spring open, causing part of the suit to snap from my sticky foot. Max draws the contraption closer to his amplified body. His face, maximized to cover my entire pussy. Me, minimized for his taking while he adjusts the machinery like the interactive segments of the exhibit. He switches our magnifications up and down to see which size is best— so when he plunges his dick, it won't shoot through my gummy shoulders or my head.

Both gigantic in size, Max leans in and flickers his tongue to taste. He sloshes it to and fro in slow, licking strokes. My juice splashes onto the wall behind us. Some flicks into the air. Some line the fullness of his lips like raw honey.

"FUCK!" Max cries out.

His roar violently vibrates every nut and bolt, shaking everything composed of matter to tremble at the sound of his voice. Max convulses in a seizure—he jerks his body in demonic postures to handle the dose of sugar on his tongue. His pants drop to the floor like a boulder. Max inspects my lips and spreads my rubbery labia,

adjusting the levers once more. Max darts his tongue at the mini dick staring at him; my swollen, edible muscle is ready for his consumption.
He spreads my legs further apart and touches me.
Tasting his fingertip.
Sucking on it like he was giving his digit a blow job.
Rubbing its syrup on the head of his dick for lubrication.
Contraption adjustments again.
Max rushes the magnification when he spits on my pussy for more wetness.
It douses me like a bucket drench, splashing his saliva like busted water balloons.
Max hoists his cock into his hand and circles my opening with the head of his shaft.
Only putting the head in once or twice.
Hearing the gumminess separating my creamy opening.
He pushes in a little more, savoring the trip.
Then pulls his shaft out, bends over, and tastes it.
He lets the suck of his pull get good to him.
Giving himself some head.
Max flickers his tongue and starts sucking slower.
Not letting anything go to waste.
Deep throating his cock to get every drop.
"FUCK!"
Ejaculation fills his mouth like milk.
Max wails as he stuffs his cock down his open mouth and throat, gagging in self-satisfaction.
He swallows his semen to gain more power.
Max stands upright and quickly pulls the apparatus closer to him.
Feeling his way.
All the way in.
Until the device can't go anymore.
The measurements are perfect now.
Max pushes it away.
Generating each stroke.
Back and forth.
Feeling the fit.
Slower, then faster.
Pounding his frustration into me.
Rubbing his thumb along my clit and his massive plug of flesh.
He lifts the apparatus, turns me over, and sodomizes me.
Changing the percentage of taste-buds on his tongue.

First, drowning my asshole with spit.
It widens the chute and cleans out the shit.
He pushes and pulls as his tongue scrubs it out.
I feel my kidneys and my liver pop, then liquify.
Screams of agony echo the space.
Turning me over again.
Plunging his dick deep inside of me.
Titillating my clit with another growth of cock-meat.
Fucking me faster.
Grinding on my soft, gelatinous tissue.
We cum together and dissipate globs of climactic secretions.
His, creamy and thick, injects into my love canal and leaks out.
Mine, watery and abundant, dissolves into a sticky residue and
intertwines with his.
Semen, feces, urine, gum, nectar, and death.
It mixes.
It disgusts.
It feeds.

For days, I'm at their disposal. Spirits dart out from the tunnel
and swoop in to feed from my seeping crotch. Some hover to govern.
At one point, hundreds swarm the room. Women spirits. Men spirits.
They bite and chunk away at the mound of organic custard piled on
my belly and crusted along my inner thigh and pussy opening, still
oozing from my hole. The spirits fed often, and when there wasn't
enough, the faceless spirit with needles came out to have me cum.
Her tongue is so wicked I climax in twenty strokes or less.

Spirits chip away at the coagulated mound of nut stuck to my
opening and almost healed thigh. One of my eyelids is partially
complete. I can see it regenerating from the inside. The mechanical
connection of neurons communicates their signals to reform. Even
though one eye is bald, the other takes on a different restructuring.
Even closed in its lid restoration, my vision is clear to see. The
computerized border gives a layered synopsis of the situation: the
temperature in the room; other things like blurry colors pulsing in the
corner; and faint silhouettes of objects that don't make any sense. I
don't know what to focus on to remember it later. Swirls. Different
colors. A multitude of dangling crystals.

The rubber slides from my hair more. I can shake my neck
around a little bit. Still stuck in an upside-down position to the
apparatus, I move my leg to see if I have regained more control.

The one spirit that floats by me daily plays one role. She watches close, but not too close. She observes my progress from above, circling from afar and masking her face with her mystified presence. I take a closer look at her from my juxtaposed position. One-eye jacking to focus on her whereabouts in the spacious room. The tethered sheet of incomplete skin over my eye keeps her masked from my discovery.

She notices my curiosity.

One day, she circles and decides to ride in closer, slowing her rate of speed, and rocks her head as she glides nearby in her taunt and flight. She suddenly stops in front of me. As she floats, her image is inverted to mine. The needles that tinker at her feet and initiate tiny sparks when they hit one another spit flares into my face. I look at their crystal precision, all ten inches, as they fire off. Lashing her tongue, she extracts it to taste my pussy again. She, too, puffs up in satisfaction. Her ghostly shadow suddenly flashes in my face. Haunting and skeletal in her image, her demonic face flashes sharp teeth that scream her death wail at me. Her ear-piercing shrills cry out at a clenched decibel, screeching as she devours a chunk of my dried, sweet orgasm and darts off into the dark hollow.

It seems like weeks, but the disconnection with time confuses the reality. Other parts of the rubberized enclosure dissipate from my body as it marches on. My newly formed skin and aching bones signify their calcified reformation. Being stuck in this convex position gives my body remembrance of just how long it's been. Only my gluteus parts have me bound to the surface. My arms and legs suspend wildly. I resemble a dead ant smashed against a window.

I peel away from the surface a little bit more every day. Once released, I look around to see where to land, and a black abyss awaits my fall. There is no end. It disappears into nothing. Then suddenly, one of my ass cheeks detaches from the apparatus like Velcro, followed by the other.

"Ah!"

I tumble down its curved decline at a rapid rate of speed and fall into the black void that echoes the horrid screams of death all around me. The empty tunnel vibrates my body as I fall. Hands dart out from every side, and as I descend, they grab at my hair, slap on my ass, and poke at my body. Every section I go through takes me deeper into hell. Maybe I'm the one that fell out in church, not the organ player. I pray there is a bottom to this pit that will startle me to wake up, and Sister Ida is splashing my face with holy water.

I suddenly stop in my fall. I land in an all-white room at the bottom of the endless drop, instantly floating with graciousness. Godly and now draped in a sheer gown. I feel renewed. I am whole. I can blink.

Max collects my lantern at the bottom of the chute and whisks me away. Enclosed within a glass case, Max carries me off quickly. As we swoop into the air, the gown material tightens against my body as we fly.

He soars across the infinite room and passes numerous hanging stations with the same enclosures. The dots go on forever. Other scantily clad women are banging their hands against the glass when they see us approaching.

From an aerial view, the dangling stations resemble flattened flowers. Gold wires hang from each petal, with other women dangling in their windowed hell, too. They sparkle like crystal icicles. Maneuvering in between them, and from above, I notice the suspension in mid-air—spinning at times, as women watch us fly by, and I, catch a glimpse of the others in their turmoil.

One woman looks ready to pop. Her belly is oblong as she prepares for birth. We pass another, her encasement full of morning sickness. The vomit splatters the glass with neon chunks of rotted food. Another woman struggles in the throes of childbirth. Blood is everywhere, at least two gallons. She looks faint in color, gaunt-like. Her exhausted face glistens with bubbling snot running from her nose and mouth as she screams in hysterical desperation.

A dark-complected woman with a blonde afro looks up as we approach. Her capsule shakes uncontrollably to get Max's attention as she sees us draw near. Her frightened eyes fill with gloom as we approach.

"No!" Rochelle screams frantically from behind the encasement, and we lock eyes as we zip by her. I place my hands on the glass in solidarity. She beats the capsule until it cracks. Max turns back at her in mid-flight and zaps her trinket with his eyes, instantly igniting her delicate grave. Rochelle explodes like a grenade. I scream as I watch her body ricochet from the fractured glass, fighting the burning flames melting her skin.

"No!" I cry as I bang against my crystal shell.

"Worthless bitch's tubes were tied anyway, *and* she was vaccinated! Fucking mutant!" Max yells in anger and his words vibrate against my transparent casket.

He redirects his attention and flies to an open compartment, petals away. Max places me into an empty slot where he latches me to the wire for security.

There is a space between another woman and me. We hang collectively in groups of fright. Classical music plays over a loud intercom. He hovers in front of my encasement to see how my body has healed and pleasures in how the fabric suctions to my skin like a glove. Its mutating sheet adheres to the curves of my body to seal in the freshness. It penetrates my skin like mesh.

As he turns to look at the others, he appears content in our assembly. He nods in satisfaction, retrieves Rochelle's engulfed lantern, flies into the white mist, and disappears.

My sorrow hangs for months as I watch bellies grow around me. The image of Rochelle replays in my head. Her hands melted like chocolate against the fireworks-engulfed enclosure. Her hair blazed between the flames like a fiery ball of death. Rochelle's tomb was filled with blood and black smoke like a pot of African soot.

The glass enclosure is too thick to permeate any sound outside of its boundaries. I try. The woman in the pod beside me tries. One lady hanging from another petal attempts to rock her pod, hoping to make Max reappear as she silently screams Max's name.

All around me, I see women in their different phases of fetal incubation, frantically moving their mouths in trepidation and wiggling their arms and legs wildly. While their torsos are strapped around their bellies to secure them, only pantomimed gestures are received. Their "get me the fuck of here" goes unheard.

We witness a woman die in her pod. Her birth canal not wide enough to deliver the breached child within her. I watch her gag and plead for help. She punches her stomach to force it out, her silent cries of agony are on display for us to see and never forget. She attempts to pull the fetus from her canal but stops when the pain is too much. After a while, she gives up. The foot hanging from her vagina finally stops moving, and so does she.

My heart races with anxiety. We move around in chaos, teetering our capsules in fear, and screaming from the top of our lungs. Tears of death drown our faces. Terrified eyes pop from sockets. Our exclamations are locked in silence within the soundproof trinkets.

As we watch the floor open below us, fire shoots out from the cracked opening, wild and free. The fire rages its power and fury in a blazing display. Finally able to breathe from underneath the ivory barrier, the wall of fire moves across the floor and opens to the pits of hell.

We scream in terror! The heat humidifies our cases as we hang in limbo above the furnace of eternal demise. The tips of the flames snap against the glass. Condensation droplets form at the base of our goblet tombs, releasing blistering bubbles of hot steam.

The room, now a brazen glow of orange, engulfs the view. Then, there are clanking noises. Her pod slowly opens from the bottom, unclamps from around her waist, and releases her. Her screams follow close behind. Seconds later, her pod unlatches from the station and falls into the burning lake below. Any proof of their existence evaporates as they dissipate into black puffs of smoke. The bottom moves back across the floor and seals with a hammering clench.

More time passes, and bellies are still growing. Thirty more pods fell victim to the fiery lake, and my stomach hasn't changed like the others.

I glimpse Max forming from sheeted molecules in the middle of the room. He morphs into a bodily form of chocolatey, 24-karat gold blackness. His face looks disturbed as he flies around me.

CHAPTER 25
Time and Patience

It weirdly struck Max when he noticed Gianna wasn't progressing like the others. He never had an issue with production, but his time to multiply was probably running out. The last four petals were duds and had to go. Their deformities had sealed their fates. Some had malformed faces, while over thirty offspring had male and female sex organs.

Max felt like he was right back at square one. That wasn't his fault. He didn't understand that ten had scarred fallopian tubes. He didn't realize five had tilted vaginas. Max unknowingly selected women with mutilated wombs, scarred by numerous abortions. Max suspected some were tied into his bloodline courtesy of his pappy. If so, it wouldn't have surprised him at all.

That's how a few ended up at the exhibition. Max didn't want a repeat cycle. Sean was right, but Max had to produce. He couldn't afford to be choosey or wasteful in his selections. Some women were sterile from promiscuous sex. The bacterial infections ate away at the cervical cup and destroyed their vaginal walls.

Max didn't know how much longer he could continue. Each ejaculation left him weaker and weaker. Securing numerous fetal cycles had become tedious. This cycle was Max's eighth, and he hoped this was his last. Not that he didn't like it, but he was tired of eating pussy. It had lost its savoir faire. The crackish addiction was not such a fiend anymore. It had become an imposition, a job he was no longer interested in working, and Max was ready to quit without giving his two-week notice.

For one reason or another, capsules were disintegrating at an alarming rate. The solstice was shifting, and time was of the essence. Max was initiating bodies left and right, trying to recoup his losses. Passing between the horizon, Max failed to locate his amulet each time he traveled to this dimension that was tied to the agreement ages ago.

Max went through stacks of amulets explicitly designed for the bearer and his assignment. As Max barreled through mounds of dirt and coal, the ancient discoveries opened crusted wounds from the past. The generations of turmoil Max went through, the digging and opening of rotted tombs with calcified skeletons. He shoveled deeper into the nutrient-rich soil to locate the weather-torn satchels that would end this curse.

With only minimal time to find his amulet between Gianna's casting, Max darted back and forth between realms to catch her for the next phase. He shifted dimensions behind the plane during Gianna's initiation. Her pregnancy submitted to the cause, manifesting that Gianna would complete the cycle, and he would be set free. Max's life could continue—with or without her. If this panned out, Max's assignment finishes as well. In essence, Max knew he was killing four birds with one stone. He satisfied everything: his father's assignment, his assignment, his mother's curse, and the Trevallier Decree that started this mess.

Taking Gianna repeatedly through the process was disappointing. He hoped one of his sperm caught an egg, but the results were nothing each time: dipping and dunking, waiting for the spirits to feast from the scalloped leftovers, anxious for Gianna to heal and incubate, and then fucking wait.

Max waited close to three years before realizing his efforts were in vain. Forgetting who she was, ignoring the red flags, and wasting all his time. So enamored by how big Gianna's ass is and her juicy-wet entry, Max loved the plumpness of her pussy friction. Max, caught up in making her his own, failed to register their reality from the beginning. Yeah, he thought about the possibility it posed and knew the facts of the matter. Max acted like they weren't related and forgot their similar genetic disposition with whose bond they share— his father's. Max subconsciously blocked that detail out on purpose and without remorse. He fought a losing battle with time, the heartbreaking truth, and Gianna.

"FUCK!"

Max wanted to kill himself. The next time the floor opened, not wishing that it would, he imagined jumping in, pulling his last parachute, and disappearing forever.

If it was possible, Max's lineage would die like a dream and become a puff of smoke like the others. Max's hell was continual. Suicide was not an option and the Declotae would just revive him back to life so he could relive his foolish death over and over.

They slashed his back and carved chunks into his flesh for remembrance. Max attempted once before, a decade ago, before the Declotae etched their faces into his back like a tramp stamp. Marking their territory as they saw fit. They were pimping out their ho. The chunks of skin sewn into intricate patterns mimicked their ram horns and wide, angled eyes that smiled back in their seductive anger. The Declotae threatened to sew a pussy to his forehead and titties to his cheeks the next time he returned to serve his time. Label him a true pussy bitch.

None of the encasements produced anything in the first two petals. All sixteen wires vanished. Max spent a lot of fucking money on wigs and those butterfly-ass-lashes in their cycle to end up with not one offspring. They had the worst-looking pussies from having so many children naturally, but they tasted like strawberries. It didn't make sense to Max either. He knew they would conceive, and when none of them produced, it punched Max clean in the gut.

There was one pod hanging from the third petal, two in the fourth petal—which Max was proud of considering they were mother and daughter, four sprinkled between the sixth and seventh petals, and Gianna, his queen, hung from the eighth.

Max's mission would be complete if eight remained from the initial planting. Max had to find his coin and vanish from this horrid realm forever, but his timing must align perfectly to escape. He only needed eight conceived pods continually, which took a lot of fucking. Women are on different wavelengths, and not everyone ovulates together. But Max learned when a house full of women live together, eventually, they ovulate at the same time. Sean was right. If Max looked at their panties first, he would know precisely when they were creamy and ready to impregnate.

Some years created a bountiful harvest of infants for the Guff, and others were dry as bone. Lately, Max's harvests are unpredictable. What enticed his loins, demised his quest. As the numbers continued to decline, desperation weighed on Max's heart heavier than before.

Gianna just had to nest. All of Max's eggs are in her basket now. The miraculous conception of the seven before her is proof there was still some supercharged semen hiding in the cut of his hulkish loins. Those sperm would connect with the top-shelf compositions dangling from their crystal tombs to multiply for his purpose fruitfully.

Max knew Gianna was a top-tier bitch, because they were the same. His daddy's blood ran through her veins. But that she, too, came from his father's testicles posed a real problem. Her womb may be diabolically cursed, like this assignment.

Impregnating her became an intricate anomaly drowning in damnation. What if her egg had a thousand babies inside, and hatched like spiders? Then what? She couldn't have those offspring here or in their earthly realm. Did he have to acquire his coin and slip into space's universe with her? Is earth's pressure too tight for Gianna to conceive? Is this realm's attachment to hell keeping her pussy closed? Those numbers both seduced Max and worried him. It was possible for anything to occur and that excited and concerned Max a great deal.

Gianna's incubation needed a unique touch; it had to swerve his mama's curse, satisfy his daddy's shit, and meet his needs. Max could hear Declotae laughing in his ear again, probably calling him all kinds of stupid asses and foolish. Max knew who Gianna was, and if she were with child, it would be deformed—another fucking dud, and unfortunately, Gianna would have to go into the fiery lake with it.

The thought of losing Gianna to hell infuriated Max. It was too much to fathom. That information must be wrong. Max was missing something and could not put his finger on what it was.

CHAPTER 26
Keep Your Enemies Close

Decades of preying, performing fellatio, spending money, dick pounding, waiting, slipping, moving, pulling the parachute, and disappearing into other realms were taking their toll. The frustration was driving Max crazy. He knew if Gianna didn't conceive this time, he would have to cut his losses and bounce.

But he couldn't. He was too far in.

The time invested in Gianna had to pan out. Max knew there must be another way to make her his own. Max understood their dynamic now. They were siblings, and how powerful they would be together in the next tier. And with his other sister, Dedrias, together with Sean, they could create a super race of pure-hearted souls and a more potent Trevallier DuBois bloodline.

Though peculiar, their broad offspring would create a new lineage of royalty to the family name. Their sole purpose would be to please, to make everything right. It would humble them before the Earth and all creation by judging the unrighteous, evildoers, and slackers. Their joint assimilation could destroy the Declotae's vicious cycles forever.

"Order is rooted in a pure heart. The ignorant vanities of man defile with greed and power when his lineage is compromised. What stands pure in its origin, is no outside blood to taint the strength of his family legend. Procreate with thine own kind to secure its uncontaminated power. No warrior would have to hold the Orb, and no other man would fall victim to the Declotae's psychotic executions." Max versed the code to himself. A reminder of his subconscious loyalty to the family code. It gives him hope for another day and selfishly, carries on.

Max's mission to acquire Gianna was contingent on finding his amulet. Maybe that was why she couldn't conceive; Max's sperm was damn near dead binding to his father's coin. He was invisible in the spirit realm, as were some of the spermatozoa. Weakened by every nut he expelled; their flagellum was too paralyzed to propel their journey to create life—everything Max needed. Switching his coin to hide from the Declotae backfired in the end. Max could almost hear his mother laughing as well. Her hawk toenail tapping the wood floors, the heaviness in the room, and her impatience whizzing past his eardrums.

It was clear to Max that the piper was coming for payment. The failed births were the signs. He would have to impregnate Gianna from their realm to make it work. That was the only thing he couldn't do there either, not without his amulet. Max needed to locate his coin, which meant digging up his father's shame.

Max did not want to see his father's penis cursed to stay hard in a state of humiliation from long ago. It would be another reminder of what he occasionally endures. It meant defacing his father's body before the last night of the solstice.

"Ugh. There must be another way."

Max had to work the aged and withered dick scraps here, bearing his father's amulet, but the longevity of their lives was fading. Some sperm did not die off so quickly, slowly decaying with his father's energy alignment. Time was ticking its time bomb. His production and ball sack would soon become dust if Max did not devise a resolution. Max calculated only a million good swimmers clinging to the time they still had left, and that bomb ticked louder than the screams from the women in the capsules. Max needed his other testicle for the mission and came to terms that he could not take this on alone.

Sean was required, and at times Max knew that he would be, but Max realized Sean had no desire to return to this God-forsaken place. Sean bitched and complained about each trip, but that didn't matter to Max. Sean was at his disposal whether he liked it or not. Max did not feel worthy enough to carry the Orb of Life—not that he wanted to, but it was just the significance of it. Holding the world on your shoulders is heavy, especially when you end up at the bottom of the sea for serving your time and holding mankind in your hands. Thank you, Declotae. Bitches.

Max felt defeated and less than a man with his missing nut sack. Max was the one walking around with one ball, not Sean. Max freezes and recalls Sean's moves in his memory, suddenly realizing he's the one that's getting played by his whole crew.

"Oh no." Max thought as the pieces clicked together; it was another part of the puzzle Max did not have. "He has them all. Sean has all the balls." Max cringed as he thought about his father's testicle stitched down the middle to look like two when he placed his loincloth around his thigh and crotch, just like Sean's flap of skin between his legs. "Dirty bastard!"

Another player entered the game without knowing they were playing, or did they?

Sean liked to push Max's buttons around others, taunting his upper hand that many didn't know he had. Max felt like Sean was trying him on purpose to see how far he could go, like the baby brother testing his value in the family, assuming Max was a weak nigga and didn't deserve to be in the position he was in.

Sean became increasingly pompous with Max as the universe hung from his crotch like a superpower. Max sensed Sean wanted to break their accord to prove his strength and worth, and he was right.

Max almost regrets accepting Sean into their fold. At times ducked off with him, binding their personal secrets along the way to keep Sean's mouth shut, Max felt obligated even more. Max sensed deep in his bones that Sean wanted his position, and for a while, Max allowed the cat-and-mouse game to play out to keep Sean close. Until Max found Sean's twin or once his testicle was back in his possession, there was nothing else he could do.

The gift wrapped with the curse was perfectly packaged with a sparkly, gold bow. Fucking different women at night, spending the money they robbed from banks worldwide, jumping through time, and getting close to Max to learn his skills. He was learning from his older brother how to move like a Trevallier man.

Max's stomach was turning.

It was nice initially, but partying and filling the Guff is a huge gig, and the glitz quickly wears off. Sean even threatened that he could push actual petal production with no duds. Better offspring and stock. Sean ragged on Max's retarded-ass kids that never made the cut. Digging on Max's curse, his mother, and his dusty lineage.

Max busted Sean to the white meat for his disrespect, dragging his feet across broken glass and whipping his back to remind his ass of who was in charge. Sean, responding with cockiness, said the Declotae were and not him. Sean knew how much that got under Max's skin and started using his cheese to reel Max into reality.

The reality was, Sean had a one-up on him. Sean had one of Max's balls and had him by it. Sean started using that leverage more and more. Telling Max what he wants in return for his services. Sean shared his disdain for the craft and how much work it involves; but owned up to what was required to be with Dedrias—he was obligated as Max's craft man, Kim's assistant.

Max did not budge because of his agenda. He ignored Sean like his demands didn't matter. Max had a Guff to supply and wasn't worried about Sean's punk-ass needs. Sean was feeling froggy, and for Max's shit to pan out, he had to appease him on some level. The last bout in the truck told Max it wouldn't be long before Sean tried him for real. Max thought about his missing testicle held hostage and what he must do to regain it. Sean threatened to disappear with it if he didn't get what he wanted.

"At this point, he can have the motherfucker." Max thought to himself. He didn't mean a word of his outburst. He was just frustrated with everything. His ball was at stake. The value of his sperm sack was on the universal line.

This trip took a toll on Max. He was sick and tired of hitting U-turns to recover his shit. His amulet, his offspring, and now, his held-hostage ball. Max was between a rock and a hard place.

Sean was feeling himself—walking around with three nut bags Kim tailored to the middle of his crotch. One full of Sean's DNA, one deflated like a raisin and possibly their father's testicle, and the other was Max's.

Max debated back and forth with himself. He needed his living sperm to do their job, and they were attached to Sean's ass. Max contemplated the unthinkable and had to decide. Appeasing Sean with something, Max had to give a few inches.

It degraded Max. The times at coronation, the twig punishment, when he was hitting Sean from the back, and sodomizing Gianna with his tongue—it was too much to deal with. Even the thought of doing it again made his stomach earl.

Max regurgitated liquified slime into his mouth when recalling the smell that freshly wafted under his nose. It was too fucking much. All Max could smell was boo-boo once the gross thought entered his head. The shitty paste it leaves on Max's shaft is like peanut butter. Having to squeeze Sean's shit from his dick opening like toothpaste grossed him the fuck out. He would have to soak his extremities in vinegar and bleach for days.

"Damnit!"

CHAPTER 27
So Now What?

With all this miraculous time jumping they were doing; Sean didn't think it was an impossible request. Sean didn't care how the extra ball came, and when Max needed Sean to surrogate for him to hide his testicle, it was a perfect trade off. It had to be hidden and preserved. With Kim being the seamstress of his pack, she attached everything accordingly.

Dedrias complained about not having her needs met, and it played in Max's head while he fucked her husband. She was making baby threats, too. The art shows and fancy clothes spoiled her. Not that she never had nice things; she just became addicted to them. Kim was upset because she needed more of whatever she was complaining about. Everybody was getting on Max's nerves with their demands and selfish requests.

Dedrias craved masturbation. She often sat on the toilet with a bowl floating under her in the water and watched her orgasm drip from her sweet pussy walls. She often scooped the slick resin with a spoon like honey and savored herself with each swallow. Her fellatio compulsions helped to back up her needs and Max's dwindling supply of pods. Dedrias' nectar kept him alive during interims of drought and the disappointment of dud ass babies. Their incestuous relations stemmed from their father's weird religion.

Dedrias believed she was the bottom bitch. She had access to everything. When they moved around, they needed each other until the hoes started coming around to see what the deal was. The easy bitches came first. They were usually the CNAs, the women at the gym, and the churchgoers. When everything was on pause while Max counted his harvest, they fed from each other. It was something they practiced, producing for him. Max would shrivel up like Sean's testicle without enough pussy nectar.

Dedrias fussed about not having a fresh supply to sup from herself. Not that the sessions with her brother weren't exhilarating, but anything done in repetition can lose its flair once it's predictable.

The thrill was over three realms ago. They were sneaking around, acting as if someone would tell on them. Their dynamic was different, and so was their purpose. Their obligations were not to this world; but to the incestuous legacy of the Trevallier Negus DuBois family name and the Declotae.

Max needed a fresher supply of pussy, too. He was sick of his sister complaining about his dick. She knew what the deal was when they moved here. She had to play wifey until his planting began in that city. Period.

Dedrias wanted someone other than her brother to ride. His moves had become predictable. His dick almost destroyed her labia from its circumference. That's when Dedrias drew the line and told Max she had to save the rest of her chopped liver for someone else to eat. Dedrias had enough of Max taking advantage of their situation, sometimes forcing her to have relations with him during menstruation, to satisfy his ungodly needs. He had defiled her in the most vulgar way. It left the bitter taste of revenge on her tongue and the foulest odor because of their sessions. The brown, chaffed skin peeling from her walls smelled a little fishy. Dedrias was tired of the UTIs, the medication that came with it, and the yeast Infection disinfection after. Max, disowning the scent, or the vaginosis, coming from him demanded it is a part of her job, and for her to go douche the funk out. He never considered the bloody actions that dishonor her as a woman. Max didn't give a fuck about the blood, but instead ate her out to get the milligrams of sugar and nutrients he needed to stay strong. Max has done way grosser shit than that to stay afloat during dry seasons.

*   *   *

Many moons ago, Max and Dedrias moved to Nevada for a time and decided to break from the normalcy of incest to scour the city for fresh meat.

The out-of-town soirees and limousine fleets in Vegas always steered plenty of women and men in that sector. The girl's trips, the bachelor parties, car shows, and cannabis conventions were yearly swanks and stomping grounds.

Dedrias was determined not to supply Max anymore, forcing him to scout for new bodies. Trolling casino spots for prospects one evening, an older woman was choking on a hot dog on the strip, and the Heimlich had failed to eject the obstruction. They didn't want to draw any attention to themselves and sat and watched the woman suffer. Max had watched women suffer before; it didn't bother him one bit. They heard the frantic cries for someone to help her, which Max had heard before, too, but couldn't care less. It wasn't his place to save her.

"Her fat ass should have been eating a piece of fruit." Max thought to himself.

Across the room was Sean. He was a single man on vacation from his meager paramedic employment and watched to see if the lady he saw helping would be able to get it out before he acted.

Her eyes rolled to the back of her head, and her consciousness faded fast. The constant dinging of machines echoed in the backdrop. Kim, a sparkly little thing, had heard the calls and rushed from her machine to assist. She cleared the area, grabbed a firm hold of the woman's arms, and attempted her thrusts. Huffing in her movements, Kim lost the woman as her knees gave way. Then, she tried to lift her leg onto the table but failed.

Now recognizing his assistance was needed, Sean watched Kim attempt to hoist the woman's two-hundred-pound leg onto the table again. After numerous failures, Sean ran over to assist. He picked the woman up, laid her across the table, and prepped her for an emergency tracheotomy.

Sean screamed for a sharp knife, a straw, a pair of tongs, and a fork. Kim shouted for dental floss, some toothpicks, and a lighter. They knew these essential items were present with as many people in the room.

Kim focused on the incision while Sean held her body on the table. The jagged steak knife made the cut difficult, but opening her airway was more critical than aesthetics. Sean, now taking over, sliced through the different layers of the epidermis, muscular, and mucus membranes. He was able to locate her esophagus and cut through to extract the lodged dog obstructing the airway behind it.

As he was cutting, he turned his head to his shoulder and began talking to himself. He was standing there having a full-blown argument with the formed hump of tissue at his side, apologizing to it for his need to help the dying lady. Cursing at himself for what he was about to do. Sean flicked his fingers at the hump on his neck, confusing Max and Dedrias. They thought his ass was crazy. Like, who was he talking to and what did he just flick that still wiggled around by his shoulder?

But as they looked closer, they could see its tiny eyes and ears. Its mouth still flapping in plea mode, shaking its neck like a spring. It was contesting and fighting to stay where it was. Everyone else was too focused on the blue whale suffocating on the table to notice it arguing in Sean's ear—not until Sean twisted the structure from his shoulder and Max could hear the tiny screams it cried as he ripped it from his flesh and dabbed the flowing blood from the woman's incision. The small, vacant space left by the hump in his neck was now void of its resident. Max questioned Sean's identity after witnessing the impossible. Where the lump was detached, was the same place where his mother cut the two-headed doll before she dropped it into the jar of egg water.

From there, Sean executed CPR. Kim, noticing the air bubbles, placed the straw into the incision to provide oxygen flow to her brain and lungs. After five compressions, Kim blew into the straw, resuscitating the dying woman. After the cheers, Kim wrapped the dental floss around one end of a toothpick, then another, and told the woman that she had to close the openings. She lit the end that was going in and burned any bacteria present. Sean leaned against her for support, squeezing the woman's hand as shallow breaths vibrated from her chest. Her feet jerked in positions to tolerate the stinging nerve discomfort. She tapped on Sean's hands to let him know she was okay. Kim's meticulous stitch work was in perfect alignment, closing the wound. It left Dedrias and Max in pure awe as they cheered them on with the crowd. They knew they had just discovered the missing pieces in their puzzle. That's how Sean and Kim became a part of their twisted fold.

*　　　　*　　　　*

Sean was slowly introduced to things as the occasions arose. Mold a cast together. Plaster the walls to seal the new addition to the estate. Permanently dispose rotting bodies that failed to showcase at their one-night exhibitions easily. Throw boiled cloth over the bodies to achieve a bubble-like effect and to make their defiled nipples pop.

Max would have Sean close his eyes, imagine a place he had never been, and POOF! They magically appeared POOF wherever they desired, shocking Sean each time POOF, and he succumbed to every one POOF of Max's needs POOF!

Max demonstrated with his father's amulet that the coin must be precisely parallel with the skyline to slip through it and enter other realms. He showed him how it opens the ambit like a key, and once the amulet clicks into the microscopic slit, he must turn it counterclockwise to drag the realm open. Sean watched how it dissipated like cream being stirred into coffee when he turned the dimension, and they walked through time.

Kim oversaw the embroidery aspect: fold and stitch some material to make Max new loincloths, cut patterns of their flesh to cover up others, and threaded facial expressions to give Sean's art an abstract appeal. By lifting the skin to sew the eyes closer together for Sean to smooth over missing chunks of flesh. Kim pulled the ropes through their feet and gathered their legs with wire—basic seamstress stuff. She often sewed a ringlet of her golden blonde hair somewhere on their bodies to sign her contribution—common psycho shit.

CHAPTER 28
Two Heads Are Better Than One

As Max walks around us, he stops at my capsule. He flicks the encasement to see if I am alert, teetering the crystal shell to wake me.

"Wake up." He taps on the glass and watches me sway sideways. "We're going on a little trip." Max plucks me from the petal casing, hooks me into one of his three-holed earlobes, and we disappear into a white mist. Flashing through time, Max arrives at Sean and Dedrias' home with regret puffing from his nostrils.

Sean welcomes him with open arms. Their conversation is muffled, but their actions are clear. Sean grabs Max's ass as we enter. Max, pulling Sean close, presses his face against my enclosure and Max's ear, and kisses him on the cheek. Max pushes Sean over to the dining room table and gives Sean exactly what he wants.

The pruning of Sean's manhood happens right before Max's eyes as he watches the three sagging sacks jingle with each thrust like bells. Max leans back to look at his selection while thrusting his dick forward. I move with him and dangle sideways, jerk with Max's moves, and catching the circumference of Sean's asshole stretch and grip Max's cock with ease. The hairiness of Max's ball set it apart from the others. It hangs like a globe covered with snow-white peach fuzz. Perfect in size and shape, it forces the other two closer to Sean's left inner thigh, tebowing the tight space. It is superior to the others. Sean's deflated cushion of skin between them divides their purpose. Smelling the backdraft of shit as Sean's pubic hairs snap like whips against his shaft. One flies into the air like a wiry boomerang. As it turns in the air toward me, it reflects against the candlelight and hits the ear I hang from. Max aims for Sean's nut sack correctly but misses, his fingernail slicing into Sean's leg more accurately.

"Sss," Sean hisses in satisfaction.

Still moving his hips slowly, Max aims for it again and misses. Sean calls out as the intensity of the cut slashes into his butt muscle.

"Yes!" Sean joyously takes what his master gives him, finally satisfying his needs and making Sean want to please his master more. While jacking off his own dick at the same time, whatever Max wants him to do, he will do. There was no need to reiterate anything else.

The first time Sean had to fill in, it left him fucked up. His balls smashed; only one survived and reinflated. His testicle flattened like a pancake; raisin cryptology, wrinkled, mazed, and destroying his millions of offspring. Sean screamed like a bitch the whole time, complaining about his role and why was he playing Max's, too? Why did his right ball have to pay the price? That wasn't what Sean signed up for. He just wanted what Max owed to him, Dedrias. That was the trade-off—Max's sister for Sean's testis.

As time went on, Sean agreed to help. His artistic gifts used to manifest the artwork in a way that confounded onlookers. They questioned whether the bodies were natural specimens or not. Guests touched body parts they couldn't believe were disfigured or brutally beaten. No one would get caught. Sean took different sheets of skin from one hoe and sewed them to another dumb hoe. That created a mysterious puzzle no agent would figure out. When Sean added liquid concrete to the hot wax and tar to his boiling emulsion, it instantly dissolved the women's fingerprints when he wrapped them. Sean needed a way to vent his sexual frustrations for unmet needs, and when Max asked if Kim could sew his one ball to hide it from the Declotae, Sean jumped at the opportunity.

Sean hated his mother for letting her new husband watch him when she went to work. After a few months, he began touching Sean's private parts. By the age of ten, Sean was sodomized. He made him bend over, suck his wormy penis, and dared him to say anything.

The forced anal thrusts started other problems. Sean began to develop a small crater in the grove between his neck and shoulder, where the stepfather used to bite when he bent over and ejaculated. Over time, as it healed, it developed a tiny keloid that sprouted into a mole. Sean told his mother he fell off his bike going down a hill when she noticed the gash.

The mole grew over time, and as it did, started whispering to Sean.

It told Sean not to be afraid.

Quietly talking in his ear.

It didn't want to scare Sean.

"Sean," the mole whispered.

"Who's that?"

It told Sean how to get rid of his stepfather for what he was doing to them.

It told Sean to stab his stepfather in the throat.

"There's an ice pick in the garage," it revealed. "Stab him when he takes you to school," the gummy tube of skin ordered Sean to drive the long way behind the lake and jab him quickly to catch him by surprise. "That's when you wrap the garden hose around his neck with the boulders."

Sean's stepfather threatened to slit his mother's throat if he ever told. The anomaly told him to keep quiet about its growth and what it was saying in his ear. So, Sean said nothing to no one.

The mole talked to Sean every day after that. It aggravated Sean's back when he taped it down during school. No one knew the abscess was there, the way Sean controlled the warty composition to hold it in place. Rubbing cough medicine over it to keep it knocked out for as long as possible. The pliant skin plug allowed Sean to press it flat. It started rustling under his shirts, often breaking the stickiness of the tape that held it down. It bothered Sean so much that it squealed to get on his nerves.

One day, Sean stabbed his stepfather exactly as it ordered just to shut the thing up. That morning, when they pulled off, it gave Sean detailed instructions. His stepfather was slumped over the steering wheel by the next stop sign. Sean drove to the lake, wrapped the rope with the heavy rock to his head, and pushed him over the bridge.

In high school, Sean liked the choices he had sexually. During his freshman year, he sought the hardness of football players. Many were undercover homosexuals and wanted to keep their perversion quiet. By his senior year, when Sean needed the nurturing softness of a female, he went to one. That choice was often mostly to fit in with the hetero members of the team. Sean was the tight-end receiver; his illusion had to look the part for both sides of his façade.

Sean liked the comfort the cheerleaders provided. They catered to his well-being and filled the void his mother failed to give. They made him feel loved. The more Sean yearned for the loving kindness of a female, the less he urged for the hardness of a man.

One summer, his mother found an old pair of Sean's underwear with shit stains in the front part and questioned him. That's when he mustered the courage to tell. Sean told her that's why her husband went missing. His mother didn't believe him and told him to prove it. She pleaded with him to show her where he dumped the body, and when Sean refused, threatened to put him out unless he made her lonely nights better.

"Since you killed him, you must fill his place," she ordered whenever she wanted fellatio.

Sometimes, she forced Sean to stay there for hours, catching lockjaw, in the process. He hated his mother for the years of abuse he endured. He often turned to building sculptures to release his pent-up rage. Two of Sean's pieces were featured in the high school arts festival and won first and second place.

Sean was good at what he did and knew his worth. He crushed their faces inward to accentuate their cheekbones. Sean imagined bashing his mother's face in. He dipped their feet into concrete blocks, hanging them to dry. It dislocated their hips and ankles. Before Sean disposed of their rotting corpses, he pulled their teeth to erase their identities.

Sean's role was to paint, prop, lift heavy shit, and hide evidence. That's it, not storing a ball sack for some man-god on a selfish, dick-ego trip. Sean eagerly hid Max's ball to feel like a whole man again. Max owed Sean a testicle, *his* ball sack. Sean didn't care how it came. Max needed Sean to surrogate for him and hide his testicle. It had to be hidden and preserved. With Kim being the seamstress of his pack, she attached everything accordingly.

A Premature Harvest

*"Family can change how they feel about
you at any time. Blood relation means
nothing. When the choice is between you
or them, guess who loses?"*

—MRM

CHAPTER 29
All In

So, they traveled after Sean had his fill, and Max told him what he needed to do. Max still needed to swoon. No matter how tired he was of it. Max needed everything to go off without a hitch this time.
Stopping in San Francisco to Pride.
Flying to Amsterdam for a tranny to get them both off.
Stopping in Sitges, Spain for the Organic Nude Experience.
Max was returning to the island where he only had days to pass through and meet his numbers.
Max unhooks me from his ear.
Where the process starts over again.
But now, Sean stands between my legs and adjusts the lever.
Pounding his dick into my worn-out pussy.
Apologizing for his abuse over and over.
He rambles on about his nut.
How he feels the sperm rushing through his vein.
He pumps harder and faster.
He explodes his custard of sperm into my rotting walls.
And here come the spirits to feast again.
I'm falling.
I'm waiting.
But something is different this time.
My pheromones and vomit alert Max's arrival.
He appears from the mist.
Switching his vision to an x-ray.
Scanning my pod from all angles.
Discovering the pooch in my belly is ready to drop.
Exhaling.
Waiting.
Breasts enlarged.
My stomach becomes oblong and tight.
My back aches and starts to burn.

My water breaks. The pod clanks and adjusts, rotating its hinges to open, and prepares to release me. As I look down, the floor shapes and shifts, unsure of its need. The device relaxes its grip, and I plunge my feet first. My arms and legs move wildly, but I place my legs together and protect my stomach. Landing in a pool of blue water, I travel through a winding chute. The painful contractions ripple through my body like jolts of electricity. My muscles seize in cooperation while my bones crack and pop, adjusting to the opening of my pelvis.

The intensity of the contractions blacks me out, and the sound of haunting voices suddenly awakens me. They chant my name in synchrony.

"Gianna."

The transference of space confuses my mind as I attempt to regain consciousness. From one horrid reality to another, I try to process the mental fractions of space and adjust to the time. The blurriness of my eyes masks the death surrounding my body.

"Ah!" I call out in agony as another contraction shocks my system. The room's temperature increases like a wall of fire and quickens my eyes to open in shock.

"Get the sticks!" Max shouts before throwing the twigs to the floor, engulfing the fire with more ferocity. His goliath stride quickly moves across the room—his swift choreography flashes across my dilating pupils like an invisible mist of white air.

"GOD, HELP ME!" I cry out as my heart races. Fear takes over in my mind. Another contraction develops, and I wildly grab onto Max's skin and pull hard. His skin stretches with me like elastic, weakening my grip as he moves.

"God can't help you now," Kim confidently states as she glows like liquid gold.

Her blonde hair coils like springs as she teases with her movements. Her hair dances against the twinkle in her amber eyes. Her teeth shine like sticks of butter and melt from her gums like hot wax when she speaks.

Kim taunts me by extending her pinky finger into the air.

"Watch this." Kim threads a string of fine wire through a hole drilled at the tip of her nail. She carefully punctures into my flesh and embroiders through each link of Mr. Willy's necklace still hanging from my neck.

"Ah!"

Dedrias pushes down against my shoulder to assist Kim's tailoring. The piercing jabs of pain dart up the side of my neck and face.

"I'm sorry." Max turns to look at me. His eyes are lifeless and black as night. Their hypnotic death darkens with vanity to justify his selfish position.

"No!" I scream, gagging to catch my breath, and terrified as I watch Max's back widen into a man-ram-beast.

His growl is hungrier. His breathing is heavier.

"Ah!"

Kim continues to push down on my head while she pierces the exposed corner of my tight neck. The puncture pops through my skin as the thread zips through my warm, raw flesh. She stitches through the jewelry on the other side of my neck, where a steady stream of blood saturates down my back. I break free and swing my arms wildly.

"Quit moving!" Max yells as he turns and forcefully strikes my arms away, and they backfire in my face. A blast of thunderous heat radiates from my cheekbone, through my nose, and across my eye. The sound mimics the cracks of crushed bone. It copies my crusting blood in microscopic shatters.

"Oh, please stop!" I cry out as another contraction takes control of my body.

"Cut the damn baby out before I do!" Max demands, flicking his pinky nail high. "I'm not going to wait much longer!"

My vision is blurred. My face burns in agony. Then, Dedrias pushes down on my stomach with force.

"Push!" Kim yells at me.

"Push now!" Dedrias scowls.

I blink my eyelids and focus on the women stepping from the canvases on the wall. My heart races faster. One woman steps out from behind her crackling sheets of material that once bound her, too, shedding her hardened shell to break free. Her face is pure, golden, and creamy. She moves with grace, stretching her ligaments to awaken her hibernating body. Her bones snap and pop as if this Mastiqulation was longer than expected.

"That was me you were touching. If you said something, we might not be here now." She floats past me and talks with her eyes. Every word she utters is clear as if she spoke their horror from her glazed lips. She softly brushes her fingertips across my genitalia, rubs the coagulated tissue between her fingers, and flicks the blood joints from her tips. She proceeds to the center of the room, where Sean sets fire to the pile of twigs. Each woman breaking from the wall places her twig wrapped in yellow ribbon into the white flame. Each wrapping encourages a whiter burn and a brighter glow. Max encircles the women with a boundary of brick dust and sand.

"Push!" Max demands.

My eyes fill with tears as I cry uncontrollably. The contractions are ripping through my body like bolts of lightning.

"Shut up!" Kim smacks my face and pulls harder on the thread to seal the seam. "Funny-shaped bitch. How would you like your smile to be, hmm?"

Kim mimics cryptic smiles before she pierces her nail into the corner of my mouth and pulls the wire. My cheek draws into the upper corner of my face near my eye. The skin around my neck on the opposite side of my face pulled tighter. Kim jerks on the thread, and my shoulders follow suit with every yank.

"I think a closed mouth would suit her best," Max taunts with a smirk of his own. "Turn it up higher in the corner some more." Max jerks his head back and laughs. "How does *this* make you feel, Gianna?" He stresses. "*Does it frighten you?*" He imitates my voice in perfect pitch.

Realizing everything Max said was a mysterious liaison to his dark script. The chords played haunting strings of death in the backdrop of his manuscript. Max does not love me; he used me. I replay the red flags repeatedly, reaching out to myself from this side to stop my actions on the other before they happen.

Don't look back at the store!

Don't leave with him!

My breathing is erratic. Someone presses on my stomach and reaches inside of me.

"I told you about fuckin' with them pretty, light-skinned hoes!" Sean hollers over my earth-shattering shrills of agony. The roof and crushed exterior frame of the house start falling like dominoes. The moonlit sky shines against the exposed brick that melts away like molten lava. Sean turns to scold Max as he uncovers a large, white canvas. "I told you I'm tired of painting motherfuckers!" He slams some materials down next to it.

Another needle sticks me by surprise. I wiggle around but have nothing to give. As I lie in a pool of blood streaming down my face and legs, Kim sews my lips together, and half-stitched lips break my blubbering whimpers. My nostrils fail to inhale the oxygen needed. A warm rush of liquid enters my vein, and the room starts moving in slow motion, restraining my faculties.

"Hurry, the baby is almost here," Max utters.

My body goes numb.
There is not an ounce of fight left within me.
The pain is subsiding.
I'm goin' down.
"Spread her out."
Frantically, I shift my eyes to focus.
"Pull it out!"

I feel the tingling warmth of the pain blocker travel from my legs, through my stomach, and toward my heart and lungs. My eyes open and close, fighting to stay awake for as long as possible in fear of never waking again. Then, suddenly, I feel empty. I hear faint cries that are innocent and weak. I see the blurry figure pass by, flailing little arms and feet in chilly convulsions.

"Clean it off!" Max orders. "I have to see!" he yells impatiently at Dedrias.

Another woman breaks from her shell and allows the orbiting air to guide her feet. One by one, loosening from their prisons. One by one, they encircle the burning twigs wrapped in their yellow ribbons. I am taken from the table, wiped off, and swiftly placed upright, standing horizontally with my arms stretched wide.

"Here's your savior," Sean teases as he looks back at Kim while fastening my arms to the canvas. "You better pray hard," he whispers before he hammers two nails into my palms.

"Mmmmm!" My throat wails from the piercing pain.

The women lift their arms in unison and release a shrilling decibel of cryptic screams filling the room before it sonically vibrates into the night sky.

"Declotae!"

The women magically transform into a state of renewal. It takes everything inside of me to survey them. One...four...seven of them, I count. All metamorphosed from their casings and held to their cocoons no more. They position themselves as the goddesses they once were. A heavenly countenance basks with them as they encircle the white-hot fire. The women hold hands, with Kim and Dedrias standing with them to guide the way. Sean dips a long piece of cloth into a bubbling white emulsion and raises the smoking sheet of material to me like an offering of vinegar for parchment.

"This is gonna burn," Sean says before he plasters it to my skin.

My screams were stifled between dried blood and perfect stitching. My face resembles a joker with jackal humor.

"Just think, when Max finds another easy bitch like you, you'll be able to see her again," Kim instigates. "You'll never escape us," she says in a haunting voice. "I can't believe how many of you left with him! Who does that stupid shit? Who in the fuck goes to the Bahamas with someone they don't fucking know?" Kim stresses as she sews my big toes together and ties a bow for completion.

"Stop hurting me! Help me, God! Jesus, save me!" They take turns mocking my cries of pain.

Sean smooths over the scorched material with care. A crease here. A fold there. Making sure I beautifully curate to the hot, defiled cloth.

"You should be used to this by now." He places hot tar on my lips and over Kim's stitches. "I bet your ass wishes you had said nothing *that* day," Sean teases as he pauses to manipulate my lips. He adds another layer of bubbling linen and plaster to my body, slapping it on in sheets to add thicker layers of death.

I wish the same thing and scream with closed lips. The rolls of hot air scratch my throat as it tears through my windpipe. Sean leans closer to my frame with his ears and laughs in his high-pitched gurgle.

"What? I can't hear you. You wish that, too?" he agitates. "Is that what you're trying to say?" Sean throws his head back and claps his hands.

I look at how they stand together, fused as one. Everyone speaks as a legion.

"Eight!" They close their eyes and loudly chant in their minds.

The sound is vacant at first until the beating drums break the hypnotic silence. It immolates shallow valleys and electric oceans. Sean continues to shape my stomach, tucking the cloth into my pussy hole to cauterize the inside and seal it shut. The scalding heat from the tar turns into a lubricating coating over my lips, filling the inner and outer holes. Sean then leans against the wall and jacks off. He plops his semen into a bowl that sits nearby. Sean soon dips a small paintbrush into his ejaculation and then into a tray of red glitter.

"How's that look?" Sean stands back to admire his work while forming and patting the glitter precisely—the sparkly sheets of shine flash from his satisfied eyes.

"Beautiful," Max says as he steps into my eyes view. "You and that fucking red lipstick."

"She looks like the whore she always was to me." Kim walks by and pinches the glitter more securely as it adheres to my lips forever. She twists enough to distort my already jangled face. She smirks at me like the bitch I always knew she was.

"Don't touch my shit!" Sean smacks her hand and reapplies the glitter with frustration.

As I mold to this canvas, the sheets of material vacuum to my body, dry into my flesh and harden instantly. I feel a warm stream of tears falling down my disfigured face. It rewets the material and quickly cements it dry. My eyes focus on Sean as he splatters acid along my chest to make my nipples rise from under the cloth, sandy rock, and tar.

"Mmmmnn." I moan as the concoction burns clean through my flesh, bubbling the raw skin.

"Damn, I'm good." Sean pinches the material together to form its shape. He smooths over my collarbone to hide uneven surfaces, delicately molding my melty flesh. "Just the right temperature. Come feel," he beckons Max to come over and see. He adjusts my necklace so the pendant dangles freely, closer to my birthmark. "Damn. See you next time. I'm sorry for what I did," Sean consoles me, like his morality is saving face.

"I thought you said you were a smart girl and knew when to bow out?" Max stands in front of me. "Don't look too intelligent to me." He animates his fingers like a camera box, scanning me for my future exposé. "Perfect."

Then Max kisses me, places a toothpick between his lips, and goes to stand in the center of everyone present. In the center of the room, the flames shot up from the brick dust and fallen wood chips. Max raises his hands and begins chanting. His strands of muscle fiber are tense. His broad back, now facing me, is covered in glowing tattoos. Goat heads, hieroglyphic slashes, and his number eight illuminate with vibrance and horror.

"Declotae," Max calls as he stretches his hands high. He is proud. He believes his journey is complete.

I shift my eyes and focus on this hell I never imagined in my worst nightmare. There Max stands, shining like some arrogant god emitting light from the middle of the floor. They chant my name as they praise, torture, and abuse me.

"Oh, Gianna, we thank you for this new life! We will be forever indebted to you!"

As I hang from this canvas, the stabbing pains of regret flood my soul. Max reaches for the baby as if to sacrifice it, lifting it high enough for all to see. Max inspects the new fold of life to see if he can find it. His white, hot flame tickles its feet and startles the infant to cry. The more he looks at the infant, the more frustrated he becomes. Max turns it over to its backside, noticing the female organs, and yells, "Yes!" then scans her arms and shoulders; finally, his eyes locate what he couldn't believe he was looking at.

CHAPTER 30
Heartbreak

"No!" Max yells in defeat.

Sean's etching is this dud's flaw. Near her ear, in the groove of her neck and shoulder, Max notices a mole. A bright pink mole that sprouts two heads—the same albino-ass-colored mole as Sean. The same mole he twisted from his body to sponge the excess blood from the woman's neck that day. The very mole Dedrias plays with when Max spies on them when she straddles him fucking.

Max throws the cursed blob of new life down into the white flame beneath his feet and blasphemes his efforts.

"FUCK!" Max cries out in desperation. "THIS CAN'T BE MY LIFE!"

Sean jumps from his position in front of me and reaches for her before she turns into a puff of smoke and disappears. He flashes past me in slow motion. His arms stretch as far as they can, and his grunts extend his reach to save her.

"She's mine!" Sean roars as he springs into action, retrieving her right before she enters the flame.

Sean punches Max's bad knee back to weaken his stance. Failing to protect his skin, he burns part of his hand and arm. Sean shields the baby's face by cupping her body close to his chest, tumbling forward and away from the burning glow of the fire. Sean abhors more hate for Max as he sticks his landing. Flares follow their tumble into the wall. The mirrors, crashing their reflective beauty, shatter to the floor below.

"You're getting weaker by the day. Why don't *you* go back and do *your* fucking time," Sean stresses as he tosses his baby to Dedrias, who quickly wraps her in her flowy skirt.

My placenta is still attached to her belly button, beating my motherly nutrients into her tiny body. Dedrias smells her skin and cradles her. She whiffs at her privates for assurance and licks her face for sweetness.

"And then *you* can come back when *I* say, bitch!" Sean adds as he pulls something shiny from his right pocket.

Max stops dead as Sean flips his token piece into the air, showing it off. All eyes are on Sean. Max notices something more when the coin catches the light with every turn. The rich color of the nickel. The unique engravings. The number eight was branded with his oxidated blood. It was his amulet. Max's eyes, now protruding from their sockets, see the unbelievable. *How does Sean have my amulet? How did he find it?*

"You really are a stupid ass. You know I can hear your thoughts," Sean reveals. "I'll tell you how…" Sean mimics Max's exact thoughts, too stuck in Max's throat for him to speak. "I had it. That's why your dumb ass couldn't find it. Not that it's of any consequence, but it's nice seeing your ass squirm for once." Sean flips it again before he places it back into his right pocket. He shakes his leg to remind Max of the upper hand that he now holds. "You ain't the only motherfucker around here moving through time."

Max is stunned by Sean's bold announcements. He jumps from the fire and positions his stance in a silent rage. Mind-blowing betrayal was spearing darts of fire in a sky-darkening attack. Sean's seven-foot frame intimidates from across the room. He looks more gigantic as he fills the space he occupies. His heated stare blazes wrath as he snatches one of the lion's heads from its base, and slings it at Max.

Max ducks and quickly snatches Sean from where he stands in retaliation. The distance, ten feet or more, surprises me with its swiftness. As Sean lunges at him, his shabby attempt to swerve Max's elastic grab causes his own feet to entangle within Max's snatch. Max's laugh only instigates the situation and infuriates Sean more.

"Sean! *Damboule!*" Max orders him to stop as he shakes him around like a ragdoll and attempts to control his movements. "*Stop it, I said!*" He focuses on his hand work, jabbing Sean in his side to knock the wind from his lungs and boulders Sean clean through another wall.

In full fury, Sean jumps up and charges at Max. Upon impact, he knocks Max over like a ton of bricks and pounds him brutally. He stomps on his shoulder in hammering steps. Then Max grabs his size fifteen foot and flips Sean to his knees. Both jump up simultaneously, but Sean mistakenly twists his body and faces the wall, not face-to-face with Max. Using Sean's error to gain control, Max uses the wall for traction and leverages his position. Max grabs Sean by the head and pulls it back with extreme force.

Sean's mole starts squealing, and Max is agitated when the appendage begins biting his shoulder and arm. Max chomps down on the lumpy mold of skin and bites it from Sean's neck.

"Ah! Motherfucker!" Sean yells before grabbing a gold vase within his reach and attempting to swing, but Max reaches over him and extracts it right from his grasp.

Max spits fire into the deep gash. It springs from the hole and catches the gold drapes on fire. Now more angered by Max's childish antics, Sean twists his body and lunges at Max, connecting quick jabs to his jaw. They punch and throw each other from one side of the room to the other. The wailing lump seizures on the floor in erratic jiggle movements.

They knock over statues and hanging globes. They crash through windows and fly into the house's upper level, which opens to the night. Passing through the already obliterated construction, their powerful punches and super-sonic movements make it hard to shut my eyes and give up the ghost. They'll likely slam into this wall, and my concrete bondage will shatter upon impact.

Dedrias shifts positions and makes her way around the room. Her unassuming stance is predatory as she stalks into play. Her devotion is unknown. She looks over at her brother and cuts her eyes. I feel the hatred in her stare. If her eyes were lasers, Max would be a ball of flames. Her aim is dead on. Then, Dedrias looks up at her beloved Sean and sniffs the air. Her neck jerks in quick retraction to catch the scent, smelling Sean and Max's fears. I could sense their anxiety. She was tasting Sean's desires through the fibers of the air, still silhouetting in their battle. Dedrias knows their moves. The matrix of time slows with each step that she takes.

In mid-stride, she looks over at me and exposes another face. A heckling spirit smirks back with its erratic displacement right underneath her sheet of face skin. Its skeletal horror deflects death and emits the horrid chill of hell. It tilts its head just enough to let me know that it sees me, too. It taunts me with Dedrias' every move. The spirit is cunning, demonically smiling as Dedrias lurks between the other women and the flying disarray of objects circling the room.

It's watching me watch her.

Her neck is turned to the side as she maneuvers forward, twitching her nostril with each breath and chomping her teeth in quick bites. Everything around her is bubbled in a womb of vibrations as she floats between them. Her bubble beats silently for the strike. As she approaches, the vibrations move her through the chaos with ease and patience. Then suddenly, time elapses, and I brace for her impact.

In a swift movement, Dedrias attacks Max from the side. She charges with her teeth and gnaws away at his arm, and part of his forehead as she zooms by.

Her stare never breaks as she attacks. Her anatomy moves with its natural boundaries of physical matter while her heckler entertains my engagement from the inside. It makes 'Ooo' faces when she lands her blows to his chest. The whole time, the demon spirit watches my reaction to her chomping on his skin and spitting out the chunks. It rotates its head and widens its mouth, revealing a blacker hole within her. Dedrias then maneuvers her neck to see my startled reaction. Her eyes flash back at me when her two entities fuse together while her body attacks Max in a heated rage.

I twist and moan underneath the dried plaster, hearing faint crackles with each twist. Dedrias waves her hands between them for fun, exploiting her pass into their matrix choreography and pound work. They destroy everything around them. Pictures fall from the walls that are left. Dedrias continuously swings at Max. He is shocked by her turn-coat actions and ducks to avoid her shots. He retracts and stands confused, heartbroken by her betrayal.

"Dedrias!?" Max calls her name. "*They must be smoking crack.*" Max thought to himself about the way they were acting.

"We're not smoking crack. Aren't you tired, brother? I'm tired," Dedrias pleads as she floats between them.

"But you know what we must do, Dedrias," Max professes. He was tired, too, and was ready for this nightmare to end. Max wanted a normal life. He could taste it on his tongue every time he ate Gianna's pussy out.

"We've been going in the same circle for a long time. Sean can end this shit for us. Just let him complete it. I want out!" Dedrias yells.

"I want out, too! I want my fucking ball!" Max growls.

Sean and Dedrias switched up on the source that supplies both of their raggedy asses. Attacking Max, who they so frogly forgot, has the keys to their ungrateful lives and could throw them both into the pit if he fucking wanted to, or the Blaque Dimension, where their asses would never return. The fortress of trust, broken by deceit and betrayal. All Max's hard work appears dismantled right before his eyes.

Max speedily gathers his thoughts and jumps into the air as Dedrias charges at him once more. She swings her arms in a turning wheel, quickly landing blows to Max's head, face, and chest. Spittle splatters from his lips in a ricochet, slapping Dedrias back in her face. Max couldn't believe what was happening. His nose bleeds from the severity of her tumbling swings. His flesh and blood turned against him for an outsider, but Max questioned that. Is Sean an outsider or a traitor? Or was Sean attempting to take this nightmare over? If so, he can go right the fuck on and take it. But Max changed that retarded thought. Sean is a cursed seed, and his destiny lies in Max's hands. Sean wasn't no special nigga; he was just born at the wrong time. This brotherly betrayal threw a monkey wrench into everything. Max thought he would get out of this sticky situation without anyone knowing they were all siblings. Now everybody wants Max's position. It was one blow after another. Max's world was caving in all around him.

Sean climbs over a broken vanity and hurls at Max in grandeur. His arms spread wide to absorb the most energy before impact. Max's height was a challenging target, needing leverage and acrobatic skills to fight him. Sean had to play a dirty game to win. Sean ventures into territory from which he cannot return.

"I'll cut it from my ass and eat it before you get it back, nigga!" Sean clings from the edge of a wall and whirls his body from the broken structure. Sean hurls towards Max in mid-air and flashes his pinky nail with a DING!

It catches Max by surprise and takes his focus away from Sean, jumping onto him like a wrestler. He slices Max's shoulder just inches away from his jugular. Sean didn't alert Max of him growing the nail. He kept his finger tucked in most times, telling Max it was an arthritic condition that kept his finger bent in that position. Growing his fingernail took some creativity and wit. He would trim it back when it became too long to hide. He covered it with band-aids during patient care in the ambulance rides.

Max could not understand why they were deceiving him like this after decades of hard work and looking out for one another. They spent intimate moments consoling each other's needs outside their incestual obligation and promises, making sure they both wouldn't die. How could she? And for a goon-ass-looking nigga like Sean? Dedrias fails to realize Sean won't be in the picture for too much longer. The sooner Max gets rid of Sean the better. His life needs to move forward, and Sean's doesn't matter.

"Why?" Max questions in sadness as he dislodges the metal pole from the gas stove.

"The fuck you mean, why? I figured out who you are. It seems you've been playing me the whole fucking time!" With untamed aggression, Sean jumps on Max's torso; they crash onto the floor and against the marble fireplace. The impact crumbles the wall beside it.

Then, they grapple to and fro, rolling back and forth, de-leafing plants, and demolishing everything in their path. Alternating over the white flames and rustling a dust cloud that attempts to blind me; so, I close my eyes as they pass by. The potash burns my face as I turn. I hear the grunts and woofs. The hollow gurgles that stuff their mouths as they pound each other in the stomach magnifies with every threatening fist.

My eyes can see through the closed lids. They tingle in focus, creating a framed picture of their battle. They karate kick each other in the kidneys and neck. Max roars like a lion as he thrashes his arms against the ground and causes a piano wave effect on the floor. It cripples Sean's stability and knocks him high into the air before slamming him dead on his ass. Sean jumps up quickly, ready in his stance, and rides the returning wave.

"I had to keep you close! I couldn't afford to lose you! Not now!" Max calls out.

They stop to look at one another. Sean's mouth hangs in the balance with every word Max speaks.

"You're the other baby in the jar! You and Gianna are my assignment!" Max confesses.

"Me and Gianna?" Sean pauses in his actions and looks at me confused.

CHAPTER 31
Brotherly Love

Images flash of the times Max prepared to impregnate Gianna with failure after failure, and Sean got it on the first try. It pissed him off that Sean's one *good* ball decided to pump sperm that fuck. The odds of Sean's sperm traveling through its crushed veins and an unknown pathway were improbable, but how Max's luck was going, it didn't surprise him that Sean's odds were being favored.

Then, the vivid memories of Sean losing his manhood flash into his head. He was making another motherfucker happy in his quest while he suffered in silence with his. Sean suddenly realizes how important he is to this game they're playing. Even the shit he suffers in his path of passive ignorance has its limit, and Sean was at his.

Yeah, it was blissful until Sean found someone else's jewelry in his biological father's coffin. It didn't match the photo left in the envelope for him. The markings were different and so were the numbers. He didn't know what the two stood for, but now he believes it stands for him and Gianna. It had to. Nothing else made sense. Sean, not knowing his natural origin and being the bastard son of a no-good deacon, was asked to come to Las Vegas to pick up his insurance check. Along with it came a list of instructions sealed with candlewax that Sean should have gotten on his eighth birthday.

Sean's deformity must have scared his mother. Who knows what the extra plug of skin resembled then? Birthing a two-headed baby is frightening, especially when the streets are dark, and no one can help soak up the gallons of blood. The vague memory hazes across Sean's memory: blurry dots of white light, black skies, and moaning. Sean remembers lots of moaning.

Sean hocks and spits into Max's eye, pissing Max off more.

"Fuck you!" Sean curses at him.

They punch each other with built-up tensions. Both think of the women they lusted after together. The nights they hung from quarter moons above London Bridge eating kettle popcorn. Sean was pissed because he had been dicking down his half-brother and his half-sister Dedrias the entire time! She wasn't a trade-off for his testicle!

"Motherfucker! What type of sick games are you playing, nigga?" Sean starts pounding the air with anger.

The wicked menagerie of incest was Trevallier Deacon Rickdick Negus DuBois' legacy. Slicky Ricky is what they called him. The Dick Slinger. The daddy/slash uncle/slash brother to all his kids and his grandchildren. He was every relative in his incestuous web of immediate family.

That's how he satisfied the Declotae's needs and fed the Guff. Everybody is related by blood anyway. Fuck it. Because they share a genetic code, it greatened the chance of retardation within the demented lineage. Sean wanted to meet the bitch that cursed his natural father's loins, his birth mother, and get rid of Dedrias' ass. Sean was over the bullshit Max had running. He wanted out more than anyone else.

It angered Max because he wasted time investing in a dead agenda. Why was he working overtime for something no one desired anymore? What for? The women are independent and don't need men. The others are either lesbians or don't want shit to do with men—let alone want babies. It wasn't going the way the universe had planned it. The shit was crumbling and wasn't worth saving. Max was over it.

With each punch, they faintly swing at one another as their stamina wears out. The fatigue didn't register. They took mini breaks to lean on the busted bar stools, drank water, and throw various objects at one another within reach. They huffed like tired, old men. Calling each bitch, worn-out, and fags. From both sides, justified cut-downs bolted from their tongues. Neither backs down until the other surrenders.

"Your baby is a dud! She's worthless!" Max yells in spite, causing more angst between them. "She has two heads for crying out loud!"

"You liar!" Sean cries out in anger as he catches his breath. Then, he throws a wooden block at Max's face.

Dedrias adds to the frustration with her wild advances that take Max by surprise. Not wanting to exile Dedrias into the Blaque Dimension for her misguided treason, Max forces her face back with his hand and warrants her to "Stop!"

He shoves her across the floor, where she stumbles over her feet and lands ass-first into a chair. Sean charges at Max and back-elbows him in the jaw. Both pant and grunt as they swing. They were cursing at one another in continuous rotations.

"Punk!"

They spit and slap one another; Sean rips chunks of Max's beard out his face, and Max bites holes in Sean's back and shoulders. Fighting through destroyed structures and slamming against the window frame shared with missing glass, they continue to scuffle.

Unexpectedly, laser beams shoot from Sean's eyes and shock even him. He barely misses Dedrias and his new offspring when he starts zapping shit left and right. While aiming for Max's fast-moving feet, Sean focuses on the number eight tattoo at the top of his spine and then the ram head tramp stamp near the crack of his ass.

"Bitch!"

Sean zeros in on Max's moves and flashes his eyes into the night, attempting to force the rage from the undiscovered sockets of power.

Sean felt like a superhero:

Flying through the sky.

He disappears in a flash with Max's magic coin.

And shooting lasers of fire from his eyes that gave him villainous flair.

At random times, the beams shoot from his pupils, he squints as he targets Max's feet again, scorching the floor by mistake and setting it on fire. Max, just as surprised, jumps into a grasshopper karate move with a finished tumble. He quickly grabs the gold shield in the corner of the room to protect him from Sean's ill-targeted aims. Sean tries to spark the lasers at Max but catches the center of my hand. The fire shoots through my palm and blisters the gold drapes behind me.

As Sean lunges at Max and rigorously pounds on the metallic shield, he envisions Max pulverized to chopped liver underneath the solid composition. The collapsed sheet of useless gold traps Max to the floor.

"You get on my fucking nerves!" Sean reaches down and extracts the shield from Max's grip, slinging it across the room and into the star-lit sky.

Max huddles into a ball to protect his face as Sean's blows come at him continually. Sean kicks him over and stomps on his back with a vengeance, leaving Max bawled up like a baby, unable to defend himself. Sean snatches Max by the carotid chunks of skin hanging from his back and hammers on his spine.

"Ah!" Max cries out in agony.

Sean's pounding thrusts vibrate the ground. Max screams out from the nerve-stabbing pain that shoots down his legs, instantly paralyzing his movements.

The gathered cloak of women, antsy in their deliberation, grow more confused. The skies are open but to where? Their freedom is a blink away. Some were missing for a decade or more, longing to return home. Others do not know where they are or who they are. The hell that casts them in bondage keeps their floating limbs frozen in place. The women's gaze focuses past the commotion flying in the room and outside near the coastal edge. I shift my eyes and notice the ocean cresting the wall in a turning wave.

CHAPTER 32
Play Gods

A gravitational shift clocks everyone's slanted position, weightlessly lifting our arms as we turn. The tilt elevates everything off the floor. The women are free to fly about the endless space, sparkling their nudity and fluid movements gracefully. My enclosure, leaning with the tide and undried plaster, drips like inverted marbles.

Max flusters for his father's amulet. His fingers frantically feel for its circular definitions. His back cracks and pops as his agonizing shrills of pain move with him. His seven-foot stature suddenly fails him without reason. Unable to stabilize his rotation to straighten his body, the amulet slides from his pocket and flips into the air. Max desperately reaches for it and misses.

"No!" He cries out in anguish as it slips from his fingers.

I hear Max pleading for Sean to stop his repetitive blows. Sean swings from a hole in the floor like a monkey as he kicks Max's chest in a steady rhythm. Sean punts the amulet further from Max's reach, causing it to spiral without direction.

Small pockets of the horizon open from the other side. My stomach rolls, noticing the holes they leave and the nightmare that lurks behind them.

This time, the shift rotates us like a crooked carnival ride, jerking our movements robotically and fractioning our turn. Twitchy but controlled, the disjointed delays throw off our balance. Sean holds on to the jagged structure of brick that clings to our gravitational adjustments along the wall and floor.

Our bodies hang sideways and away from the ceiling. As we rotate, the grounds flicker the butterflies from their grassy nest outdoors. The midnight shimmer of the ocean rolls against the inversion of the moon, staining the sky like broken glass. As the amulet dings against Sean's nail, he flicks it by accident and boomerangs the coin into the inverted night.

Each click rotates in ten-degree angles until we reach a complete one-hundred-and-eighty-degree flip and stop. The rotation dangles us like bats. We cling to our savior of choice:

A destroyed wall.

Something nailed into the chipped ceiling.

Jagged windowsills with their shards of pointed glass.

Kim clings to the bamboo leaves on the ceiling fan. Her hand wraps around the stem like rubber, forming a seal to safeguard her grasp. The seven women soar into the atmosphere. They swarm towards the moon, which spins with more spatial definition and purpose. Whistling in its rotation, my eyes, still closed in this disarray, see clarity glowing from its whirl as the diamonds, encamped from the white fire, fly towards its destination.

The silhouette of a strong man holds the white sphere in position. His wide arm curl secures its globular turn. His neck, bent forward, creates the space required for circulation. He has an infinite number of lives weighing on his shoulders, waiting to birth a lie.

A fortress of baby skulls shields the outer layer. It protects the first fruits of embryos from damage. The next layer of the sphere is numerous dots of light sparkling intermittently. Blocked in sections, they twinkle like stars and flash their cosmic energy of new life. In the center is a winding ribbon whizzing protection around an enormous brilliant diamond dazzling with power.

With a glow of light that encourages the way, the flashing dots travel sections of the Orb. The twinkles of new life must pass through a lake of wondrous galaxies. Then, they transform into snowflakes before the infants shoot from the starry tunnels like silent bombs. Flying sheets of skin form into clumps of matter as the objects eject.

The Guff, an entangled sphere of infant souls, rotates with purpose. It releases the infants from the spinning globe at will. As the offspring extract, their cries quickly escape to the heavens, but lately, the Guff spins slower, and their cries turned into moans. The life that once flourished on the planet was losing its battle with the changing times. Men were becoming women by taking hormones and getting their penises cut off, while the women were getting their pussies surgically pulled out and their breasts permanently removed. There were fewer successful pods in this generation. The Declotae was losing its grip on the universe, and so were the Trevallier.

Those of us who have made it this far hold a special flaunt. We are indeed cursed—Our decisions forced into assimilation. What should feel like a joyous occasion is a vicious cycle of bondage wrapped in vague and deathless hope of life.

An array of rainbow colors and patterns sync together in an instant. Each ribbon, connecting with its equal, twists together and unites. The covet of women from the estate connects with their young first. They must be the bottom bitches. Soon after, a conglomerate of others moves forward, awaiting their young to spin from the sphere.

As their ribbons intertwine, they embrace, pucker with the sweetest kisses, and fly off. Their time is limited. Limited before another gathering happens or may not occur. It's sad to watch—the ghosts of heartache travel with them. The longing for my baby girl aches deep within my soul. Nothing can fill my emptiness, but the sweetness of her warm body in my arms.

In the middle of flying about, the material suddenly deconstructs from my body and breaks the cast off completely. It crumbles into the night. The shell releases me, and I connect with the others. Now gracious and anew, my body trails in a flowing gown of defiled purity. Attached to the hem are yellow ribbons. They glow like the rise of the morning sun. Tiny, steel needles imbed my garment. I see thousands tinker at our feet as we float into the universe together.

The song of a shattered war cry bellows across the heavens. It echoes our pain in this ongoing hell. As I sniff the air, my amplified sensory picks up hints of her sweet essence. With the absence of sight, I hover amidst the twilight realm to smell her out. As I whip through the atmosphere, the stars guide my journey. I see the distinct markings, and colors, in everyone's ribboning through computerized lids that formulate a synthesized picture of heat and distinct radioactive movement. It identifies our bond and connects our link.

As we sacrifice ourselves continually, our bodies pang in heartache. We cast over and over for them and die spiritually with our souls. We believed Max's lies before the exposed truth. He razzle-dazzled his wealth and cooed us with his soothing voice. We looked at his hot, enlarged extremities instead of his cold, black heart.

We take this time even if it means only for these few moments of interaction. I watch the tears of our hearts form waters of joy. We bask in the purity of our love for the infants. How unconditional that bond is. A mother's vow to nurture, protect, and save is finally realized.

Here I was, looking for a man to fill this aching void, but this infant is tangible—her devotion is genuine and true. My hope is removing her from this realm of circulating trauma masked with spiritual illusions. For tradition's sake, we breed on; because if we do not, the world collapses within its vanity of sin. Satisfying the remnants of the past, we nurture what traumatizes us. The infants did not ask to be here. We created their doom and hold their bondage in our deceived hands.

The unique attachment we share will never break. My life depends on keeping her safe, the protective mama bear I become. Never to abandon her in times of need. What greater superpower is above birthing life? If that innate opportunity is taken away, then what else *is* the sweet canal of punani to do? Be a barren womb of unproductive flesh not multiplying God's creation?

We are torn between happiness and gloom here. Our existence is an evil web of production that never stops. It is an intricate assembly line of incest that replenishes within itself and has no shame or remorse. Our divine sisterhood beats with passion, and we are committed to our purpose through this assembly, which is to supply the nectar of humankind. To be fruitful and multiply. I am determined to return to my world, what is familiar to me—but with purpose. My circumstances choose me to testify that hell is alive, burns bright, and repent your sins!

No one would believe me. Everyone ignored the mental breakdown I'd been silently crying about for years. No one listened. The tears shed on stage were not a part of the show; they were surrender calls of defeat. They turned their heads and shut me out. The emotional connection was too much for them. Even when I would plead through my drunken outbursts, my sudden drop in weight from the stress of independence was exposing my broken spirit.

My voice often wailed in flight, releasing the years of pain that leaked from my heart. The weight of outward appearances that seemed together; but was collapsing on the inside from the lack of a better foundation. No one cares if I decide not to give a fuck about anything. Their agendas are all the same; people want what they want, and once they get it, fuck you!

My poor decisions led to this moment. All the stupid ass choices I made to end up here. Giving everybody what they wanted while my shit was circling the drain. Not anymore. Everybody will pay for my suffering heart. I am therefore fucked and not to be pitied. What my eyes have witnessed. What my soul continues to endure, is all with an objective.

As I assimilate to this curse, the orchestrated song of life plays its music in heavy rotation. I understand the assignment. Determined to reclaim all the enemy took; I scratched the record of discord and skipped its evil play.

A universal pulse runs through my soul. My baby mama status is now part of my story like all of us trapped here in our house of whores. As I join my loving two-headed infant, *our* coronation is happening; at this moment, the twinkling echoes of our ribbons intertwine. The delicate dance of the sheer material is beautiful to watch. The twists and turns that it does before tying itself into a basket weave pattern to lock her inside my arms is an intricate web of beautiful bondage. She immediately rubs her face against my breast and finds my jelly-pink nipple to supp from.

The first suck is frustrating. Her two faces change and display anger. Then, she tries again, snorting both sets of her nostrils across my breast to catch the scent of warm milk. She latches onto my breast, hungrily pulling the nourishing liquid from every duct as she tucks her body closer.

Our energy transfers and warps my mind in transfer. It travels through electric waves and flashes of light that document the ungodly speed of her euphoric draw. Connecting spiritually. Bonding eternally. I vow never to open my eyes to this wicked world until we are free from Max's living hell. My vision is more transparent than ever before. From the corner of my computerized eye, I see a small object propelling through the air. As it turns, the circular object begs me to reach for it. I snatch it from the air and tuck it under my other breast. Behind it, I see Max frantically sifting his arms through the sky as he flies towards me.

"That's my amulet!" Max plunders through the array of women connecting with their young. He Godspeeds his efforts as he flashes through the domain. "Give it back to me!" Max bellows in his travel, rushing towards me.

I remove the amulet from my titty fold and plug one of the holes that appear nearest to me, but nothing happens. Anxiously I try another, patting and slamming the coin into the porous pocket and turning it sideways to see if it will create an opening. A break. A crack. The tiniest slit is all that's needed. Fucking something!

""I'm going to get us out of here, baby girl," I guarantee her with my tender words. "Come on! God, please!" I scrape the coin back and forth to create friction. A groove. An impression. I'm dying here, Father!

Max gets closer and quickens his haste. His charcoal black skin intensifies with heat and ashes into a glowing beam of white light as he travels.

"Stop!" Max screams. "Don't do that!"

There is a slight separation of the inverted dominion beside me.

"He's close! Gianna, hurry," the opening beckons in a haunting voice.

I look back at Max as he flies closer, then back at the slit gesturing for me to quicken my urgency.

"Turn it this way," the opening whispers as the realm starts liquifying counterclockwise to unlock.

"Please, Lord." I tuck her into my arms and pray as I insert the amulet.

"Don't do that, Gianna! It's not what you think!" Max yells in his flight.

As I turn the coin with the swirl direction, my hands nervously shake. Max reaches out and suddenly grabs my wrist before his amulet fully engages into the slot. Max hopes to retrieve his coin before I completely turn the lock counterclockwise. He stretches through the opening and grabs my hand, forcibly unturning the dilation of my hand. His exposed flesh unexpectedly bursts into flames, burns his hand to fine dust, and disappears like the wind.

"My fucking hand!? No!" His disappearing appendage infuriates him with more anger. Max bellows as he pushes in further, screaming, fighting to grab his amulet with his other hand, and burns his entire arm to ash before being forced to retreat.

"No! I'll find you, Gianna!" Max's voice leaves a threatening trail of terror as it dissipates into the vanishing swirl. The realm sucks his burnt, ashy skin away with him as it spins into a tiny black dot and disappears.

"Thank you, Father," I whisper to the heavens as we travel through flashes of time and escape the realm of Max's damned. My eyes, still absorbing this world through my eyelids, tear as they console my promises. "We made it, baby girl." I kiss both of her juxtaposed foreheads and breathe sighs of relief. The smaller head nestles close to my breast and sucks her draw with tenderness.

Now, I have other things to worry about. I don't even know how to stop this crazy ride. So many periods in time are zipping by us that I don't know when to remove the coin to make it stop. I don't want to end up in another fucked up dimension. Maybe if I thought of a place far away from the hell we escaped, we would magically be there. My mind draws a blank, thinking too hard of a destination...anywhere but here...

My mother. Rochelle. The beach. Max fighting on the other side with missing body pieces. The seven women. My twin, Sean.

Then, Max jumps through the vortex with force and startles with his frightening presence. He stretches the realm wide to his body frame and reaches through the entry, quickly rebelling against the burning chunks of ash that fall from his vanishing structure. "Don't turn that dial!" Max's regenerated limb grabs my ankle and tries to pull me back into his death-filled world. "It's not what you think! Don't go in that dimension! Please don't leave me here!"

"No!" I scream as I kick back his grip. His outline blows away like powder the more he battles. I watch his figure fall back to dust and start thinking of a place again...

Back in Florida, at the corner store where I first met Max.

If I...if I...didn't look back, I won't end up here.

Praying hard for God to reverse time. Wailing out in fear.

"Please!" I cry out in despair. It's funny how I call on God now, when I failed to give Him any time before. But isn't that what sinners do when fighting their way to salvation? When stumbling down the narrow path of deliverance, mistakes are made. Lessons take repeat instruction to learn. When things are good, we ignore Him; but when our lives are out of control and in ruin, we beg for Him to save us like a loving father would. Snatching us from the snare and the fowler lurking in the brush, waiting for the opportunity to devour and destroy.

And as I pray another prayer, Max reaches inside again, this time, swiping his reach like a sharp knife in swing to clench any part of me he can. He latches to my calf and ankle, quickly losing three of his fingers.

"Fuck!" Max screams as his digits snap from his grip and wither like dehydrated sticks. "Ah!" Max retreats. "No! I *will* find you!" Max disappears into the realm of his multiple hell of failed attempts.

And as we narrowly escape his capture, the amulet clicks. The swirl reverses its direction to align the plane and stops. The crack pushes the shimmering gold coin out from the slit and it floats into my hand. An unknown dimension slowly opens and the voice calls out again.

"Open it my love," it beckons from behind the sparkling slit. "Here is where you will find me and all your questions shall be answered. You'll like what this realm offers."

As the vortex clamps shut, a luminous sphere opens and my eyes are filled with crocodile tears that fall like heavy rain.

"I can't believe where we are," I whisper as the realm seals behind us and I step into our new reality flourishing with beautiful women drenched in the finest gold and the rarest silks known to man. Their diamond black hair shimmers from across the water as it cascades like a sleek river of onyx glaze. Ahead of us is a man forged between two goliath steel posts holding the world on his shoulders as it spins effortlessly against the back of is mutilated skull and his neck...

To be continued

DEDICATIONS

I thank My Father in Heaven for the strength to complete this book. I will have to answer for the language used between these pages and pray Him to forgive me.

I thank my professor, Dr. Carole Cole at South College of Florida, for her credible words of encouragement and edits. She will surely need a cigarette after this manuscript. To Thorald Roberts at the University of South Florida, thank you for teaching the art of clear and concise writing. I thank him for the opportunity to write for Sarasota Magazine's, biz941, with Susan Burns during my internship. It was an honor to have my work published there. Your combined knowledge helped to craft my writing skills and facilitate this work of art.

To my mother, Barbara Hicks, thank you for reminding me of my gift with shifting storylines. I also want to thank you for putting the rest of the vision together. This manuscript was a doozy! Thank you for all your hard work and enduring my crying spells! I love you.

I give a special shout-out to Brian Hill for his creative connections! If it wasn't for you, I would not have linked up with the most fly, coldest, freehand artist on the planet! Thank you, Danielle, for your artistic gift and this dope ass illustration! It is everything to this book and to me. You both understood the assignment.

I also give a special shout out to you, the reader. Thank you for purchasing my book and entrusting me to satisfy your hunger for an excellent read. This manuscript is my baby, and I am grateful for the opportunity to share my imagination with you. Your investment is important to me, which is why reviews are welcomed, and I encourage readers to share thoughts on my Facebook page and other platforms!

Melana

About The Author

Born in 1972, Miss Morris is a Pittsburgh, Pennsylvanian native that
bleeds black and gold for her football team, the Pittsburgh Steelers.
Miss Morris grew up in Rankin PA, where she later graduated from
Squirrel Hill's own, Taylor Allderdice High School in 1990. Taylor Gang
or Die!

After moving to Florida in 1995, Miss Morris attended Manatee
Community College, now South College of Florida, and later, the
University of South Florida. Go Bulls! She has two degrees under her
belt: an Associate Degree in English, and a Bachelor's Degree in
Professional and Technical Writing, where she interned at the Sarasota
Magazine's, biz941, for her final fall semester. The magazine published
Miss Morris' articles from September of 2008 through January of
2009.

Miss Morris grew up writing poetry, short stories, and plays. She loves the neo-era of Hip-Hop and R&B. Erykah Badu, Jill Scott, and Masego are a few of her favorite artists She loves to cook, especially Italian dishes. She also has a passion for cutting hair and has devoted thirty years of her life to the cosmetology industry. Her business, Roqstylz LLC, is rooted in precise haircutting, healthy hair, and beautifying women every day.

Contact Info and Socials
RIPE FRUIT SOON SPOILS on Facebook @
www.facebook.com/ripe.fruit.soon.spoils
i.roq.stylz on Instagram
Mel Morris on Facebook
7roqstylz2 on TikTok
morrismelana@gmail.com